MURDER-ON-SEA

Pearl is rushed off her feet with her restaurant, The Whitstable Pearl. While organising the family festivities as well as mulled wine for a charity church fundraiser, Christmas cards are delivered around town – filled with spiteful messages from an anonymous writer. Pearl's curiosity is piqued but having pledged not to take on a case at her detective agency before Christmas, she agrees that Canterbury's DCI Mike McGuire should take over. McGuire goes along to the fundraiser with her where a guest suddenly collapses. Have they had too much of Pearl's delicious mulled wine – or could it be something more sinister?

Murder-On-Sea

by

Julie Wassmer

Magna Large Print Books
Long Preston, North Yorkshire,
BD23 4ND, England.

British Library Cataloguing in Publication Data.

Wassmer, Julie
    Murder-on-sea.

    A catalogue record of this book is
    available from the British Library

    ISBN   978-0-7505-4282-1

First published in Great Britain in 2015 by Constable

Copyright © Julie Wassmer, 2015

Cover illustration © CBCK-Christine by arrangement with
Alamy Stock Photo

The moral right of the author has been asserted.

Published in Large Print 2016 by arrangement with
Little, Brown Book Group

Magna Large Print is an imprint of Library Magna Books Ltd.

Printed and bound in Great Britain by
T.J. (International) Ltd., Cornwall, PL28 8RW

The author gratefully acknowledges permission
to quote from 'Catching up with Christmas'
by Edna Ferber, used by permission
of the Edna Ferber Trust

For Krystyna Green

'*Christmas isn't a season. It's a feeling.*'
Edna Ferber, 'Catching Up With Christmas'

Chapter One

Tuesday 14 December, 4 p.m.

Any fisherman would have described the wind that day as 'blowing a hooley'. The icy blast had whistled a direct north-easterly passage, straight off the Norwegian coast, arriving on Whitstable's shores at the very moment Pearl Nolan was stepping into its path. Closing her front door, she pulled her scarlet coat tighter to her body, burying her chin into its black velvet collar as she turned her back on Seaspray Cottage and hurried along Island Wall.

Wearing a black Cossack-style fake fur hat and lace-up boots, Pearl looked much like a romantic Russian heroine, and certainly younger than her thirty-nine years with her dark hair falling across her shoulders and her light frame allowing the biting gusts to propel her along the street. Daylight had already faded as she ducked for cover in the lea of Kemp Alley, where a streetlamp reflected against the stage door of the old Playhouse which was plastered with posters advertising the coming attraction of *Puss in Boots*. The sound of Pearl's own heels bounced off the alley walls as she headed for the lights of the High Street.

In her shoulder bag were the Christmas cards which she had forgotten to take with her to the restaurant that morning. Instead, they had been left behind on her kitchen table, even after she had sat up into the early hours making sure she had written every last one so as not to miss the final post before Christmas. Increasingly, it seemed that these short, bleak December days reflected a shortage of time itself.

During the summer months, the clientele of The Whitstable Pearl consisted largely of tourists – DFLs mainly (the town's acronym for Down from Londoners), keen to sample the town's famous oysters – but at this time of year Pearl's customers were generally High Street locals looking for something more substantial. The menu today had featured a Stargazy pie, a hot chilli-salmon flan and a home-made lobster bisque, served with croutons and a *rouille* sauce fired with *espelette* pepper. The dishes had satisfied a host of Christmas shoppers, but having closed the door on her restaurant for the day, Pearl had trekked home, not to put her feet up, but to deal with her forgetfulness.

On the High Street, a sign helpfully directed Whitstable's visitors to the harbour in one direction, and the station in the other, but Pearl ignored both and headed directly across the road to St Alfred's where the old church clock suddenly chimed the quarter-hour. Pearl loved the sound of church bells and felt warmed, if only from the glow of festive lights.

Whitstable's local council had abandoned responsibility for funding such non-essentials as seasonal decorations. Even the city of Canterbury, a twenty-minute drive away and the seat of Anglican Christianity, was now starved of Christmas

14

lights to celebrate the Nativity. But Whitstable's shopkeepers had characteristically risen to a challenge and used a final one-off municipal payment to provide a budget host of illuminated angels; the latter hovered above the main thoroughfare, heads bowed and hands clasped in prayer, seemingly the only figures in the busy High Street to be reflecting on the true meaning of Christmas.

Carollers' voices grew louder as Pearl crossed the road, but none belonged to members of the church choir who would gather in a few days' time around the dressed tree on St Alfred's front lawn. Nor were they the voices of churchgoers who would assemble on Christmas Eve for Midnight Mass. Instead, Pearl noticed that a bunch of enterprising kids had parked themselves at the front of the Playhouse, a school beret on the pavement as they busked their own casual rendition of 'Silent Night'.

The plaintive lyrics found their way straight to Pearl's heart, reminding her of other Christmases from her childhood as well as memories she would always treasure of her own child's wonder at a Christmas morning. It seemed impossible to believe that nearly two decades had passed since Charlie's birth, but soon – in a few days' time – he would be returning home from a working holiday in Berlin, part of his gap year from university. Pearl had yet to buy her son's Christmas present, torn between splashing out on a much-needed winter jacket or a piece of technology. She suspected Charlie would sooner put up with the cold than be frozen out by the shame of not having access to the latest apps.

These last days before Christmas were always a fraught period before the part of the holiday season that Pearl enjoyed most – preparing and providing an unforgettable Christmas lunch. Once the home-made pudding and brandy butter was eaten, the table cleared and the usual tipsy game of charades played, a spell of wonderful idleness always followed, punctuated by welcome parties, bracing beach walks and evenings spent lounging before a roaring fire with a drink in one hand, a good book in the other and sufficient time to read it. At least, that was the plan.

The dream vanished as the rope fixed to the old union flag on the church tower whipped suddenly against its pole in the bitter wind, sounding much like the loose halyards which clanked interminably against the masts of sailboats on a blustery day down at the beach. The sound also marked the end of the carol – 'sleep in heavenly peace' – and Pearl took out the post from her bag and checked the envelopes to make sure that each was stamped and sealed.

Many contained business cheques payable to her suppliers. Others held charity donations and a number of calendars featuring striking photographs of The Whitstable Pearl taken in the height of summer when there had been queues of tourists at the seafood bar, sporting T-shirts, shorts and suntans. The summer now seemed an age ago and the envelopes in Pearl's hand contained, for the most part, Christmas cards she had written to friends, family and valued customers. While it seemed that electronic greetings were becoming increasingly popular, to her mind the old-fashioned Christmas card remained a potent force. Bridging time and distance, its arrival offered welcome reassurance that established relationships remained in place, while signalling to more casual acquaintances that we still exist and might yet meet again.

Reflecting on this, Pearl checked the final envelope in her hand and dropped it into the postbox. It was stamped and clearly addressed to the man who had occupied her thoughts for the past four months – Detective Chief Inspector Mike McGuire of Canterbury CID.

Chapter Two

Wednesday 15 December, 9.15 a.m.

'Trust me, Pearl. At this time of year, just forget all about being a private detective and stick to being a restaurateur.'

The advice came from Pearl's neighbour, Nathan, delivered in the soft mid-Atlantic accent he had acquired during the twenty years he had lived in Whitstable; however, there was a certain tension to his voice and Pearl knew the reason why. She looked down at the Christmas card in her hand, noting instantly that it was the kind of shoddy card that usually came in a cheap boxed set. Its front cover featured a cheeky robin perched on a garden shovel in a snowy landscape that was scattered with glitter. The message inside was short and sweet, consisting of four simple words cut out from newsprint. "'You have...'" she broke off for a moment "'...no style?'" She frowned up at Nathan, puzzled.

'There's no question mark, sweetie. It's a statement.' His voice sounded slightly more Californian now, as it always did when he was trying to control his temper.

'But hardly an accurate one.' Pearl took a moment to study Nathan as he sat across the kitchen table from her. He was wearing a baby-blue cashmere sweater, slightly lighter in shade than his open-necked shirt collar. His linen trousers were not creased, but rather perfectly crumpled, and his brown leather boots remained pristine in spite of the weather. His designer stubble was peppered with grey but his thick, cropped hair remained a rich warm brown. For a man of forty-two, Nathan was fit and youthful-looking, his taut physique honed by regular visits to the gym. He was perfectly groomed – as ever.

'You have buckets of style,' she announced.

'You bet I have,' Nathan agreed. 'So why on earth would somebody send me this?'

But before Pearl could reply, he quickly ordered, 'Don't answer that!' He snatched the card from Pearl's hand. 'I shouldn't even have shown this to you. I don't want you trying to solve mysteries when you should be getting ready for Charlie coming home. I'm sorry I ever bothered you with it.'

Part of Pearl was wishing the same, but now she felt conflicted. In the past six months, since

18

Nolan's Detective Agency had been operating, she was proud of having solved a string of cases – including a murder. At this time of year, she may not have been in a hurry to burden herself with another case – even one whose successful outcome might help to assuage Nathan's injured pride – but nonetheless, mysteries were for solving not ignoring.

'It's probably just someone's idea of a joke,' Nathan said, although Pearl could see that he was cut to the quick.

'I suppose it could have been worse,' she suggested.

Nathan looked up sharply. 'How?'

'A homophobic message?'

'*That* I could cope with – but this?' Nathan looked down at the card again, his brow beginning to furrow.

Feeling torn, Pearl glanced at the clock on her kitchen wall and downed the last of her coffee. 'I'm really sorry, Nathan, but I have to get off to the restaurant.'

'Of course you do,' he said, coming out of his reverie. 'And I have my article to write.'

'Article?'

'The one I should have handed in last week to that women's online mag – about New Year's resolutions?'

'I thought you'd finished that.'

'Haven't even started, sweetie. I seem to have a mental block. Perhaps my own New Year's resolution should be never to write about them.'

Pearl smiled. 'So why did you take it on?'

'Why else? Christmas comes but once a year

19

but when it does, it costs a small fortune.'

'Yes,' Pearl sighed. 'And I haven't even dressed my tree.'

'So I see.' He gazed at the tall blue fir which stood only half-adorned by the window in the living room. 'It looks a total mess,' he said in all honesty. Nathan was a proponent of the unvarnished opinion, especially with Pearl whom he considered to be worthy of the truth. Having begun his working life as a talented advertising copywriter in Los Angeles, he had soon tired of using his best ideas for commercial hyperbole and instead he had taken up freelance journalism, contributing articles to magazines on varied subjects that included interior design, food and his greatest passion – film.

Pearl stared across at her Christmas tree. 'I haven't even been able to get the lights to work.'

'Tried tightening the bulbs?'

'Of course.

'Then you'll have to buy some new ones.'

'They *are* new.'

Nathan sympathised. 'Christmas is sent to try us. Come over after you've finished at the restaurant and I'll soothe you with Rioja.'

'I wish I could,' Pearl turned to him. 'But I have to meet Diana to go through my accounts. I've been putting her off for weeks.'

'I don't blame you. The woman's a dragon.' Nathan fell suddenly silent. Then he picked up the card again and frowned. 'Think she meant my home?'

'Who?'

'The woman who sent me this.'

'And what makes you think it was a woman?'

'No man would ever be so bitchy.'

Pearl offered a knowing look. 'No?'

'No,' said Nathan firmly. 'I certainly don't know a single gay man who would ever choose something so tacky.' He tossed the card onto the table and immediately wiped his hands with a paper napkin as though it was possible to catch bad taste simply by touching it.

Amused by this, Pearl ferried their empty cups to the sink, recognising that as Nathan spent so much of his time away, either working or visiting friends in Europe and the States, it was a real treat to have him home again in Whitstable – especially since she was missing her son, Charlie.

'Forget about the card and come over on Friday,' she said suddenly. 'There's a charity fundraiser at St Alfred's. You can help me chop fruit for the mulled wine.'

Nathan raised an arched eyebrow. 'Ah, but can I be trusted to do it with *style?*' He gave in to Pearl's warm smile and finally agreed. 'OK. When d'you want me?' Taking his navy-blue corduroy jacket from the back of his chair, he got to his feet.

'I'll let you know,' Pearl said as she picked up his scarf. 'I've promised to do some mince pies as well, so I'll get them out of the way first.'

Nathan allowed her to coil the scarf carefully around his neck. 'You take on too much, you know that, sweetie?'

'I know when to say no.'

'Good.' He looked pointedly down at the Christmas card still lying on the kitchen table. 'So, no more cases for you until after Christmas.' He leaned in and planted a kiss on Pearl's cheek. 'See you Friday.' He smiled and gave her a wink before disappearing out of the back door.

Pearl watched Nathan's tall frame disappearing past her kitchen windows which looked straight out on to her garden and beyond that, to the sea, but it was an unwelcome view this morning with the slate-grey estuary waters blending seamlessly into a dull sky. She glanced back down at the kitchen table and picked up not the card, but the envelope lying beside it, which bore a strange stamp. Without her glasses, it looked much like a fleur-de-lis, but before she could give it more thought, her phone rang and she picked up the receiver, listening for just a moment before she interrupted the caller mid-flow.

'Hold on. Can you say that again? And a little slower this time?'

As the caller continued, Pearl found herself looking down at the envelope in her hand. 'You don't say,' she mused thoughtfully.

That afternoon, Pearl was in her restaurant, play-ing hostess to an office Christmas party which consisted of staff from a local estate agents. These days, almost every other High Street premises seemed to house a new estate agent, prospering from the high demand for characterful homes by the sea and within only an hour's drive of south-east London. Increasingly, more DFLs were com-ing to settle on this part of the North Kent coast, and some of the estate agents' profits were ending up in The Whitstable Pearl, where those present today had sunk considerably more in wine than they had eaten in food.

From the counter Pearl surveyed her little culinary empire: strings of cherry-red fairy lights draped around the paintings which lined the restaurant's walls. Pearl was known to host the odd exhibition for a hungry if talented local artist, but mainly the restaurant was an informal gallery for the work of her son, Charlie, and her mother, Dolly. Charlie's efforts were bold, striking and graphic while Dolly's remained as always an eccentric collection of seascapes featuring various items of *objets trouvés* such as driftwood and dried seaweed.

Pearl usually turned to Charlie for design advice about the restaurant, though she always reserved the final right of approval. It was a sign of her own individualism not to match the sleek minimalist lines of other Harbour Street eateries but instead to provide an example of Whitstable's own idiosyncratic nature – particularly with Dolly's quirky work.

There were some grand restaurants down on the beach but The Whitstable Pearl remained a small but precious gem, full of charm and with a reputation for providing some of the best seafood in town. Fresh oysters, crab, shrimps and prawns were always available at the bar but Pearl also offered a selection of signature dishes in the restaurant, ranging in the summer from marinated *sashimi* of tuna, mackerel and wild salmon, to a year-round menu of squid encased in a light chilli tempura batter and sautéed scallop dotted with ginger and breadcrumb.

The Whitstable Pearl's reputation was for simple

dishes created with the finest ingredients, each course having been perfected over time – which meant that while Pearl's presence wasn't always needed at the restaurant, the quality of her food remained constant and guaranteed a steady if not growing trade. A small but trusted group of employees were treated like an extension of her family. Ruby, a once troubled teenager, had been taken under Pearl's wing to settle down as a fine waitress. Ahmed, a young Moroccan student, provided trusted help in the kitchen while Dolly's extrovert nature lent itself to most front-of-house roles, including giving restaurant recommendations to customers in spite of her innate dislike of oysters.

The business had supported Pearl while she had brought up her son as a single parent, but old ambitions had reawakened once Charlie had disappeared off to university in Canterbury, convincing her that it was high time for a new challenge. Starting up Nolan's Detective Agency had offered a fresh opportunity to use the police training Pearl had chosen to abandon on discovering she was pregnant with Charlie, and to demonstrate the detective skills she always felt she possessed. To some extent, Dolly believed that Pearl had put her life on hold for her son, eschewing many opportunities, even for romance, but Pearl had never given up on the idea of finding the right partner – she had simply found nothing among the sparks of a few short-lived liaisons to match the white heat of her first love for Charlie's father, Carl. That is, not until she had found herself pitted against a Canterbury police detective during a murder investigation last summer. For a time, Pearl had allowed herself to think that something might come of the relationship, but as summer had faded into autumn, the days had grown shorter and the memories had begun to fade of Detective Chief Inspector Mike McGuire. Almost, but not quite – as McGuire's absence had only served to pique Pearl's interest.

Now, a new season had begun, prompting Dolly to make her annual sortie to the local village green at Duncan Down, returning with ample supplies of twigs and foliage which she had fashioned into displays on each of Pearl's marble restaurant tables. In place of a Christmas tree, a striking arrangement of dogwood – spray-painted white and adorned with Dolly's favourite glass baubles collected over the years – took pride of place near the seafood counter. Dolly had a knack of making something beautiful out of nothing and had always been a natural recycler, long before it had become a 'green' responsibility. While Pearl appreciated her mother's creative talent, she herself preferred to look deeper, beyond the surface of things and people, to what lay beneath. If Dolly acted as the eyes of the town, Pearl represented its X-ray specs.

'Four cards, you say?' asked Dolly, entering from the kitchen to resume a conversation with her daughter as she settled clean oyster plates on a shelf behind the counter.

Pearl nodded. 'Yes. They all arrived today so they must have been sent in a batch.'

Dolly frowned. 'Who else got one – apart from Nathan?'

'Jimmy from the Leather Bottle and Charmaine

from the salon.'

At this, Dolly seemed instantly curious and leaned closer. 'And what did hers have to say?'

Pearl clammed up, recognising that her mother was showing far too much interest to deserve the full details. 'That would be breaching client confidentiality,' she said in a clipped manner, trying to close down the conversation.

'Don't tell me you're going to investigate,' said Dolly. 'You've got enough on your plate with this place and Christmas and Charlie coming home...'

'I know,' said Pearl, quickly adding: 'I haven't actually agreed to take the case on.'

'Then you can tell me what Charmaine's card said,' Dolly wheedled artfully.

Pearl recognised that she was trapped. 'Let's just say, it was an unwarranted comment.'

'But not unfounded?' asked Dolly with a knowing smile.

Pearl eyed her mother, who continued: 'Well, if you really wanted to upset someone, you'd put an element of truth in there somewhere, wouldn't you?'

Dolly was right, her daughter realised. Nathan's card had found its mark, as had every other incisive message for the recipients – but Charmaine's card was the most cryptic: *Look sideways at others and you will never go forward*, it had stated.

Dolly now asked a question that threw new light on the subject. 'Something about her boob job, was it?'

'What?' asked Pearl, coming out of her reverie.

'Well, don't say you haven't noticed. Charmaine's like the prow of a ship these days. That new bust of hers rounds a corner before she does. I'll bet there's not much of her that hasn't seen the knife.'

It was true that Charmaine Hillcroft had long been addicted to the cult of celebrity – and all that went with it – including a bit of cosmetic surgery. Pearl had always believed Charmaine to be somewhere in her late forties, but it was quite possible that she might be at least a decade older. Her beauty salon, Whitstabelle, was piled high with magazines about showbusiness. What the stars had, Charmaine had to have, even if this subjected her to what was known in Hollywood as a little 'work'.

'What about Jimmy?' asked Dolly.

Jimmy Herbert, the landlord of the Leather Bottle pub in Middle Wall, was a genial man who spent much of his time, since his marriage three years ago to Valerie, not pulling pints but supping them. Having relinquished nearly all responsibility for his business, he now sat back and allowed his wife to take over the running of the pub, remaining content to simply watch the large flatscreen TV in the saloon while feeding a veritable barrel of a tummy with unending supplies of bar snacks and beer. Val, as she preferred to be known, was a whippet-thin woman with a honey-coloured crop of hair, who spoiled and nagged her husband in equal measure, always taking control but forever complaining how overworked she was. In fact, it was Val who had contacted Pearl, outraged that the cheap Christmas card that had arrived for her husband had contained the words *Lazy slob* – even though these were words she had used to describe

Jimmy herself.

'Spiteful,' Pearl said thoughtfully.

Dolly mused on this before asking, 'And the last? You said there were four altogether: Nathan, Charmaine, Jimmy – and who else?'

Pearl looked across at the group of estate agents, presided over by the owner of Castle Estates. Adam Castle was topping up his own glass with champagne as his young employees stared on in admiration or merely gratitude for their substantial Christmas bonuses. Adam was a year younger than Pearl but several times wealthier due to a booming trade and a competitive spirit that had been evident since the time he and Pearl had attended school together. Adam had never excelled academically but had proved himself to be a keen sportsman and athlete who had developed a taste for winning and still took pride in doing so. His flyers and advertisements in the local press always included the personal touch of a photograph of himself, posed in a smart jacket and open-necked white shirt, not unlike a young Tony Blair, with a wide smile and an eager faun-like expression. The photograph was pleasant but there was something about the man in person that Pearl found unattractive: a vague agitation and impatience in the way that he often spoke over others as though he was either in too much of a hurry, or far too important, ever to listen properly to anyone else. In Adam Castle's world, time was money – and though he wasn't short of the latter he could always do with more of the former to increase his commission.

Pearl handed Dolly a card from her bag. Glitter

fell onto the counter as Pearl's mother eyed the snowman on the front and the message, spelled out in newsprint, inside.

'The love of money is the root of all evil,' she read aloud softly. Looking up, she saw that Pearl's attention was still fixed on Adam, who appeared to be holding the full attention of his adoring young staff as he relayed an anecdote. Dolly huffed. 'I'm surprised he was concerned enough even to mention this,' she remarked.

Pearl took the card from her. 'Well, any concerns he might have had seemed to vanish when he learned he wasn't the only person to have received one.'

A sudden burst of laughter went up as the estate agents responded to the punchline of Adam's story. For a moment, his eyes met Pearl's across the restaurant, as he became aware that he might be the subject of her conversation. But his wide Cheshire cat grin soon replaced any sign of anxiety and he raised his glass as though to toast Pearl before taking another sip of champagne and turning his attention to the attractive young girl who sat beside him.

'Any idea who could be sending them?' asked Dolly, nodding towards the card Pearl was replacing in her bag.

'No,' Pearl said honestly, though she was becoming increasingly curious about the identity of the person who had cut out so many newsprint messages and posted them all around town. At that moment, the door opened and Pearl saw two familiar figures enter the restaurant. Pearl's young waitress, Ruby, immediately showed the couple to a table and the man looked across and acknowledged Pearl as he waited for his wife to take her seat. 'I'll be right back,' Pearl told her mother.

Clasping two menus, Pearl hurried across to her new customers, neither of whom looked to be in the best of spirits, though Dr Richard Clayson managed something of an automatic smile, perfected over the thirty years he had practised his bedside manner. Quietly spoken, Richard Clayson always managed to convey a natural gravitas, having earned a good reputation as a caring and efficient local GP – the kind of man in whom Pearl might have found it easy to confide, *if* he had been her own doctor. In fact, Richard Clayson had moved surgeries some time ago from Whitstable to the neighbouring town of Tankerton.

A tall man with an angular physique, Richard had a slightly stooped posture that gave him the appearance, from a distance, of an upright canoe. Although he was not yet fifty years old, the man appeared considerably older since his naturally dark hair had turned silver overnight a few years ago.

'Good to see you both,' Pearl said warmly. 'How are you?'

'Fine, thank you,' the doctor replied politely, though he glanced quickly at his wife as he did so, as if for confirmation. Alice Clayson gave a fragile smile before accepting a menu from Pearl.

'We came into town for a few presents,' she explained, but aware that they had no shopping with them, she offered a small shrug. 'A bite to eat here seemed preferable.'

Pearl smiled. 'Well, I'm actually going to leave

you in my mother's good hands as I have to head off to see Diana.' Alice Clayson looked up at the mention of her neighbour.

'Accounts,' said Pearl. 'It's that time of year. But I'll see you both on Friday at the fundraiser?'

'Of course,' replied Dr Clayson. 'Alice has donated one of her paintings for the raffle.' Pearl noticed how he squeezed his wife's pale hand.

'A lovely idea,' Pearl said sincerely. 'It will be a lucky person who takes that home.'

As she headed back to the counter, Dolly tutted before volunteering an unwanted opinion: 'If she turns sideways we'll never see her.' Dolly was staring across at Alice whose attention was still taken with Pearl's menu. 'She's like a wraith,' Dolly murmured. 'There's something ... Ophelia-like about her, don't you think? The painting, I mean, by Millais. Pale and otherworldly.'

Pearl took off her white apron, recognising that Dolly was right: there was indeed an ethereal quality about Alice. Dolly had a point about the painting too, except for the fact that Alice Clayson was no artist's muse but a fine water-colourist herself, whose popular classes Dolly had signed up to in the late summer.

'She's still not over him,' Dolly muttered to herself.

Pearl remained unimpressed. 'You've said that a million times.'

'You weren't there, so you can't judge,' Dolly argued testily. 'That boy was head over heels in love with Alice and anyone could see the feeling was mutual.' Pearl eyed her mother but Dolly continued unabashed. 'I'm telling you, there were

31

plenty of us in that watercolour class who picked up the vibes. I've never felt more of a gooseberry in my life.' She looked across at Alice Clayson. 'In the words of Noël Coward, she was mad about the boy.'

'Hardly a boy,' said Pearl

'He was to me,' countered Dolly. 'At twenty-seven or twenty-eight years old, he was at least ten years younger than Alice.'

Pearl observed Richard Clayson trying to engage his wife about the menu. 'If you're right,' she conceded, 'why didn't she stay with him?'

'That's something we will never know,' said Dolly. 'Maybe she needs more security than a boy could give her or maybe she just came to her senses.'

Pearl considered her mother's arguments. 'Or maybe *he* did,' she suggested. 'Since he was the one who left.'

'Yes,' agreed Dolly finally. 'And if you ask me, Alice Clayson's been pining ever since.'

Dolly returned to the kitchen and as Alice stared at the menu with doleful eyes, Pearl was forced to admit that her mother, as usual, was most probably right.

Chapter Three

Pearl sat poring over a bound booklet of figures as Diana Marshall leaned in beside her.

'No chance of that detective agency replacing your restaurant business in a hurry.' Diana's expression confirmed that this was more of a rhetorical question than a genuine enquiry.

The separate accounts that Diana had prepared for both businesses showed that The Whitstable Pearl was making a very healthy profit, while Nolan's Detective Agency was barely covering its expenses. This came as no surprise to Pearl, who knew that lately she had been too selective, or perhaps 'picky' was a better word, with the jobs that she had chosen to accept. Pearl really wasn't keen on the kind of cases that provided the bread and butter income for most private investigators, cases that would have required her to spend long evenings on stakeouts, spying on errant spouses of either sex. Certainly, the added income had never been the sole reason for starting up the agency, though at this time of year, the extra money always came in handy. Having succeeded in the roles of restaurateur and single mum, Pearl hoped that she could now find new purpose for herself following the path she had always felt, instinctively, to be hers – and if she did so before her fortieth birthday arrived in February, all the better.

Coming into contact with Detective Chief Inspector Mike McGuire had reminded her that if she had made it to his rank, she would now have plenty of other officers to take on routine surveillance tasks. McGuire had earned his status and was duly given important cases to investigate, the true mysteries that required more than mere observance of a tick-list covering method, motive and opportunity. Working closely with Mike McGuire in the summer, or as closely as he had allowed, had demonstrated to Pearl that while the detective put all his trust in procedure, she still had the clear edge on him in instinct. She had therefore chosen to wait for a suitable case to come along so that she could use that instinct to best effect.

Diana handed a coffee to Pearl. It came in a mug but Pearl noted that it was still classy – white china with a gold pattern at the rim.

'It's true that the agency could do with more cases,' Pearl said, 'so I've no plans to give up on the restaurant yet.'

Diana passed her a stylish pen which Pearl used to sign both sets of accounts. As if in celebration, six chimes rang out from an elegant clock on the mantel and Pearl looked up, taking time to admire the tall Christmas tree that stood at the side of Diana's roaring fire, in front of which her Labrador, Drummer, lay sleeping. The tree was dressed with traditional gold baubles, and tiny red velvet bows were scattered on its boughs. Diana's gifts were already bought and wrapped with ribbon, the whole image summoning up the kind of Victorian elegance which marked the accountant's style.

Diana moved to a selection of drinks on a table where a fine crystal decanter stood on a silver tray, but Pearl saw her open a new bottle beside it; the label featured what appeared to be a Dutch barge sporting dark red sails. 'Sure you won't join me?'

Pearl shook her head. 'Better stick to coffee. I have too much to do.'

Diana poured a hefty measure from the bottle into a cut-glass tumbler and against the firelight the liquid took on a warm glow. Pearl was sure the drink was Diana's usual tipple of Dutch gin, which she always referred to by its correct name of 'old Jenever'. Although Pearl was no great lover of gin, she appreciated that Jenever possessed an altogether more smooth and aromatic taste – a certain smoky flavour acquired from having been aged in wood, much like a good whisky. Different grains – barley, wheat and rye – could be used in the process, which provided very different flavours. Diana loved them all.

She raised her glass now with a smile and a suggestion. 'A couple of these might help you whiz through your Christmas chores?'

For a moment, Pearl considered the possibility of doing some late-night Christmas shopping, while powered by Diana's gin. Then she decided against it.

'Friday,' she said. 'Once I've got everything ready for the fundraiser.'

'Ah yes,' mused Diana, the glass still poised in her hand. 'I should've recognised that our vicar would be making use of your skills, or do I mean taking advantage of your generosity?'

'I volunteered,' Pearl said fairly, without elaborating on the fact that even trying to provide mulled wine would prove challenging in St Alfred's church-hall kitchen. She savoured her coffee and, for a moment, the peaceful quietude of her surroundings provided a welcome contrast to the usual hubbub of The Whitstable Pearl. Diana's home was a large gabled house situated on the southern side of Joy Lane, a long road that began at the old tollkeeper's cottage at the entrance to town. It was a unique and desirable area of Whitstable with the majority of its houses built, like Diana's, on generous-sized plots that were coming under increased pressure for redevelopment for further housing.

Homes in Joy Lane were highly sought after, particularly on the northern side where gardens backed on to a sea view. The road continued straight on towards the village of Seasalter, the link route between the two towns having existed for almost 250 years when the area had been historically associated with both smuggling and farming. Much of the land that now comprised Joy Lane had been leased by the founder of the infamous Seasalter Company which, in spite of the name, had in fact been little more than a group of smugglers making use of the nearby Parsonage Farm.

Residential development had begun between the First and Second World Wars with an eclectic mix of suburban styles, a few large Victorian-style detached villas and a pub called the Rose in Bloom. While the Claysons' home was on the northern side, enjoying a gated entrance, swimming pool and sea views, Diana's house, Grey Gables, sat on the opposite side and was altogether more colonial in style, littered with artefacts left to her by her family: a rifle, inherited from her military father, hung in the panelled hallway beside a remarkable framed photograph of a group of men in pith helmets holding what appeared to be a dead python several metres long. The house was conservative in appearance, rather like Diana herself who was never more comfortable than in twin-sets and pearls. Today, however, Pearl thought her accountant appeared rather more glamorous in a pussy-bow blouse and velvet skirt which showed a trim waist for her fifty odd years. Diana's hair was usually cut into a thick bob but now it appeared longer, more styled and perhaps a little more blonde than grey. Certainly, Pearl was given the impression that her accountant had taken herself in hand for the festive season.

'Are the family coming for Christmas?' asked Pearl. Diana had never married, but her nephew, Giles, who lived in Esher, had always been treated like a favourite son following the untimely death of his young mother from a heart condition.

'Yes,' Diana replied. 'They'll be arriving tomorrow evening for the fundraiser and staying until Boxing Day.'

'Very nice for you,' said Pearl politely, though she never understood how Diana could stomach more than an hour in the company of Giles, his wife Stephanie, and their spoiled child Nicholas, who had once unashamedly told Dolly that her old Morris Minor resembled 'a clown's car'.

'How's everything going with Giles's new business?'

'Which one?' asked Diana, as she bundled together Pearl's accounts.

'The last time I heard, he'd invested in a baby-basket company – goodies and essentials for new mothers in hospitals? Sounded like an excellent idea.'

'Sometimes you need more than just ideas,' commented Diana flatly.

'Oh?'

'The bottom fell out of his baby baskets,' she went on. 'Literally. So now he's into gyms.' This time Pearl detected some tension in Diana's tone. 'Perfectly stupid to keep throwing good money after bad.' She sipped her drink and Pearl could tell the Jenever was loosening her tongue. 'We must all keep to a budget, though I'm not sure Stephanie knows the meaning of the word.' Diana sipped her drink. 'Sooner or later, lessons must be learned.'

She paused for a moment and as though recognising that she had said too much, she quickly checked the time on her watch and setting down her empty glass, said, 'I'm sorry, my dear. I have to go across and see Richard.'

'No problem.' Pearl got to her feet. 'He was in the restaurant earlier.' She had picked up her bag before she noticed that Diana was looking at her curiously.

'With Alice?'

Pearl nodded. Diana appeared to consider this before commenting, 'Well, it's good he managed to tempt her out, I suppose.' Under Pearl's questioning gaze she said, 'Let's not beat about the bush. She's clearly not over it yet, is she?'

'Over what?' asked Pearl, expecting that Diana might mention the romance with a young man in Alice Clayson's watercolour class. However, instead she said starkly, 'The breakdown, of course. It's fairly common knowledge so I'm hardly breaching a confidence. Alice has always been a victim to her nerves.'

Pearl couldn't help reflecting on her earlier conversation with Dolly but Diana gave a small shrug. 'She's very lucky to have Richard,' she stated. 'He really is very understanding.' Diana smiled serenely but her expression suddenly clouded and she muttered, almost to herself, 'I must offer him some advice.' She failed to look at Pearl but rather seemed to be confirming this to herself as if she had just reached an important decision.

'Advice?'

As if snapping herself out of a reverie, Diana offered Pearl a brief, compensatory smile. 'Financial, of course. What else would you expect from an accountant?'

Pearl indicated her completed accounts and said sincerely, 'I'm very glad I have you to sort all this out for me, Diana. I know you haven't kept on many clients since you closed your business.'

'Nothing to it,' said Diana, shrugging off Pearl's compliments. 'It's just numbers. And they always add up if you allow them to. Take something out and you must pay it back somewhere else. A balance sheet. Rather like life.'

Pearl decided against offering her own view of finance which could be summed up neatly in her own term: 'cosmic gambling'. What Pearl had discovered long ago was that if she bowled money out to someone, especially when she could least afford it, the universe invariably batted it straight back, with interest. Before she could give an opinion, however, Drummer suddenly sprang up from the fire and began barking at the French windows as motion-activated security lighting sprung on to illuminate the garden.

'Damn!' exclaimed Diana as she followed after her dog. 'Blasted vermin again!'

Pearl joined Diana at the windows to find a large fox helping itself to some food on a large expanse of well-kept lawn. 'I put those scraps out for the birds,' she fumed. 'You don't expect foxes to come calling in the middle of the day, but that one's so bold it's a wonder it doesn't come knocking on my door.' The fox glanced up suddenly, as though it had become aware of the two women observing it. Drummer barked loudly again.

'Pretty tame, by the looks of it,' said Pearl.

'Thanks to my new neighbours,' remarked Diana through gritted teeth. 'They've been encouraging it – probably just to spite me. Here, see it off, Drummer.' She unlocked the French windows, allowing the barking dog to bound across the lawn. For a moment, the fox stood its ground as though assessing the situation, but then it took off like a bullet, chased by Drummer who failed to follow it through a hole in the shrubbery at the foot of the garden. As Pearl and Diana looked on, a man's voice could be heard at a distance.

'What's going on?'

Drummer continued to bark between bouts of tearing up the frosty earth at the exit point the fox had taken through the hedge. Diana stepped straight out onto her patio, and in spite of the cold, stormed off across her lawn, calling loudly: 'I've told you before about encouraging that filthy creature. If I see it again...'

'You'll what?' came the man's reply from the other side of the fence.

'I'll shoot the damn thing!' warned Diana, without a moment's hesitation.

For a moment there was silence before the sound of creaking wood. Pearl's gaze followed the noise to see a young man standing high on a wooden structure in the trees of the neighbouring garden. He was wearing jeans and a warm sweater over a gingham shirt. He had dark, gypsy good looks with raven hair almost to his shoulders, though his accent was rather more public schoolboy than woodsman. He stared down at Diana.

'Do that,' he said, 'and you'll deserve to go the same way.' The words had not been spoken in anger but in a calm and authoritative tone, so compelling that Drummer backed away, whimpering before joining his mistress.

Diana, however, held her ground. 'I'll see you in court, Simon,' she hissed. Turning her back on the young man, she strode back towards the house. 'You see what I have to put up with?' she said angrily to Pearl. 'Why on earth did he have to leave the house to that spoiled child?'

Light dawned on Pearl and she finally understood. Diana's house backed on to the old Grange which had belonged to Francis Sullivan, a local historian and writer who had died a little over a year ago. 'His granddaughter inherited the

41

property,' remembered Pearl.

'Bonita,' said Diana, making the most of the explosive syllable. 'And that arrogant boyfriend of hers.' She glared back at the tall trees but the figure had now disappeared.

'You're taking them to court about a fox?' Pearl frowned, confused.

'Of course not,' said Diana irritably. 'I'm planning to sue them about that monstrosity in the trees. They built it without planning permission. I could hear them working on it all summer, banging and sawing away, but I didn't have a clue what they were doing until the autumn when the leaves began to fall and finally I saw that damned tree house overlooking my own garden. I complained to the council and they've issued an order for it to come down, but enforcing it seems to be another matter. They've visited and sent numerous letters that are all ignored so I'll take matters into my own hands and sue those two for lack of privacy. They've been given enough warning – now I'm going to make them pay for spying on me.'

Diana was physically trembling with rage as the two women re-entered the house and went into the sitting room where Pearl saw that they were no longer alone. Martha Newcombe, Diana's elderly cleaning lady, had just entered, dressed in a pinafore lined with cloth holsters containing various polishes and products. Martha brandished a duster in her hand but Diana ignored her and continued with her rant. 'They're meant to be hippies, but for all the talk of peace and love they spout, they have no consideration for others at all.' She paused, slightly penitent as she turned to witness

Martha's shocked reaction. 'I'm sorry, Martha, but you know how I feel about them.'

Diana then turned her attention back towards her French windows, opening them wide as she stared down towards the foot of her garden, her face set in anger. 'Bloody eco freaks!'

With no reply forthcoming, she slammed the windows shut and stormed from the room, leaving Pearl to exchange the briefest look with Martha. Clearly embarrassed, the old lady looked down at the duster in her hand as if for a response before deciding to follow after her employer. Pearl prepared to do the same but after picking up her bag, she gazed one last time through the windows towards the bottom of the garden, where a flag was now flying in the cold wind above the branches of the old yew tree. It was the Jolly Roger.

Chapter Four

Thursday 16 December, 7.30 p.m.

'Recipe for disaster,' Dolly said. It was an unfortunate turn of phrase as she had just helped herself to a large bite of one of her daughter's mince pies. Pearl had baked over two hundred of them for the Christmas fundraiser and stopped by her mother's on her way home, after settling the pastries into the restaurant pantry. Dolly was rather partial to a mince pie so Pearl had brought several with her in return for some information.

'It'll be World War Three, you mark my words,' Dolly continued, her voice muffled by shortcut pastry as she brushed sugary crumbs from her black sweater. 'Bonita was always a handful as a toddler but she soon graduated to wild child and finally moved on to fully-fledged rebel.'

Pearl frowned. 'I can't say I remember her too well but her boyfriend seems pretty spiky. Good-looking though.'

Dolly gave a nod. 'Simon's a bit of a Heathcliff – all dark and dangerous. Comes from Wiltshire or Warwickshire, can't remember which, but I do believe they met out in France. Bonita can't be thirty yet, but she's old enough to know better. I always thought she'd been wrongly named because Bonita means "pretty" in Spanish, and it was actually her mother, Virginia, who was the beauty. She married a travel writer and they settled out in Catalonia. Virginia never got on too well with her father, but she used to bring Bonita back to visit the old boy. I remember that poor child always looked like a street urchin, plain as a pikestaff with long straight plaits the colour of dishwater.'

Dolly tutted to herself, remembering. 'They stayed for quite a while one summer. Must have been when Virginia's marriage was breaking down. I thought she might come back for good then, but by autumn she was off again, trailing Bonita along with her, as usual. They went somewhere out in the Pyrenees, I think. There was talk that the old boy wanted to put Bonita in public school – but Virginia wouldn't hear of it. She was all for Montessori and Steiner, and giving children lots of freedom to follow their instincts.'

'And what happened to her? Virginia, I mean.'

Dolly grimaced. 'Died in a car crash – must be ten years ago now. Winding cliff road. Terrible tragedy.' She heaved a sigh. 'Bonita was only young, but she stayed on out there. It was her home, after all.'

'Until now,' said Pearl.

Dolly picked up another mince pie and examined it appreciatively. 'I'd heard that Francis had left the house to her but I thought she would probably sell it. She's into animal rights, I gather. I noticed a letter from her in the local paper, protesting about the live animal exports. Good for her.' Dolly took a bite of pie and savoured it before recalling, 'Someone mentioned that she wanted to start up an animal shelter. That house has a fair amount of ground so perhaps she's going to run it from there.'

'Not if Diana has anything to do with it,' Pearl commented grimly.

Dolly finished her mince pie, wiped her lips and then suddenly looked anxious. 'What's the time?'

'Nearly seven.'

'I can't sit here eating pies!' Dolly jumped to her feet. 'I've got to meet and greet!'

'Guests for the attic?' asked Pearl, amazed that her mother still managed to get winter bookings for the little holiday flat she rented out all summer.

'Guest singular,' Dolly corrected. 'I was expecting a couple but it appears the young woman's coming alone. Maybe they split up.'

'At Christmas? Bad luck.'

'Yes,' agreed Dolly. 'But all I know for sure is that she's on the 6.40 train and was planning on getting a taxi from the station – so she should be here any minute.'

Pearl took in this news as Dolly headed out into the hallway, hurrying as, that very minute, she heard a car pulling up outside. She opened her front door to see a passenger emerging from a cab to thank the driver who began to take luggage from the boot and park it on the pavement.

Once out on the street, Pearl saw that Dolly's guest was petite with a shiny black fringe showing beneath the red beret she was wearing at a jaunty angle. Matching red gloves and a black woollen jacket over bell-bottomed trousers offered an impression to Pearl that the girl had stepped out of another era – a latterday Sally Bowles.

'You must be Dolly?' the young woman said, coming forward.

'That's me,' Dolly smiled. 'And this is my daughter, Pearl.'

'Cassandra,' announced the girl in what Pearl decided was a Yorkshire accent. 'But you can call me Cassie. Everyone does.' The girl's eyes smiled while her lips formed a crimson cupid's bow.

'Have you come far?' asked Pearl.

'Hebden Bridge. It's a market town west of Halifax.'

'And you're bang on time,' said Dolly, tapping her watch.

'Aye,' Cassie nodded. 'I was lucky the snow held off.' She looked up, but the stars were masked by the Christmas lights of Harbour Street, though the canopy of sky above the beach would be studded with them on a crisp, clear night such as this.

'Come on, I'll show you in,' said Dolly briskly,

46

keen to get back into the warm.

Cassie glanced swiftly around at the quaint, colourful facades of the shops in Harbour Street. 'So this is Whitstable,' she said to herself. 'Perfect.'

Picking up her suitcase, Cassie followed after Dolly through the separate front door to the attic flat, leaving Pearl with the thought that if the girl had just split up with her boyfriend, she certainly didn't seem to be suffering from a broken heart.

If the weather had been better, Pearl might have taken the sea route home, along the promenade from the Horsebridge to the rear of Seaspray Cottage, where a wooden gate opened on to the few steps that led down into Pearl's garden. In the summer, it was a riot of blossom, with the air filled with the heady scents of honeysuckle and lavender, but the winter months were harsh, and made worse with the cold salt-laced air, and Pearl's garden now looked sad and unappealing. A small square of lawn was bare in places and the jasmine that lined the wooden beach hut which Pearl now called an office was little more than bare twigs.

Pearl took a more direct route home along Island Wall, passing by the front windows of her neighbours' cottages to spy families huddled on the sofa together, watching Christmas ads on TV or putting up paper chains and dressing trees, for this was the season for families to come together.

At any other time in winter, curtains would be drawn at dusk, but Christmas provided an opportunity for each home to show off its festive decorations; every window now sparkled with Christmas-tree lights or Hanukkah candles, signalling a time to relax and feast. It was also a time for love and companionship to block out the cold, and for the pagan symbols of evergreens such as mistletoe and holly to serve as a reminder that spring would follow in due course.

Pearl, however, was more than aware that her own home still lacked the seasonal glow of friends and family. Partly this was due to her own lack of preparation because Christmas seemed to have caught her off-guard this year. Her own cottage window was still bare of decorations, reinforcing her sense of trailing behind the festivities. Nevertheless she was determined to get back on track and extend her usual invitations for a small drinks party at Seaspray Cottage on Christmas Eve.

Reaching her front door, as Pearl took her keys from her bag, she became aware of footsteps behind her. Turning, she wondered if she could be dreaming, for Detective Chief Inspector Mike McGuire was standing before her, looking different from the image she had kept of him in her mind's eye. Though his Viking good looks remained in place and his blond hair was still cut short at the sides, exposing his high cheekbones, his summer suntan had vanished and he wore a heavy grey jacket with the collar turned up against the cold. A glance across the street to where his car was parked told Pearl she wasn't imagining him.

'Am I in trouble or is this a social call?' she asked.

McGuire offered a small smile as though stalling for a suitable response. 'I just happened to be passing,' he explained. 'Thought I'd stop and say thanks for the card.' Taking a step closer, he blew into his hands. 'Any chance we could get out of this cold?'

Pearl remembered the keys in her hand and immediately opened her front door. Entering to switch on the light, she saw that she was standing on some mail that lay strewn on the carpet by the door. It was McGuire who bent to pick up the envelopes which he handed to her. As he did so, he held her gaze.

'You're looking well.'

'Am I?' Pearl asked, recognising that McGuire had chosen his words carefully: he hadn't exactly offered her a compliment but it was on the way to one. Setting the envelopes on a table she took off her coat and hat, noticing that McGuire was staring at her.

'What is it?'

'Your hair,' he began. 'It's so much longer.'

She smiled. 'It's been months since you were here, McGuire. I'd begun to think you might have taken that transfer back to London, after all.'

'Not quite,' he replied. 'But I've been there for much of the time. A long court case,' he added. 'It's only just ended.'

'Right verdict?'

He shrugged. 'Can't win 'em all.'

'Coffee?' Pearl suggested with a smile.

'Beer if you have one.'

As she headed into the kitchen McGuire surveyed Pearl's Christmas tree, surrounded by a few unwrapped presents: some perfumed candles and boxed toiletries.

'How's Charlie?' he asked, joining her in the

49

kitchen as she plucked a bottle-opener from a drawer.

'He's been in Berlin since September, helping a friend with some designs for a T-shirt company.'

'But he keeps in touch?'

'Not as much as I'd like. He's managed to lose his mobile phone,' she said ruefully, 'and he should have been home by now but he came down with a bad dose of flu and wasn't well enough to fly.'

'Better now?'

'Apart from bronchitis. He didn't tell me until the last moment because he didn't want to worry me.' She paused. 'I managed to get him a flight on Christmas Eve. It's cost a small fortune and he won't get in until ten at night.'

'But it'll be worth it.'

Pearl softened. 'Of course. But I wish he'd take better care of himself.'

'I'm sure you'll do that for him over Christmas,' said McGuire knowingly.

Pearl felt cheered by the thought. 'He's kept on his flat in Canterbury and with a bit of luck he'll be starting a new Graphics course next September.'

'So maybe I'll see him around,' said McGuire. 'I've just moved into a little place in Best Lane.'

Pearl looked up. 'By the river?'

McGuire gave a quick nod.

'Nice.' Pearl handed him a beer. McGuire checked the bottle's label and saw that it was his favourite – oyster stout. He took a sip, savouring the moment and remembering another time on the beach right outside when the wind was stilled and he had felt warmed by Pearl's presence. He gestured at the bottle. 'I've yet to find this in Canterbury.'

'Plenty here in Whitstable,' said Pearl. 'A good enough reason to return?'

Looking at her, McGuire agreed. 'For sure.' He took another sip and noticed the many notelets pinned to Pearl's kitchen shelves, handwritten aides-memoires, reminding her about mince pies and mulled wine. As though reading his mind, she suddenly asked, 'What are your plans for Christmas?'

'I'll be working,' said McGuire, failing to explain that as Christmas was the time he found most difficult since Donna's death, he always volunteered for duty. Looking back at Pearl he saw she was now squeezing lemon juice across some plump green olives and felt vaguely uncomfortable at the thought that he was taking up her time. 'Look, maybe I should've called first...'

'You still have my number?' She looked up at him expectantly.

'Somewhere,' he replied, his voice soft.

'Good.' Pearl handed him the olives. 'Because I wanted to stay in touch.'

McGuire said nothing, taken aback by her honesty.

She leaned closer. 'I may need help with a case some time.'

'So you're still playing detective?'

Piqued by his wry smile, Pearl replied pointedly, 'Not "playing". In fact, I was contacted by no fewer than five potential clients just today.' She put an olive to her lips and scraped its flesh against her teeth, savouring the taste. 'Mmm. These are Sicilian. Try one.'

McGuire finally did so. *'Five* clients?'

'Poison-pen messages,' Pearl explained. Picking up Nathan's Christmas card she handed it to McGuire. 'What d'you think?'

McGuire gave the card a cursory glance then looked again at Pearl, unsure if she was toying with him. 'Someone's weird sense of humour?'

'Perhaps. But using newsprint like that adds a touch of the macabre, don't you think?'

McGuire considered the card once again and resorted to procedure. 'Whoever received this should contact the police...'

'And you'll investigate?' Pearl said quickly. 'I ask because as much as I'd like to find out who's been sending these, I'm not sure I can take on a case right now.'

'The details will be logged,' McGuire told her.

'And forgotten?' suggested Pearl, imagining how a string of city crimes would easily take precedence over some spiteful messages sent to a handful of people in a small backwater town. She looked from McGuire to the card then strolled back into the living room to consider her half-dressed Christmas tree. 'Nathan was right.'

'Nathan?' asked McGuire.

'A friend of mine,' Pearl said. 'There's so much to do with Charlie coming home, I haven't even managed to get these lights working yet.'

McGuire followed her gaze to the tree. 'Have you checked the fuse?'

'Checked everything.'

McGuire set his beer down and began tightening each tiny bulb.

Pearl shook her head. 'Look, I've already tried that.'

'Try again.'

'But...'

Seeing McGuire's determination, Pearl gave up protesting and followed the detective's example. 'Perhaps I should have gone for the LED ones,' she eyed McGuire as he worked deftly, careful not to miss a single bulb. 'The thing is,' she continued, 'they're such a cold light whereas these...' she trailed off as she became aware that she was now standing very close to McGuire. He looked back at her and for a moment remained happily trapped in the gaze of her moonstone eyes.

'Yes?' he asked softly.

'These are...' But before Pearl could finish, the lights suddenly sprang on and began to flash a sequence. 'Golden,' she said in awe. 'How did you *do* that?'

'Joint effort. You know what they say? Many hands make light work.' McGuire picked up his beer and took another blissful sip.

Pearl observed him before asking, 'Why did you stop by tonight, McGuire?'

'I told you. I was passing.'

'So you said.'

He looked back at her. 'Look, Pearl, I...'

'What?'

'I ... suppose you're busy tomorrow night?'

'Very.'

McGuire covered his disappointment and picked up his beer.

'Why?' she asked.

McGuire shrugged. 'It doesn't matter. I'd better get off.' He started for the door.

'Wait.'

As he turned back, Pearl told him: 'I'm actually "busy" helping with a fundraiser at the local church tomorrow. It's for a hospice. A good cause. So if you happen to be passing again...?'

McGuire said nothing but waited for Pearl to continue.

'You could come along,' she suggested.

McGuire hesitated for only a moment. 'Time?'

'Seven.'

The detective toyed with Pearl by pretending to consider this, but finally he smiled and said, 'See you there.'

Pearl continued to stare at the door for some moments after it had closed on him. She listened to his car start up and head off into the night before she picked up the empty bottle of oyster stout and looked back at the flashing lights of her Christmas tree, recognising how the detective's arrival back in her life had lit up her spirits too.

Chapter Five

Friday 17 December, 4 p.m.

'So you told this detective about the poison-pen cards?'

'Be careful,' warned Pearl. Nathan was seated with her at the kitchen table, paying far too little attention to the way he was chopping apples for mulled wine, using one of her sharpest knives.

'And he's going to investigate?' Nathan continued, chopping more carefully.

'He didn't exactly *say* that.'

'Then why was he here?'

'I told you, he was...' Pearl waited a moment. '...just passing.'

Nathan noted something of Pearl's wistful mood and shot her a sidelong glance, pointing the tip of his knife towards her as he asked, 'Is this by any chance the same detective you were involved with last summer?'

Pearl turned his knife away from her. 'We were not "involved".'

'In the murder case,' Nathan clarified. He eyed her now with some suspicion. 'Methinks this lady doth protest too much.'

Pearl picked up her own knife. 'Will you please just concentrate on what you're doing?'

For a few moments, Nathan chopped obediently but after a pause, curiosity got the better of him. 'So what's he like?'

'To be perfectly honest...' Pearl sighed, shaking her head. 'I don't know.'

Nathan took this to be a sign of Pearl choosing to clam up, but she surprised him suddenly by admitting: 'Actually he can be very annoying. Rude and positively dismissive.'

'Of you?' asked Nathan, taken aback.

'Of my detective agency.'

'Ouch.'

'Other than that, I really know very little about him,' she realised. 'He likes to play his cards close to his chest.'

'Hmm. A dark horse? Intriguing.'

'You can judge for yourself later because I've invited him along tonight.'

Nathan frowned. 'To a church fundraiser?' He gave Pearl an admonishing look. 'It's hardly a hot date, is it, sweetie? Or is he likely to get carried away with the tombola?'

Pearl was about to protest when the doorbell suddenly rang. For a moment it occurred to her that it might be another impromptu visit from McGuire so she took off her apron and tidied her hair a little before heading off to the living room. Once there, she detected a familiar silhouette framed against the glass panel of her front door – not McGuire but Phyllis Rusk. Phyllis was a well-known character in town, a herbalist who owned a health-food shop in the High Street. She had fine platinum-coloured hair that was always haloed around her head like a dandelion. A pretty woman, she was also larger than life – literally – and usually jovial, though as Pearl opened the front door, Phyllis turned to face her with sad eyes and chins a-quiver.

'I'm sorry but I need to talk to you, Pearl,' she said urgently, grabbing a tissue from her pocket and dabbing her eyes.

'Come in,' said Pearl immediately, opening the door very much wider to allow her unexpected guest inside. Phyllis was wearing a pink fake fur coat which made her appear even larger. It sported pom-poms and reinforced the memories Pearl always found hard to shake off of Phyllis as an out-sized child. At six years old, Pearl had envied Phyllis's dimpled knuckles but not the way she had found sports lessons so challenging. The girl had been heavily dependent on an asthma inhaler, puffing her way through primary school and college until finally, in her twenties, having embarked on a course in herbalism, she had managed to overcome her allergies with the aid of various natural remedies. The same could not be said of her weight, and a GP would surely have considered Phyllis to be medically obese. Her hands trembled as she pulled off her mittens and delved for something in her handbag.

'How could anybody be so cruel, Pearl?'

At that very moment, Nathan popped his head around the kitchen door and saw Phyllis pluck a card from her bag which she handed to Pearl. It showed a sleigh, drawn by reindeer, carrying Santa Claus across a range of glitter-strewn rooftops. Pearl braced herself before she opened it and read the two words inside that had been cut from newsprint. *Greedy Pig.*

Phyllis's face instantly crumpled before she

57

wailed, in tears, tumbling into Pearl's arms like a giant marshmallow. Across Phyllis's shoulder, Pearl exchanged a helpless look with Nathan.

An hour later, after much tea and sympathy, not to mention a few mince pies, Pearl had managed to comfort Phyllis sufficiently to get her back home. Nathan had driven her, the pair forming an odd couple in Nathan's vintage Volkswagen, looking a little like Noddy and Big Ears. Phyllis's card now sat beside Nathan's on Pearl's kitchen table, and the joke, if ever it had been one, seemed to be wearing thin. The mystery was compounding but still Pearl found herself with little time to give it proper thought since the fundraiser was due to take place in only a few hours.

With her cooking completed, Pearl took down several notes from her kitchen shelf and recognised that she was on her way to finishing most of her tasks for the evening's event. There was gravadlax on rye bread with sour cream and caper berries, and a vegan option of courgette noodles which she imagined Bonita Sullivan and Simon might welcome.

In contrast, Diana Marshall was an unashamed carnivore – and a good markswoman who lived up to her name as the Roman Goddess of the Hunt by shooting rabbit, pheasant, woodcock and snipe – as well as enjoying some fishing too.

If ever Francis Sullivan had wanted to set a cat amongst the pigeons, he had done so by leaving his property to his granddaughter – a young woman clearly at odds with her neighbour and destined to remain so. Reflecting on this, Pearl set the last of her chopped fruit in the fridge and headed upstairs for a shower.

With a few welcome moments to herself, Pearl considered the recipients of the cards: there was no clear connection apart from the fact that they were all local people and would therefore be known to one another to some degree. An estate agent, a herbalist, a publican, a beautician and a writer. No obvious links at all. The whole thing gnawed but Pearl tried not to think of it as she prepared for the evening ahead.

After a hot shower, she wrapped herself in a large fluffy white bath towel and padded wet footprints on to the thick bedroom carpet as she pulled out from her wardrobe a slinky red crushed-velvet dress which she decided was suitably festive for the evening's occasion. Lying on the bed for a moment, she glanced towards the window. Outside, white-capped waves were blowing up on the northerly wind, and a scattering of navigation lights glowed like rubies and emeralds on the dark sea. Pearl closed her eyes, hearing only the sound of the breakers rolling onto the pebbled shore outside…

It wasn't long before the sound of the waves merged with that of footsteps approaching on the beach and she saw McGuire standing at the tide's edge, wearing a white shirt and blue jeans, his fair hair slicked back off his face, his blue eyes reflecting the colour of the sea on a fine day. He said nothing but gave the faintest of smiles before his hand moved forward to frame Pearl's face. 'Merry Christmas,' he said gently, before he leaned in to kiss her

At that very moment, McGuire's mobile suddenly rang, loudly and fiercely, puncturing the magic of the moment. Pearl opened her eyes but McGuire disappeared from view as she realised it was her own bedside phone that was ringing. Still half-asleep, she picked up the receiver and heard Dolly's voice on the other end of the line. 'Pearl?'

'What is it?' she asked sleepily.

'Why aren't you here? It's almost six thirty.'

Pearl reacted quickly, her heart pounding like the waves on the shore. Springing to her feet, she grabbed the red dress from the coverlet of her bed. 'Set the mince pies on the table,' she commanded, 'and tell the vicar I'm on my way.'

Chapter Six

Friday 17 December, 7 p.m.

St Alfred's church hall was a large space with a stage at its far end on which many a panto and concert performance had been given. It served as a local community venue and flourished with the same spirit: even the plush burgundy curtains that fell either side of the stage had been run up by a team of volunteers after the tired old ones had become too threadbare for use. The hall was used for a variety of activities, anything from keep fit classes and farmers' markets to badminton sessions. Pearl arrived, barely an hour after Dolly's call, to find the place had been transformed.

Walls were lined with Christmas-themed works of art contributed by children from the local primary school. Tea lights flickered on tables that were already groaning with food and donations of prizes for the evening's raffle. An enormous Christmas tree, donated by Pearl's old suitor, Marty Smith, the owner of an upmarket fruit and vegetable store called Cornucopia, had been dressed by volunteers and was now glowing with silver lights at the foot of the stage. Music played in the background – a version of Prokofiev's 'Troika', summoning visions for Pearl of a carriage dashing through snowy streets before it segued into Tchaikovsky's 'Dance of the Sugar Plum Fairy'.

Pearl made her way directly to the prize display where a watercolour by Alice Clayson took pride of place. It featured the view from West Beach, not on a hot summer's day when the area could pass for a tropical hideaway, but at early dawn when an overcast sky and low tide allowed the lonely mud flats to reflect a sense of loss and desolation. Alice had managed to create a powerful work of art from her barren subject-matter, but one which offered to Pearl a hint of tragedy about the artist herself. Alice was, after all, a talented and beautiful woman but it seemed clear she had felt some resonance with this bleak coastal scene. For a moment Pearl dwelled on this, remembering all that Dolly had told her about the young man from her summer watercolour class. Pearl now wondered if perhaps Diana had been thinking of Alice's affair when she had spoken of Richard Clayson being an 'understanding' man, but before she could properly connect the two thoughts, a voice rang out. 'Pearl!'

The Reverend Prudence Lawson was heading across to greet Pearl with the warmest of smiles. A tiny woman in her late thirties with a peach-like complexion that made her look as though she had been scrubbed, Rev Pru, as she liked to be known, always smelled of incense but wore surprisingly short skirts for both her profession and the season. Pearl always felt that Rev Pru had a compressed sense of power about her, like a charged battery. Since arriving in the parish five years ago, Whitstable's new vicar had fired the community with her enthusiasm and supported a number of charitable causes with her dynamic fundraising – rattling a few cages of the more conservative members of the community with her radical style.

'Sorry I'm late,' said Pearl quickly. 'But everything's prepared and all I have to do is mull the wine.'

'Super!' beamed Rev Pru. 'I think we have everything under control. Will you excuse me while I greet the Scouts?' She then headed off, exposing a clear view for Pearl of the stage on which a large familiar figure was stepping out from the wings, attempting to secure the wide black patent-leather belt on his scarlet Santa suit.

'How do I look?' asked Jimmy Herbert, straightening a cotton-wool beard with one hand while with the other he pulled up a red hood to hide his cropped black hair.

Pearl gave him an encouraging smile. 'You should fool the kids, Jimmy.'

The Leather Bottle's landlord accepted this

with a nod. 'Good. At the end of the day, that's what it's all about.' Jimmy took his seat by the Christmas tree and drew a large black Santa sack towards him. 'Any word yet on who sent that card?' he asked.

Pearl shook her head. ''Fraid not. But one thing I can tell you – you're not alone.'

Jimmy looked surprised.

'Five so far,' Pearl said. 'And those are just the ones I know of.'

Jimmy considered this, easing the girth of his belt. 'Well, I've been called worse than lazy in my time,' he said philosophically. 'And it really doesn't bother me as much as it does Val. It's her that's taken offence. If you ask me, it's not a good time of year to be looking sideways and suspecting neighbours, so maybe it's all best forgotten?' He jerked a thumb at a banner that hung across the stage. Decorated by local children with angels blowing gold trumpets, it bore the message: *Peace to all and goodwill to all men.*

'Yes,' agreed Pearl, accepting his well-made point. 'Perhaps you're right, Jimmy.'

A little later, the hall was buzzing with the arrival of new guests. Pearl was in the kitchen but heard families taking advantage of an early start before children's bedtimes. She was just tasting her mulled wine and adding yet another pinch of cinnamon when Martha Newcombe entered bearing a tray of used mugs which she began quickly washing up at the sink. Her presence in the kitchen might have gone unnoticed by anyone other than Pearl, who sensed that Martha's inconspicuousness might be the result of decades spent scuttling around other people's homes, industriously performing her duties as invisibly as possible.

As Martha dried her hands, Pearl stirred her mulled wine and asked, 'Would you like to try some?'

The elderly lady turned in some surprise and observed both Pearl and the pan bubbling on the gas ring, a heady aroma of herbs and spices rising from it. She quickly ducked her head like a naughty schoolgirl.

'It really isn't too strong,' Pearl reassured her. 'The heat will have burned off most of the alcohol.'

'No, thank you,' Martha replied. 'Best if I don't.'

Knowing that Martha had been a committed Christian and devout lifelong worshipper at St Alfred's, Pearl wondered whether it might be religious views which prevented the woman from trying the wine, but the elderly lady explained, 'It does things to my blood sugar and I have to be careful these days.'

She then darted out of the room, and as Pearl stared after her, Rev Pru suddenly entered. 'Is she OK?' Pearl asked.

Rev Pru glanced back towards the door. 'Martha, you mean? Yes, I think so. She wasn't too well for a time – blood pressure, I think – but she seems almost back to her usual self now, though I gather she's lost most of her cleaning jobs.'

'She still works for Diana.'

'And the Claysons, I believe. I'm always very grateful that she helps out so much here too. At one time, I was actually thinking of offering her the job of churchwarden but I think that it would be too much for her now.' Rev Pru looked inquisitively towards the large saucepan on the stove. 'Could I possibly try...?'

'Of course,' said Pearl, filling a glass and handing it to her.

Rev Pru took a sip and Pearl waited for a response. The vicar's face creased into a slow smile. 'Mmm. That's so delicious I think we'll double the price.'

The hall was now almost full to capacity. Several stalls were peddling local produce: cakes, jams and even homemade Christmas puddings, reminding Pearl that she still had so much to do for her own Christmas. Dolly was orbiting a captive audience, selling copious numbers of raffle tickets for an array of prizes which included some of her own pottery oyster platters that were used at The Whitstable Pearl.

'You Brits really know how to pull off this kind of thing, don't you?' whispered Nathan's voice in Pearl's ear.

Turning, she saw that he was dressed impeccably in a smart houndstooth check jacket and black trousers, his hair slicked back so that he looked much like an English gentleman from the 1930s. It was a style Nathan liked to adopt from time to time, such was his affection for all things British.

'Going swimmingly, eh what?' he ventured, much like Bertie Wooster.

'Looks like it,' Pearl agreed. She was looking for McGuire, but since he was still nowhere to be seen, she began to wonder if he had been caught up with work or another engagement. Taking out her mobile she saw, with a sinking heart, that there were no messages. Then someone spoke.

'Pearl?'

It wasn't McGuire but another man who stood before her. He was in his mid-forties, although the blazer he wore and his golf-club tie contributed to the style of someone much older, as did the premature thinning of his hair.

'Thought it was you,' Giles Marshall said, looking around. 'Any sign of Auntie Di?'

Pearl noted that Giles was scanning the room like a lost child, which in many ways he always seemed to be without his aunt's presence.

'She's here somewhere,' Pearl replied cagily. 'The vicar mentioned she's donated a bridge night for the raffle.'

Nathan piped up at this. 'Dashed generous of her,' he said half-mockingly, slightly ruddy from the effects of Pearl's mulled wine. Pearl gave him an admonishing look and Nathan took the hint and moved off, but at that moment, they were joined by Giles's son, Nicholas, who was eating a large chocolate cupcake. The charmless boy said nothing but simply crammed another bite of cake into his mouth as his father sipped mulled wine.

'How about you, Giles?' asked Pearl. 'Have you donated anything?'

'No,' he said, boldly and unapologetically. 'But we'll buy some raffle tickets, I expect.'

'No time like the present!' announced Dolly, popping up beside him with a book of tickets. 'How many would you like?'

As she waited expectantly, Giles patted his jacket pockets and looked around for his wife, Stephanie.

An imposing woman sporting bobbed fair hair and county-set clothes consisting of a tartan skirt, beige twinset and boots, she was eyeing Alice Clayson's watercolour on the prize table when Giles finally spotted her.

'Steph has all the loot,' he explained. 'I'll be right back!' He made a quick escape, leaving his son still standing in front of Pearl. Nicholas was at that awkward age when teenage acne had taken hold. The boy seemed to have inherited the worst physical attributes of both parents: his mother's broad hips and his father's narrow shoulders, giving him the appearance of a lead-bottomed toy. He surveyed Dolly with some fascination as she wore a white fur bolero jacket and a pair of flashing Christmas-tree earrings. 'Do you still drive a clown's car?' he asked bluntly. Pearl sensed danger as her mother's eyes narrowed but Nicholas merely took a last huge bite of his cupcake before dumping its wrapper on the table and heading off in search of his father.

Dolly stared after the teenager as she picked up the wrapper, screwing it tightly in her hand as though it might have been Nicholas himself. 'What a precocious little...' She stopped herself from delivering an expletive and instead hurled the wrapper in a litter bin. 'Only to be expected from spawn of Giles and Stephanie,' she snapped. 'How Diana puts up with them I'll never know.'

Before Pearl could comment, Dolly steamed off and Pearl stared after her until another voice sounded.

'Sorry I'm late.'

It was McGuire. Wearing a heavy dark overcoat,

he was cleanshaven and exuding more than a hint of expensive aftershave. It was clear he had made an effort.

'No problem,' Pearl said softly, pleased that he had finally arrived. 'Let me take your coat.' As McGuire shrugged it off, Pearl looked in the direction of the cloakroom to see that its entrance was obscured by a swarm of children. The local Scouts were mounting a stall offering pledges of various duties such as babysitting and dog walking, and at least a score of boys were queuing to hang up their own coats. Pearl decided to direct McGuire to the kitchen. 'This way.'

Once there, she hung up McGuire's coat on a hook by the door, noticing how the smell of Calor gas rose from the cooker, reminding her of childhood caravanning holidays. 'You made it,' she announced, relieved. 'I'll reward you with some of my mulled wine.' She moved to the saucepan which still sat on top of the cooker and McGuire observed her as she carefully poured a hefty measure of wine for him while following up with one for herself. The wine was filled with fruit and the sweet smell of cinnamon which Pearl sniffed approvingly before raising her glass to him. 'Thanks for coming.'

'Thanks for the invitation.'

For a moment Pearl felt slightly self-conscious as McGuire's glass met her own. She hadn't had time to put on any make-up apart from a slick of scarlet lipstick to match her dress, but McGuire's interest was taken with the silver locket around her neck, the one that always caused him to wonder whose image she carried with her in that heart. Pearl savoured the mulled wine, satisfied that she had achieved the perfect ratio of spice and fruit. Thinking of Nathan's words, she felt the need to explain.

'I can promise you nothing more than parochial fun and games tonight,' she said. 'The usual bout of carol singing, a raffle and a few of these.' She raised her glass again.

'You don't say.' McGuire smiled and sipped his own wine before commenting, 'You look...' he gazed at the red velvet dress that clung to her slim figure.

'Yes?' she asked expectantly.

'Very festive.'

Pearl smiled lamely, keen to hide her disappointment but before she could reply a familiar voice addressed her from the doorway.

'Am I interrupting something?' Diana Marshall had just entered, shrugging off a cashmere coat as she stared pointedly between Pearl and McGuire.

'Not at all,' replied Pearl, coolly. 'Diana, let me introduce you to Detective Inspector Mike McGuire from Canterbury CID. McGuire, this is Diana Marshall.'

McGuire smarted slightly since he was actually a Chief Inspector and felt as though he had earned the title twice over, but he offered no correction, not wanting to appear either a prig or a pedant.

'Police?' Diana frowned, not proffering her hand to shake his. 'Has there been a crime committed?'

'Of course not,' Pearl said pleasantly. 'The inspector happens to be my guest.' But Diana seemed wholly unimpressed, her mood betraying some tension which McGuire instantly picked up from her body language and the tone of her voice.

'I'd like a word in private, if I may, Pearl,' Diana continued.

Recognising that the atmosphere had curdled with her accountant's arrival, Pearl opened her mouth to respond but McGuire saved her from any apology.

'I'll go and take a look around,' he said tactfully, and left the kitchen. As she stared after McGuire's retreating figure, Pearl wished that Diana had not barged in when she had. She stood before Pearl, dressed in a chic maroon dress with festive rubies at her throat, but the shoulder bag she carried looked wholly incongruous with her outfit.

'What is it?' asked Pearl, hoping that whatever Diana had to say would be worth it.

'The subject of booze,' Diana replied. 'I hear there's only wine and cordials, so I used my initiative. Don't take it personally, but is there any chance you might have a decent glass for this?' She plucked a bottle of Jenever from her bag. Judging from its label it appeared to be the same one she had opened the night before, only now it was two thirds full. 'Should do me for the evening,' she went on.

Pearl found a highball tumbler on a shelf above the sink which she handed to Diana, who filled it. Pearl looked on as she did so. 'Would you like me to put the bottle in the fridge?' she asked.

'Sacrilege!' uttered Diana, horrified. 'Jenever is always drunk at room temperature. I'll leave it right here.' She set the bottle down on the kitchen top by the door and took a large sip from her glass.

'That's better,' she sighed, but made no attempt to move back into the hall.

'Giles and Stephanie are here,' Pearl informed her.

Diana gave a casual shrug. 'I know. But I don't think they've noticed me yet and I'd like a few minutes to myself.'

'Fine.' Increasingly frustrated by Diana's difficult manner, Pearl picked up her glass of mulled wine and made to leave. Taking another sip of Jenever, Diana smiled, slightly crookedly, giving Pearl the impression that she might well have had a few drinks before arriving – and was certainly set to have a few more.

Children from St Alfred's Primary School were just coming to the end of their rendition of 'Little Donkey' as Pearl emerged from the kitchen. The hall erupted with applause and Rev Pru mounted the stage, clapping along, while Pearl looked around for McGuire. She finally spotted him standing alone by the Christmas tree, his attention fixed on the stage as Rev Pru addressed them all. 'What a truly wonderful turnout we have for a very worthy cause,' she grinned. Pearl took this as her cue to rejoin McGuire, but no sooner had she begun to move off in his direction than a figure blocked her path.

Charmaine Hillcroft was tall and abnormally leggy in her designer diamanté high heels. Her perfect complexion was fixed and expressionless, like that of a doll – an impression further emphasised by the particularly shiny ponytail gathered high on her head. The overall impression was that almost everything about her was false.

'I hear there's been more,' she said.

'More?' echoed Pearl.

'Cards, of course.'

Pearl had realised immediately what Charmaine Hillcroft had been referring to but she had been distracted by the sight of the beautician's improbable bosom, encased in a figure-hugging sequinned top. Dolly's comment had been right: Charmaine did look much like the prow of a ship.

'There's been a whole spate of them,' Pearl informed her. 'So I don't think you should take it personally.'

'Oh, but I do,' bridled Charmaine, 'which is why I asked you to investigate.' Charmaine's speech was clipped, revealing her mood which was less angry than controlling. The slightly nasal tone to her voice was one that Pearl found as difficult to listen to as the idle chit chat that she knew always circulated in Charmaine's beauty salon – the kind of schoolgirl gossip which some women never grow out of. Charmaine herself openly revelled in having an enemy or rival in her sights, usually another woman who had attracted her envy rather than disapproval. Pearl found that for all Charmaine's glamour, there was still something ugly about her, neatly summed up by the message in her Christmas card: a general lack of satisfaction drove her constantly to look sideways in order to compare herself to others, rather than forward to follow a path of her own.

Pearl took a deep breath, reminding herself of everything that Nathan and Dolly had said. She phrased her reply very cautiously. 'Charmaine, I really would like to get to the bottom of this mystery for you, and for everyone else who has received one of these cards, but I really don't think I can begin this until after Christmas.'

Charmaine sneered, 'You mean you're just going to let them get away with it?'

'No,' countered Pearl, torn. 'I'm just asking you to wait until the New Year.'

'That's easy for you to suggest but you haven't received one. I thought you were meant to be a detective.' Charmaine looked Pearl up and down, taking in every detail of Pearl's attractive yet simple style before issuing a disdainful sniff and turning on her high heels to mince off into the crowded hall.

Pearl heaved a small sigh and looked towards McGuire, who was still sipping his mulled wine. He seemed to be listening intently to Rev Pru who was reading out a list of achievements of the local hospice which the fundraiser was intending to help. Casting an eye around, Pearl also spotted Giles Marshall engaged in conversation with Adam Castle, brought up short for a moment as she hadn't been aware the two men knew one another. It was possible they had just been introduced, but certainly not by Diana who had yet to leave the kitchen. Pearl observed the two men chatting and considered that in some ways there were similarities between them, since both were entrepreneurial and chasing material success – though it was clear to Pearl that Giles would never match Adam's achievements as his many business projects had all ended, so far, in failure.

At a young age, Giles had been packed off to a

smart public school at which he had seemed to acquire the notion that he was born to rule but, thirty years on, the sad truth was that Diana's nephew had yet to manage even to cut loose from his aunt's purse-strings. Diana had spoken in frustration about lessons having to be learned, but Pearl wasn't sure that Giles would ever learn them. Instead he seemed destined to remain what he had been for the past four decades: dependent upon Diana.

Pearl made her way across the hall and spotted Phyllis enjoying a large bite of one of Pearl's mince pies. Jimmy, still in character as Santa, was tucking into angels on horseback by the Christmas tree but Nathan appeared to have vanished – for which Pearl was quite grateful as she sidled up closely to McGuire. 'About those cards I mentioned last night,' she whispered.

'Cards?'

'The poison-pen Christmas cards,' she clarified. She frowned, clearly conflicted. Then: 'You're right. I'll tell all the recipients that they should come to you to investigate.'

McGuire wondered where Pearl's competitive spirit had vanished to, but Pearl knew it was Charmaine's reaction that had caused her to relinquish total control of the issue. 'The thing is,' she went on, 'some people are upset – and rightly so. Will you promise to give it proper attention?'

McGuire registered the sincerity behind her question. 'I promise,' he agreed.

Feeling a strange mixture of relief and disappointment, Pearl gave her own attention to Rev Pru, who was just reaching the conclusion of her speech on stage.

'...and so I have pleasure in beginning the raffle for which St Alfred's has received so many generous contributions.'

A stir of expectation went around the hall as the vicar picked up a large red box containing the raffle tickets. She looked into the audience, squinting against the footlights. 'I was thinking that it might be nice if I called upon one of our visitors to help with this.' She paused for a moment. 'Pearl?'

Pearl reacted to the mention of her name, but Rev Pru then added: 'Might I ask your friend there to select the winning numbers?'

McGuire saw that all eyes in the room were trained on him. But Rev Pru's suggestion was already generating a round of hearty applause.

'That's right, everyone,' she boomed. 'Let's give him a big hand.'

'Go on,' whispered Pearl urgently. 'No one's allowed to refuse Rev Pru.' She now joined in with her own applause, while McGuire recognised he was hostage to the vicar's expectation. He knocked back the rest of his mulled wine, handed his empty glass to Pearl and joined Rev Pru on stage.

'Thank you so much...' the vicar left a suitable gap for McGuire to fill in with his name.

'Mike,' repeated Rev Pru, confident that she had recruited the right man for the job.

Pearl was still enjoying McGuire's embarrassment as Nathan leaned in to her, and murmured, 'I'm guessing that's your "dark horse" detective?'

'Kidnapped by the vicar,' said Pearl, amused. 'Where have you been?'

'Getting some food, but the dragon lady, Diana,

75

caused me to lose my appetite. She's complaining about the cakes being too sweet.'

Pearl frowned. 'What – my mince pies?'

'Not sure. She's in a truculent mood and looks like she's half-cut already. I made an excuse to head off to the raffle prizes. Have you seen that watercolour? It's a fine piece of work.'

'Donated by Alice Clayson,' Pearl explained. 'The doctor's wife.' She nodded to where Alice stood with her husband, looking on with everyone else in the direction of Rev Pru and McGuire on the stage.

'What a sad-looking woman,' Nathan commented. 'Queen Guinevere.' His description was an accurate one, for Alice's red hair flowed loose over her shoulders, and the long purple dress she wore, with a gold chain around her hips, was reminiscent of a Pre-Raphaelite medieval style. Nathan glanced away to the raffle-prize table. 'If I don't win that watercolour,' he said, staring down at the tickets in his hand, 'I may just treat myself to some of her work for Christmas.'

Over the next fifteen minutes, McGuire acquitted himself valiantly, plucking tickets from the vicar's red box to announce the numbers. A few small prizes of chocolates and liqueurs went to grateful recipients, but there was considerable excitement after the selection of a number caused a familiar voice to ring out from the back of the hall.

'Here!' called Dolly, her legs moving like pistons as she beetled her way through the crowd and up on to the stage.

Once there she waited expectantly as the vicar opened a well-sealed gold envelope to finally read out: 'A gift voucher for three yoga sessions.'

'Superb!' exclaimed Dolly. In spite of her general dislike of all authority figures and her special nickname for McGuire of 'the Flat Foot', she found a warm smile for him. 'Thank you,' she said, both gratefully and graciously, before heading off with her token as a light flashed from somewhere near the front of the stage. Pearl noted that it was Cassie who had just snapped Dolly with her camera.

'What's *she* doing here?' asked Pearl as Dolly joined her.

'I thought she might like to come along,' said her mother innocently, studying her gift voucher before adding knowingly, 'that's surely the same reason you invited the Flat Foot?' The question was left hanging as McGuire's next efforts resulted in a bottle of French perfume for Marty Smith.

Laughter rippled around the hall as Marty held the bottle aloft. 'I'll be the best-smelling fruit and veg man in Whitstable!' he boasted. His eyes met Pearl's for a moment, both of them aware that only a few months ago, the perfume might have found its way to Pearl if Marty had not finally given up his long pursuit of her and taken up instead with a florist, Nicki Dwyer. In spite of Marty's dark good looks, he had failed to light Pearl's fire and had been astute enough to recognise a rival for her affections in McGuire. Now he shook the detective's hand and left the stage while the next prize – a donation from Pearl of a lunch for two at The Whitstable Pearl – went to estate agent, Adam Castle.

Judging from the number of tickets Adam had been checking throughout the raffle, he had clearly

77

speculated to accumulate as usual and his strategy had paid off. His secretary, Paula, hung devotedly on his arm – and every word – while Pearl also spotted her waitress, Ruby, in conversation with her new boyfriend, Dean. Pearl prized her independence but it was true that Christmas spiked a sense of expectation in which romance always played a part. It was difficult to be single at this time of year.

Looking towards McGuire, Pearl recognised that the evening thus far had presented only a series of obstacles to keep them apart.

'Only two more prizes to go now, Mike,' Rev Pru informed him as she offered him the box. McGuire chose the penultimate ticket and Rev Pru called it out boldly. 'Fourteen!' Pearl reacted instantly as the number was always her favourite choice. Charlie's birthday was 14 April.

'Here!' she called excitedly, raising the ticket high above her head before hurrying up on stage.

Rev Pru opened another gold envelope and reacted to the voucher prize inside. 'How wonderful,' she commented, increasing Pearl's expectations before revealing the surprise. 'A bespoke facial – at Whitstabelle!'

Pearl's smile remained in place but was now fixed by sheer willpower since she could see Charmaine looking on proudly from the audience as everyone applauded Pearl's apparent good fortune. The thought of having to spend her valuable time in Charmaine's salon, emerging possibly to look like its plastic owner, was not an idea Pearl welcomed. Nevertheless, she gave her thanks as she accepted both the voucher and a chaste kiss on the cheek from McGuire.

As she stepped down from the stage, Cassie's camera flashed once more. Rev Pru offered the ticket box back to McGuire. 'And now, Mike, if you wouldn't mind, we have one more prize: a superb watercolour of the view at West Beach, donated by Alice Clayson.'

Applause rippled around the hall, followed by an expectant murmur. It was clear that the final prize was of interest to many, so McGuire paused for effect before he finally plucked the ticket from the box. This time, Rev Pru nodded for McGuire himself to announce it.

'And the final winning ticket is...' he checked it in his hand, leaving a long, suspense-filled pause, 'number a hundred and twenty-two.'

Much checking of tickets followed, particularly by Nathan, who strode across to Pearl to grumble, 'Why am I so unlucky at these things?'

But Pearl failed to answer, picking up on the fact that nobody seemed to possess the ticket – until a voice finally piped up from the crowd: 'I have it.' Heads turned to observe a young couple making their way to the front of the stage.

'Well well,' breathed Dolly. 'I can hardly believe it. That's Bonita Sullivan.'

It would have been impossible to recognise Bonita from Dolly's previous description: the dishwater-coloured plaits were gone and instead a mane of blonde hair tumbled down the girl's back. There was a Scandinavian look about her high cheekbones, pale blue eyes and tall, slim figure, encased in faded blue jeans and a flowing blouse made from vintage silk scarves. Silver bangles jangled at her wrists as she handed her coat to her companion. Pearl recognised him as Simon, the young man from the altercation in Diana's garden.

Bonita mounted the steps of the stage, graceful and confident, accepting the watercolour from McGuire while Pearl experienced an unexpected pang of jealousy as he leaned forward and kissed the girl's cheek. Applause broke out and this time Cassie's camera flash popped several times as she recognised an opportunity to take various shots of the assembled guests during the highlight of the evening's entertainment.

'That's some makeover,' Dolly commented, watching Bonita descend the steps of the stage to re-join her partner. 'The proverbial ugly duckling turned swan at last.' She tutted quietly to herself in disbelief before she noticed her empty glass and moved off to get another drink. As she did so, Pearl was reminded of Diana and looked around the room, catching sight of her, standing beside Martha but looking on at Bonita, the winner of the final and most desirable prize. Diana knocked back the Jenever in her glass and went back into the kitchen to get herself what Pearl felt sure was another refill.

With the main event over, Rev Pru seemed far more relaxed as she approached Pearl with a large glass of wine in her hand. 'I honestly believe that things couldn't have gone any better,' she said. 'Thanks to your friend.' She cast a glance back to where McGuire was just now stepping down from the stage. 'Nice fellow,' she commented. 'Handsome too.' She gave a knowing smile before hastening away.

McGuire didn't get very far before his path was blocked by the rotund Scout master, Owen Davies, who was supervising the Scouts' stall. As Pearl approached, a young Cub looked up at her hopefully, indicating a large drawing on the wall showing a rough equine figure with a long broad snout and antlers. 'Pin the tail on the reindeer?' the boy asked. He was offering a piece of frayed rope while indicating a sign which gave the price of £1 a go.

'How about it?' asked McGuire. Pearl looked back at the young boy's expectant face, reminded that Charlie had been a Cub Scout for only a short while before skateboarding entered his life.

'Go on then,' she smiled, rising to the challenge. McGuire took the blindfold from the boy while Pearl slipped it on, feeling the detective's strong hands upon her shoulders as he gently turned her in a full circle before positioning her in front of the badly drawn reindeer.

'I should have taken a better look,' she protested.

'Too late now,' said McGuire. 'Use your instincts.'

Pearl did exactly that and raised her hand, trying to see in her mind's eye the drawing before her. She launched herself forward and stabbed the wall with the pin. 'How did I do?' she asked excitedly, ripping off the blindfold. Before her, and to McGuire's amusement, the reindeer's tail hung absurdly from its antlers.

'Do you think you can do any better?' challenged Pearl.

'Not sure that I can,' admitted McGuire truthfully.

He found himself smiling, caught in her gaze, enjoying the opportunity to be with her, but with no expectations. Since Donna had died he had made the mistake of trying to fill the physical void of her absence, only to find that a greater void still existed. Ending a few brief flings had disappointed not only the women involved but McGuire himself, and these days it seemed increasingly easier for him to be alone, or to fill with work the empty space that was left behind with Donna's absence. Only when he was with Pearl did McGuire allow himself to think that he might not remain alone for ever.

As he turned away, Pearl caught his mood. 'What is it?' she asked.

McGuire shook his head. 'Nothing,' he said quietly. He paused, catching sight of the mistletoe that was hanging above their heads.

Pearl was used to taking the lead, especially in the restaurant, but something in McGuire's look silenced her. He leaned in a little closer, leaving her unsure if he was about to kiss her or whisper a secret ... but once more the moment was broken by the sound of a raised voice near the stage.

'How dare you have the effrontery to come here tonight – and after this?'

It was Diana speaking. A small crowd had gathered around her, and as Pearl began to push her way through it, she saw that Diana was now bellowing at Bonita while brandishing a card in her hand. Bonita stood her ground with Simon by her side.

'I really don't know what you're talking about,' the girl said, in a calm tone that seemed only to increase Diana's frustration.

'You know damn well what I'm talking about!' Diana snapped. She indicated the banner strung across the stage. 'Peace and goodwill to all men? What a joke! You've revelled in making my life hell ever since you moved back.'

At this, Simon took a step forward in Bonita's defence but the girl held out a hand to stop him. 'You'll be wasting your time. Just ignore her, Simon.'

'Yes,' he agreed, turning to face Diana. 'It's obvious you've had enough for one night, so why don't you just sober up and go home?'

Diana's mouth gaped at this. 'How dare you...' She swayed on her feet but Rev Pru suddenly thrust herself between the warring factions and attempted to bring a peaceful end to the situation.

'Diana, please. Calm down.'

Giles instantly left Stephanie's side and moved forward to assist his relative.

'Rev Pru's right, Aunt Diana.' He lowered his voice to an embarrassed whisper. 'You're causing a scene...'

Diana shrugged him off. 'Of course I am. And I'll have you know that my New Year's resolution is not to put up with nonsense from anyone – *including you.*'

Giles gaped in hurt confusion while Stephanie now marched up to them, shocked to the core, by the treatment being meted out to her husband. 'You have no right to talk to Giles that way,' she scolded.

'Put a sock in it, Stephanie, I have every right,' Diana scowled, taking another sip from the glass in her hand. 'I can promise you a Christmas of home truths, some of which you are not going to like.'

For a moment, Diana cast her gaze around the room, appearing to fix everyone with a warning look. Then she gave an unexpected toast. 'Cheers!' and swallowed the last of her drink. She had begun to walk off, unsteady on her feet, when she put out a hand for balance and by accident dropped her glass. It smashed loudly on the floor and she stared down at it, confused, managing to take only one further step until she began to sway again, like a tall building, before collapsing heavily on to the floor.

Everyone present, including Pearl, remained rooted to the spot for a split second, unable to believe what they had just witnessed. Then a murmur spread like wildfire. Dr Clayson and McGuire hurried over to the fallen woman. Pearl shared a shocked look with Giles who knelt close to his aunt while the doctor gently slapped her cheek.

'Aunt Diana!' called Giles loudly. At this, Diana opened her mouth and appeared to murmur something before her eyes rolled back in her head. Dolly slid close to Pearl.

'Out for the count,' she commented in a loud whisper. 'I always thought she had a hollow leg as far as booze was concerned, but it was bound to catch up with her sooner or later.'

Diana lay motionless while Richard Clayson felt for her pulse and laid his head close to her chest. As the church clock chimed midnight, something in his expression rang alarm bells for Pearl.

'Call an ambulance,' he said tersely, as Diana began to hyperventilate.

McGuire reacted quickly, taking out his mobile phone as Pearl noticed something lying close to her feet. It was the card that Diana had been waving in her hand. Glitter was scattered around the shards of her broken highball tumbler on the parquet wooden floor. As all eyes remained on Diana, Pearl picked up the card and saw that it bore a familiar design: a snowman in the front garden of a Victorian home. Opening it, she was taken aback by the prescient message cut out in newsprint inside. *Lose your temper – and you lose everything.*

Chapter Seven

Saturday 18 December, 9 a.m.

During summer mornings at high tide, the soft breeze that blew in across Pearl's sea garden would have smelled cool and fresh until around midday, when the aroma of barbecued sea bass, sardines and spicy sausages would invariably waft its way into her own kitchen from the beach. By contrast, on the cold winter's morning that followed the Christmas fundraiser, the tide seemed stapled to the horizon and only the smell of rank seaweed rose from the shore.

In summer, Pearl might have taken her dinghy out to sea, sailing beyond the shingled bank known locally as the Street to gaze on the wind-farm sails turning on the warm breeze. However, an icy wind still blew its way down from the north-east, even more bitterly today, and she chose instead to head on foot, westwards in the direction of Seasalter.

The low tide matched Pearl's mood. She felt drained by the events of the previous evening. Calls to Dolly had provided nothing in the way of news concerning Diana's condition, and a message left on McGuire's voicemail had gone ignored. All Pearl could be sure of was that with the arrival of an ambulance at St Alfred's church hall, Giles had accompanied his aunt to hospital while Stephanie had returned with Nicholas to Grey Gables to await further news.

To Pearl it seemed almost impossible to believe that such a self-possessed woman as Diana Marshall could have allowed herself to become so out of control, and at such a public event – but perhaps Dolly had been right and it was Diana's penchant for Jenever that had finally caught up with her.

Pearl had only an hour or two before she needed to head to the restaurant, but today of all days, she felt the need to clear the cobwebs from her mind and being close to the sea always helped. Having departed Seaspray Cottage from her garden gate, in no time she had passed the distinctive landmark of the Old Neptune – the timber-framed pub that stood upon Whitstable's beach. Just beyond it, the pretty row of colourful cottages at Marine Terrace came into view; they always captured the full attention of inquisitive tourists in the summer months. Visitors peered through the front windows as they were apt to do at Pearl's back garden, but in spite of living under this scrutiny, the cottages were highly prized by homeseekers, changing hands for almost half a million pounds while beyond the old tennis courts, the larger four-storey terraced houses at Wave Crest sold for more than double that sum. The view from their sea-facing windows was stunning in the summer, especially at sunset, but during the winter, the Wave Crest area, and beyond, always seemed to Pearl to be somewhat cut off from the rest of the town. A small parade of beach huts prefaced the land before the old caravan park at West Beach, behind which lay the golf course that offered for many, especially dog walkers, a scenic short cut from the beach into town.

Today, however, with the cold north wind still blowing in off the sea, Pearl couldn't help reflecting on how vulnerable the town was to the powerful combination of high winds and tides that had threatened the area throughout history and would continue to do so.

Pearl's grandfather, William Nolan, had been only ten years old when his father had taken him to gaze out at a frozen sea. It was during the winter of 1940, when icebergs almost two metres high had been left marooned on the beach as the tide moved out. William had told the story to his own son, Tommy, who in turn had painted a word picture for his daughter, Pearl, of the day every oyster boat had remained ashore and the beach had been littered with the bodies of frozen birds.

That image had haunted Pearl as a small child

and returned to her again just as she realised that she had walked almost as far as the furthest parade of beach huts. On this part of the beach, the huts seemed distinct from those at the more populated easterly end at Tankerton. To Pearl, they served as sentinels in a no man's land between the old West Beach caravan park and a 'millionaire's row' of beach-front properties at Seasalter. It was part of Whitstable's peculiarity that such contrasts could co-exist so easily, side by side, and Pearl now remembered that one of these beach huts was in fact used as a retreat by Alice Clayson.

As Pearl crossed a timber groyne in its direction, a woman called out, stopping Pearl in her tracks. 'Hi there!'

It wasn't Alice Clayson but a young girl who was waving from the beach. She looked familiar but it wasn't until she had come closer and removed the knitted red beret she wore that Pearl realised it was Dolly's Christmas guest, Cassie.

'Sorry,' said Pearl. 'I was miles away.'

Cassie was dressed casually in jeans and a bouclé vintage jacket that smacked of early Chanel. Her cupid's-bow mouth eased back into a pout from its pretty smile as she said, 'Have you heard any more about the woman who was taken ill last night?'

'Afraid not.'

'What a weird way for the evening to end,' Cassie went on. 'It was a bit like a soap opera, wasn't it?'

Pearl had to admit that the girl was right: there had been an air of unreality about Diana's collapse, as though the event might have been scripted, but before she could comment on this, Cassie continued. 'Horrible for the family. They looked distraught, didn't they?'

'Yes,' Pearl said sadly. 'And they'd only just arrived for Christmas.'

'I know,' nodded Cassie.

Pearl looked at her enquiringly and the girl explained, 'I talked to them. Your mum introduced us. She seems to know everyone in town.'

'True,' agreed Pearl. Noticing that Cassie was staring out towards Seasalter, she asked: 'Are you heading somewhere in particular?'

'Yes. I'm trying to find a place called...' Cassie broke off, taking a map from her pocket which had a note attached to it. 'The Battery?'

'That's right,' said Pearl. 'It's less than a ten-minute walk from those beach huts. I'll show you, if you like?'

'Cool. I thought I'd take some shots there.' Cassie indicated the camera bag across her shoulder before producing one of Dolly's many local history books that were so familiar to Pearl from her childhood. This one featured photographs of the landmark wooden naval building which had been erected in the nineteenth century as two large wooden sheds. One had housed cannons while the other had formed a drill hall for sailors – but for many years now the extensive beach property had been the home of an artist who sometimes rented it out to guests and for creative workshops.

'Was she in bad health?' Cassie asked suddenly, rounding the path from the old caravan site to the beach huts. 'The woman who was taken ill, I mean.'

'Not as far as I know,' replied Pearl, aware that Diana appeared not only to be healthy but extremely fit since she played both golf and tennis on a regular basis.

'I must admit she looked pretty tanked,' commented Cassie frankly, taking out her camera and framing a shot of the western horizon towards the Isle of Sheppey. 'And she didn't seem to be making much sense, sounding off like she did to that pretty girl.'

'Bonita,' said Pearl. 'She's Diana's new neighbour.'

Cassie was quiet for a few moments as she photographed the coastline with a series of swift shots. She then hooked the camera strap back across her shoulder and had just begun to move on when Pearl halted in her steps.

'What is it?' the girl asked.

In the distance, Pearl had caught sight of someone, huddled on the porch of a beach hut. Cassie's eyes narrowed as she followed Pearl's gaze. 'That's the doctor's wife, isn't it?' She asked.

Alice Clayson's head was lowered, as she appeared to be studying a sketchpad in her hand. Engrossed in her work, she failed to notice anyone approaching but Cassie suddenly exclaimed, 'Wow! What a great place. Must have a fantastic view from that porch.' And before Pearl could stop her, the girl began bounding across the beach like a young puppy.

Alice immediately looked up as the sound of pebbles crunched underfoot, and on seeing her unexpected visitors, her expression clouded with what looked to Pearl to be a mixture of confusion and fear.

'Sorry to disturb you,' Pearl said gently, noticing that Alice had been sketching the seascape stretched out before her. 'I didn't expect you'd be here on such a cold day.'

Alice flashed a nervous smile. 'I needed some air.' She held Pearl's look for just a moment before Cassie strode forward and ran up the steps of the beach hut, invading Alice's space.

'That watercolour you donated to the raffle was superb,' the girl enthused. She waited for a suitable response but under her scrutiny Alice merely looked helplessly at Pearl.

'Cassie's staying at Mum's attic over Christmas,' Pearl explained.

'How nice,' said the artist automatically.

Cassie beamed. 'I'm a photographer. Do you think I could possibly take a few shots from your porch?'

Alice was clearly troubled by the request but offered up a resigned shrug.

'Go ahead,' she said, giving in to Cassie's enthusiasm. Abandoning her sketchpad, she thrust her hands deep into the pockets of her jacket and moved from the protective shelter of the hut and on to the beach with Pearl.

'I'm really sorry to disturb you,' whispered Pearl, staring back towards Cassie who was already snapping the view from Alice's hut. 'I happened to meet her on the beach.'

Alice glanced back. 'It's OK,' she said finally, giving the ghost of a forgiving smile.

In the harsh winter light, Alice's complexion

was like that of an alabaster sculpture, though a scattering of pale cinnamon freckles remained as a reminder of a summer long gone. Nathan was right, Alice was indeed a beautiful woman – tall, slender and as Dolly had rightly judged, with a look about her of a doomed Ophelia.

'Have you heard any news?' Alice asked now. 'About Diana?'

Pearl shook her head. 'None.'

Alice considered this. 'I tried calling Giles this morning but there was no reply so I left a message on the answerphone.' She sighed. 'I do hope she's OK. She was so angry at Bonita, wasn't she? Diana's a spirited lady, but I can't say I've ever seen her as furious as that.'

Pearl was about to comment when Cassie stepped down from the hut. 'Thanks so much,' she grinned. 'I've taken a few of your hut too, so if you want, I'll give you some prints?'

'Thanks, but there's no need,' said Alice flatly.

An awkward silence fell before Cassie finally recognised that she was overstaying her welcome. 'Well, I ... suppose I'd better get off. Don't worry, Pearl, I'm sure I'll be able to find my way alone.' She headed in the direction of Seasalter but wasn't too far away when Pearl's mobile rang. Checking it, Pearl saw that the caller was McGuire and she moved away to answer it.

'You got my message?' asked Pearl, under her breath.

McGuire gave a terse reply. 'I have to make this quick.'

Pearl recognised the urgency in McGuire's tone. 'What is it?' she asked.

For the next few moments, Pearl listened very carefully to what McGuire had to say, then asked: 'Are you absolutely sure of this?'

In the pause that followed, Alice registered the change in Pearl's tone and glanced up with a questioning look while Pearl continued talking to McGuire. Ending the call, Pearl remembered Alice, still looking on, waiting for information.

'Diana,' said Pearl. Dazed, her eyes finally met Alice's. 'It appears she was poisoned.'

'Poisoned?' echoed Alice in a startled whisper. 'Are you sure?'

Pearl gave a nod and added slowly: 'She's dead.'

The words seemed to hang on the air for a moment before a gust of wind sliced its way between the women. In a split second, Alice's eyes flickered and closed. Like a flower cut down by the wind, she suddenly collapsed. Pearl quickly knelt down and took Alice's hand, which felt cold and limp in her own, then she looked up and called out desperately across the beach for help. *'Cassie! Come back quickly!'*

It was almost an hour later when Alice's husband, Dr Richard Clayson, descended the stairs to Pearl who had been waiting anxiously in their sitting room. Because it was outside surgery hours, Pearl had called Richard immediately, knowing that it would take him only minutes to drive from Joy Lane to the car park which served the West Beach caravan site. Richard had duly arrived to find his wife recovering from her fainting attack, and had then taken all three women back home with him in the car. Now he stood in front of Pearl, who

93

rose quickly to her feet from the comfortable sofa and asked, 'How is she?'

'She'll be fine.'

Pearl exhaled with relief

'It was just shock,' he said confidently.

'Of course.' Pearl nodded. 'It was a shock to us all.'

He looked directly at Pearl. 'There's no mistake, I suppose – about the police findings?'

'Unfortunately, no. The police were alerted by the hospital. Following on from Diana's symptoms, there were toxicology tests. I don't have all the details,' Pearl added sombrely, 'about whether there were any suspicious circumstances...'

Richard broke in tersely. 'What on earth do you mean? If Diana was poisoned, it was surely an accident.'

'I don't know,' said Pearl honestly. 'There'll be a police investigation to find out exactly what happened.'

Richard shook his head in incredulity. 'But we were all there, we *saw* what happened. She'd been drinking, and far too much by the looks of it. She lost her temper and collapsed.'

'Yes,' said Pearl, not wishing to argue with the facts. She left a suitable pause as she saw Cassie approaching the house from the garden. 'I was with Diana just two days ago,' said Pearl. 'She said she was coming to see you that evening?'

Richard frowned, vaguely irritated by Pearl's question but he became distracted by the sight of Cassie at the open doors to the kitchen, staring back towards the swimming pool. 'What of it?' he asked.

'Well, did there seem to be anything on her mind?'

'I'm not sure what you mean.'

'When I left her,' explained Pearl, 'she was clearly upset with Bonita and her boyfriend, Simon. They'd had some falling out over a fox.'

Richard exhaled in exasperation. 'They'd been driving Diana to distraction. Invading her privacy with that damned tree house. They did everything they could to provoke her. She couldn't stand them. But other than that, she was absolutely fine and...' He trailed off as he saw Cassie coming towards them.

'I do hope your wife's feeling better?' Cassie's question caught the doctor off-guard.

'Yes, thank you.' Seeming a little confused, he said, 'I'm sorry. I'm afraid I've forgotten your name.'

'Cassie Walker.'

Richard gave a polite nod then took a step towards the front door – a move which signalled a cue for both women to leave. 'I really must get off to the surgery, but I thank you for taking care of Alice.'

Pearl offered an understanding smile which Richard returned, fleetingly, before she and Cassie left the house. As the door closed after them, Cassie looked back at it.

'What a place,' she said starkly. Pearl turned to see that the girl was rooted to the spot, staring up at the Claysons' home. 'It's beautiful, isn't it? Swimming pool and everything. Must be worth an absolute fortune.'

Pearl was taken aback by the inappropriateness

of Cassie's remark. The girl was proving to be pushy, intrusive and tactless but she was also Dolly's guest so Pearl bit her lip and said, 'Yes. I suppose you're right.'

Chapter Eight

Saturday 18 December, midday

'So you've already spread the news?'

McGuire was standing across the seafood counter from Pearl, waiting for a reply as a group of customers came forward to take their coats from Ruby. Only after Pearl had wished them goodbye, along with the season's greetings, did she turn to give her attention back to McGuire.

'I assumed that if you wanted it kept secret, you might have told me.' She was looking at him challengingly, in that checkmate way of hers that always had McGuire searching for a suitable defence. In this instance he knew there was none because she was right.

'The hospital released the news to the family,' he said.

'Giles?' asked Pearl. 'Of course – he was the one who went in the ambulance with Diana.' Suddenly realising she was failing as a hostess, she said, 'I'm so sorry. You look all in. What can I get you?'

'Coffee. Black. Plenty of sugar.' McGuire slumped on to a stool and Pearl eyed him as she poured a squat cup of thick black syrupy coffee

96

from her cafetière. 'You didn't get much sleep by the looks of it.'

She was right again, but McGuire had been kept awake not by policework but the late-night licence that had been recently awarded to the bar close to his new apartment. He could have complained about the noise but he rather liked the idea of there being a place nearby where he could find a drink or some company after a late shift. He had also made a judgement to keep a low profile in his new neighbourhood regarding his police status.

Pearl handed him the coffee. 'So what happens now?'

For an instant McGuire was thrown as he stared into Pearl's grey eyes but his concentration rallied with a sip of coffee.

'An investigation,' he said briefly, hoping the caffeine would sharpen his wits.

'Which you've begun,' she prompted. 'So what can I do to help?' As he held her look, Pearl made a sudden realisation. 'Of course! *You* can't lead the investigation, can you? You were there last night so you're a witness.'

McGuire wasn't sure what irked him most: the fact that Pearl had just accurately described the situation, or that his presence at the fundraiser now prevented him from taking charge of a possible murder case. Instead, the investigation had been given over to Chief Inspector Tony Shipley, another sour note for McGuire since the young man had only recently been promoted from Detective Sergeant by McGuire's superior, Superintendent Maurice Welch. The latter seemed intent on overlooking McGuire, an outsider from

London, in favour of his local team and the situation increasingly rankled, not least because Shipley's own shortcomings as a Senior Investigating Officer were perfectly evident to McGuire.

'What is it?' asked Pearl, curious now.

McGuire escaped her enquiring look by glancing quickly around the restaurant. 'Pearl, you know this town – and the people in it. You even knew the deceased.'

'Yes,' she said ruefully. 'And less than forty-eight hours ago I was actually having coffee with her. You see, Diana was my accountant.' She lowered her voice as more customers took their leave, waving to her from the door. 'There's no mistake, is there? She *was* definitely poisoned?'

'By ethylene glycol,' said McGuire starkly.

'Antifreeze?' asked Pearl, shocked. 'Possibly the perfect poison,' she murmured. 'Odourless ... no bitter taste.' Then something else dawned on her. 'Of course,' she said, almost to herself. 'Diana mentioned it.'

'Mentioned what?' McGuire asked, feeling increasingly excluded from Pearl's train of thought.

'The sweet taste. She thought it was the cake.'

'What are you talking about?'

Pearl gathered her thoughts and explained carefully: 'Most people drank my mulled wine – including you. But Diana brought her own bottle. Dutch gin. It was her favourite but she grumbled to Nathan about the cakes being too sweet, possibly even my mince pies.'

'Nathan?' asked McGuire with some suspicion, noting this was the second time Pearl had mentioned the name.

'I told you, he's a friend of mine,' she went on quickly: 'You met Diana. She was in a difficult mood and clearly unsteady on her feet by the end of the evening so everyone assumed she was drunk – but that could have been from the effects of the ethylene glycol.'

She looked at McGuire, who frowned. 'How do you know that?'

'Because I happened to train as a police officer, remember?' Pearl was being disingenuous since she had learned nothing about ethylene glycol during her training at Hendon. However, she did recall how a series of local cat deaths had been attributed to someone maliciously setting down saucers of antifreeze for the animals to drink. At the time, Dolly had feared for her own cat, Mojo, who had been imprisoned indoors until the incidents had stopped.

'Diana left the bottle of Jenever in the kitchen. I gave her a glass so she could top herself up, but anyone could've tampered with the bottle. It was sitting there all evening and–' She broke off suddenly before asking, 'Has it been found?'

'The bottle?' McGuire was finding it a challenge to keep up with her.

'You'd better tip off the investigating officer quickly,' Pearl ordered. 'Today is recycling day and the lorry's always here by early afternoon.'

McGuire took this in then checked his watch and threw the last of his coffee down his throat. Taking out his mobile, he headed for the door, looking back once at Pearl. 'Thanks!' And with that he was gone.

Pearl gazed down at McGuire's empty cup and

mused on the pattern of grounds left in the bottom. If she had been Dolly, who read both tea and coffee cups, she might have sworn there was a clear image of a question mark staring back at her. Before she could give this any further thought, a text arrived on her phone – from Giles Marshall summoning her to Grey Gables – as soon as possible.

Having recruited Dolly to cover for her at the restaurant, Pearl managed to find a parking space not too far from Grey Gables. Usually, she would have walked the fifteen minutes or so required to reach the house from Island Wall, but Giles's text had sounded urgent.

By 4 p.m. the light was already fading and the wind had come up again, bitingly cold. As Pearl approached the driveway it seemed impossible to believe that only two days before, she had been arriving to discuss with Diana the prosaic affair of her annual accounts. The latticed windows now glowed – not with Diana's Christmas decorations but the light of a single candleflame. Pearl rang the doorbell and after a few moments, she moved to peer through the front window. The house seemed empty, cold and unwelcoming, but a figure eventually became visible through the stained-glass panel of the front door, and as it opened, Pearl came face to face with Stephanie. Giles's wife looked not grief-stricken but stunned by shock as she invited Pearl inside.

Stepping into the hallway, Pearl caught the faint aroma of eucalyptus and cinnamon wafting from an infuser on the window ledge.

'I'm so sorry for your loss,' she said sincerely.

'Thank you,' Stephanie replied. 'And for coming so quickly.' She took Pearl's red winter coat which she hung on a stand in the hall. 'Giles is upstairs,' she said in a low voice. 'I don't think I've ever seen him like this. He slept in Diana's office all night – if he slept at all. He really is quite bereft.' For a moment, Stephanie Marshall seemed uncharacteristically lost.

'I could come back another time?' Pearl said gently.

'No.' Stephanie pulled herself together. 'He's determined to see you. Follow me.'

She led the way upstairs and when the two women had reached a closed mahogany door, Stephanie visibly braced herself before tapping on it with a single rap of her knuckles. Opening the door, she poked her head around it. 'It's Pearl,' she confirmed, taking a step back before telling her: 'I'll be in the sitting room if you need me.'

With that, she moved off, leaving Pearl to open the door wider to find that Giles was not seated at his aunt's desk, as she had expected, but standing with his back to the door as he looked out of the window. He failed to react to the sound of the door closing and only seemed aware of Pearl's presence when she spoke.

'Giles?'

At this, Giles suddenly drew the burgundy curtains and turned to face her. He looked distracted, his hair was ruffled and his cardigan had been buttoned wrongly. Pearl couldn't help but feel sympathy for him, not just for the loss of his beloved aunt but because he was, as his wife had described, clearly bereft.

'Please sit down,' he said, indicating a chair. Pearl did so but Giles failed to join her and instead thrust his hands deep into his cardigan pockets as he paced up and down, trying to collect his thoughts. 'The police have been here all day,' he said. 'A detective called Shipley.'

'Has he been able to tell you anything?'

Giles frowned at Pearl's question. 'He confirmed that she was poisoned. Hospital toxicology reports.' He looked at Pearl, his expression suddenly hardening. 'But he couldn't, or wouldn't, tell me anything else. That's why I needed to see you, Pearl. You're a detective too – you know about these things. I have to find out what happened, do you see? I owe it to Aunt Diana.' He wiped his face with the palm of his hand as if to erase any possible show of weakness.

'The police will investigate,' Pearl reminded him. 'I understand they're already doing so...'

'I don't care,' said Giles testily. 'I don't trust them to give me answers so I'll pay whatever it takes, Pearl. I can't rest until I know what happened. You understand, don't you?'

Pearl felt instantly conflicted. Nothing had changed since she had turned down the investigation into the poison-pen Christmas cards – except for the single fact that Diana Marshall was no longer alive. The restaurant was still busy and Charlie expected home for the holidays, his present remained unbought and Christmas was only days away – but the determined look on Giles's face revealed the urgency of the situation and the importance of the issue at stake.

'Will you help me, Pearl?' He looked at Pearl

imploringly like a lost child and Pearl came to a decision.

'I'll do all I can, Giles.' She paused before adding an important qualification: 'As Diana's friend.'

Giles took some time to assimilate this before he began to nod slowly. 'Thank you, Pearl.' Her response seemed to have given him a measure of peace, and to lift some of the responsibility that weighed heavily upon him as Diana's sole relative. Perhaps, thought Pearl, he might now be able to get some rest and re-order his thoughts for a fresh day.

A short while later, as Giles led the way downstairs, Pearl glimpsed Nicholas sitting on the floor in front of Diana's TV in the sitting room, comfort-eating a large tub of ice cream. Lights now blinked from Diana's tree, conveying the image of a normal family Christmas if only Diana had been present, glass in hand.

'One thing,' said Pearl, turning to Giles as they had almost reached the front door. 'Did the police fully investigate the house today?'

Giles nodded. 'They went through everything, even took away her laptop.'

Pearl stared towards the sitting room. 'And the bottles on the drinks tray?'

'Everything,' Giles told her.

'Thank you,' said Pearl, considering this.

As she stepped out of the front door, Giles surprised her by putting out his hand. If she had accepted the case on a professional basis, Giles might have been seeking to seal their association with a handshake, but instead Pearl felt instinctively that he was simply in need of some physical contact. She responded by taking his hand and laying her own upon it, and Giles held her gaze for a moment before closing his eyes in an effort to force back tears ... but the moment was broken by Stephanie's voice cutting into the silence.

'Goodbye, Pearl,' she called, appearing in the hallway as she dried her hands with a kitchen towel.

Giles opened his eyes and in an instant broke away from Pearl to resume his usual stilted tone. 'Thank you,' he repeated. Stephanie came to stand at Giles's side at the front door as Pearl made her way down the York-stone pathway, passing the Victorian lamp-post in the front garden. Looking back, she saw the front door had closed.

Once she was sure that Giles and Stephanie were no longer watching, Pearl took the narrow alley that ran alongside Grey Gables and led to Francis Sullivan's old property. The Grange was a house of considerable size with mature trees towering over the alley wall. In contrast to the staid order of Grey Gables, a colourful nesting box had gone up above the door of the Sullivan property and wind chimes sounded from a large fir tree on the front lawn. A formal sign that had hung for years above the door had been replaced with a ceramic heart on which the house name had been painted – features that might have looked more in keeping on a charming cottage than the imposing Edwardian property in which Francis Sullivan had lived out his years. It seemed clear that his granddaughter and her partner were now staking out their territory and adding their own indelible stamp to the place. They had stood their ground in the face of Diana's threats, and the construction of the tree house now seemed to Pearl to have been less of an unintentional threat to their neighbour's privacy as a declaration of war – an assault on Diana's suburban sensibilities.

The house was in darkness apart from a single light in one of the upper windows, silhouetting a feathered dream catcher resting against the pane. Pearl was familiar with the story of the Native American tribe who believed that the dream catcher acted as a filter for nightmares, trapping them in its web until they evaporated with the light of day.

As Pearl looked up at the house she imagined that perhaps Bonita and Simon might sleep peacefully now. They may well have considered Diana Marshall to be a kind of nightmare – but if so, she would never be troubling them again.

Chapter Nine

Sunday 19 December, midday

'Don't tell me you've taken on a murder case.' Nathan offered an arch look and a large glass of Rioja Reserva – which Pearl declined. It was only midday but that didn't stop Nathan, who took a large sip and waited for her reply.

'I only said that I would help,' she clarified.

'Which means precisely what? That you'll find the murderer and let Giles Marshall off a bill for your trouble?'

They were sitting in the living room of Nathan's beautiful Island Wall home which was described as a cottage though its interior boasted something much more roomy and refined with a large extension creeping into the garden area. Nathan's books lined the walls from floor to ceiling and his ginger tomcat, Biggy, lay curled on a blanket on his comfortable sofa. Nathan's laptop, however, was in 'sleep' mode – no sign of an article on the screen.

'And the detective?' he probed. 'I can see you've been holding out on me there, sweetie. I expected something in a tired old raincoat, but he's hardly Columbo, is he? Rather more James Bond.' He eyed Pearl across his wine glass.

'I'm sure McGuire would be very flattered to hear that,' Pearl said, as Nathan, a stickler for detail, shifted a bauble to a different branch of his white artificial Christmas tree.

'If you ask me, the man's been having handsome lessons.'

'Can't say I've noticed,' lied Pearl.

'You notice *everything*,' countered Nathan, turning to her. 'And I'm sure that empty space on his wedding finger hasn't passed you by either. What's his story?'

'I don't know what you mean.'

'Everyone has a story, Pearl. What's his? Married to the job?'

'I honestly don't know,' she said, truthfully this time. 'I told you, he plays his cards close to his chest.'

'And you're just the woman to prise them from him,' decided Nathan. He was about to take

106

another sip of wine when he saw Pearl staring at him and asked, 'What're you thinking?'

'That poison is such a terrible way to die.'

Nathan considered the glass in his hand then shrugged. 'Is there ever a good way?' He savoured his Rioja and Pearl continued to observe him, suddenly curious about something.

'Where were you?' she asked. 'Last night – when Diana collapsed?'

Nathan thought for a moment. 'Standing not far from the Christmas tree with a perfect view of you and Detective Heart-throb.'

'So you also had a clear view of Diana?'

'I was actually more interested in what was going on with you.'

'You mean you were spying on me?'

'Yes,' said Nathan unashamedly. 'I'd spotted the mistletoe when I came in, and the way things were going, I thought you might need rescuing – but then Diana started braying at that lovely young girl...'

'Unprovoked?'

Nathan paused in an effort to recall then gave a shrug. 'I really don't know what started it. One minute they seemed to be talking and the next, Diana had kicked off and hit the deck. I assumed it was the booze. Didn't we all?'

'Did you happen to see what she'd been drinking? Was it a clear liquid?'

Nathan shook his head. 'I can't remember, but she was quaffing from a large glass that covered her nose like a trough.'

'Nathan...' Pearl admonished.

'I'm no hypocrite, sweetie. I really didn't care

for the woman, though I wouldn't have wished her dead. But somebody clearly did.'

Pearl reflected on this. 'There may be an investigation underway but it hasn't yet confirmed her death as murder.' Nathan looked up and she decided to remind him. 'There's always a chance it was suicide.'

'Oh come on, Pearl. Would anyone really choose antifreeze for a way out? Whatever else Diana Marshall may have been, she couldn't be called a quitter. In fact, there was something of your Mrs Thatcher about her, don't you think? Oh-so-strident and those pussy-bow blouses?' He gave a shudder.

'Maybe,' agreed Pearl. 'Except she was dressed rather differently last night, wasn't she? Rather glamorous, in fact, in that maroon-coloured dress. And when I saw her about my accounts the night before, she looked...'

'What?'

'More feminine,' Pearl decided. 'As though she'd had a re-style.'

'Short-lived,' said Nathan flatly. He finished his drink and eyed her with a look that Pearl rarely saw from him. His mood was generally flippant but the usual charming gleam in his eye had vanished and his voice took on a serious tone. 'If it really was murder, Pearl,' he said. 'Be careful.'

McGuire was making headway from the car park in Pound Lane along St Peter's Street against a tide of Canterbury shoppers. They were always there, whatever the season, a mixture of tourists, locals and those making consumer pilgrimages

108

from small towns in the environs – like Whitstable. For the last hour, a fine rain had been falling and the pavements were glistening, though the buskers and young beggars were still in place, huddled in doorways against the cold.

McGuire's mind was filled with Pearl. At this time of year, he always wished he was far away, somewhere hot and preferably unChristian so he didn't have to think about Christmas and all that accompanied it. In terms of family life, he had none to speak of. His parents were dead and a few elderly aunts had moved on without bothering to inform him of their new address, since he had patently failed to maintain proper contact. He blamed the force for that: too many weekends spent working on cases until Donna's arrival in his life had allowed him to think that he might, one day, create a family for himself – a proper unit into which he might fit. But almost two years on from her death he was still alone, the move to Canterbury CID having failed to create the right working environment for him – though he blamed that on no one else but his new boss.

Welch was a small man in every way, his intelligence limited by a narrow viewpoint which rarely allowed him to see the bigger picture. However, he had played a good game of politics within the force and had manoeuvred himself into the role of Superintendent rather than having earned it. The one thing McGuire's move from London to Canterbury had given him had been an introduction to Pearl Nolan. Although he had lost touch with her for several months, the arrival of a lone Christmas card at the station had supplied him with a suitable cue for him to re-establish contact.

During the summer he had tried to convince Pearl to give up on detection and concentrate on being a restaurateur, but that was before he had discovered what an asset she could be to a police investigation. In fact, he had learned that Pearl possessed both a breadth of local knowledge and a natural instinct for people that was invaluable in crime solving – the only complication being that she had used both to take over his investigation.

McGuire liked to think that he wasn't bothered by finding himself in professional competition with a woman. He didn't consider himself to be a chauvinist in any way, but neither was he a 'blokey' pack animal who needed the company of other men when he was gambling or drinking – which he was apt to do in equal measure. In fact, he was a sociable loner who enjoyed his own company as much as that of others, and though he played the odd game of squash with a few casual acquaintances at the local gym, he hadn't found much time to do so recently since the London court case had ended and he had moved into his new flat in Best Lane.

He had been hoping that the Christmas period would provide the perfect opportunity to settle into his new home and allow space for visits to his favourite haunts, but this hadn't yet proved possible. He hadn't been to a race course for months, though he had placed a few Internet bets to lighten the boredom of the court case. Lately he had come to realise that gambling was, in the main, something he only resorted to in times of stress, a habit he had acquired after Donna's death. It was a coping strategy, like the drinking. He had managed to get a handle on his reliance on alcohol, which he had always previously put down to having simply too much of a taste for Bourbon. Time had moved on – and so had McGuire.

One senseless incident had robbed him of Donna. Two drugged-up kids had mown her down in a stolen car one cold, rainy night on the streets of Peckham in south London – and from that moment on, life had never been, and never would be, the same. But the itch to gamble was still there to scratch: the need to play a hand of poker, to place a bet, to engage in a game of pitch and toss merely to see which way the dice would fall, perhaps in the hope that luck might return his way eventually, as it had always seemed to do when Donna was alive.

Gambling remained McGuire's way of exploring how much influence he, or anyone, might ultimately have over events; as such, it represented an analogy for the greater game of life itself. Until Donna's death McGuire had been a winner, easing his way up the ranks: collecting promotions and accolades on the way while making progress and plans for the future. But it was a future that had been snatched from him, together with the luck; a sense of things always having fallen his way until that fateful night on the dark streets of Peckham. Now, events seemed increasingly random, including the way Pearl had come into his path last summer. He had been investigating what had appeared simply to be an accidental death, although Pearl had sensed otherwise – and her senses had proved to be correct.

McGuire had underestimated Pearl – but why on earth would he have expected that a cook and restaurateur could possibly eclipse his own abilities for crime solving?

'Clues for a murder are rather like ingredients for a recipe,' Pearl had told him. 'Put them together in the right way and the results can be very satisfying.' She had said those words in the Hotel Continental, in the same bar in which he had sampled his first oyster stout. He had quickly developed a taste for the beer – and Pearl – then promptly lost contact with her until the card had brought them back together. She had written only a simple message inside: *Merry Christmas, McGuire. Maybe one day you'll return – for a native.*

It was now the season for the Whitstable's native oyster but McGuire suspected it was also the season for murder. Though he was excluded from the official investigation into Diana Marshall's death, he was still owed a few favours at the station and had used them to discover that two capable sergeants had retrieved a Jenever bottle from the recycling box at St Alfred's church hall before it had been taken away. The residue inside had matched traces found in the shards collected from Diana Marshall's broken glass – ethylene glycol from the same industrial source. The question remained: how had it got there?

McGuire had just reached the wrought-iron gate that led into the courtyard where his new front door was situated. He glanced at the fast-flowing River Stour and saw the rain piercing its surface like fine needles. Entering his apartment, he decided he would have a hot shower, change his clothes and strike out in a new direction. Taking a deep breath, he pulled his mobile phone from his inside pocket and tapped out a short message. *Can you meet me in the Continental at 7?*

Seconds later, Pearl's message appeared on the screen. *See you there.*

Pearl switched off her phone. 'Sorry about that.' She smiled at the person before her.

'No problem,' said Rev Pru. They were sitting in her study at the vicarage. 'Where were we?'

'You were saying ... about the bottles?'

'Oh yes. The police managed to get to them before they went off to the recycling plant. In fact, they went through the whole church hall with a fine-tooth comb.' She took a sip of tea. 'It was a particular gin bottle they were looking for.' She frowned in confusion. 'Though I can't think how they knew that.'

'I wonder,' said Pearl, without further comment.

'It could have been far more distressing,' continued Rev Pru, 'but poor Martha was nevertheless in quite a state. She had cleaned for Diana for years, and she still helps out on a voluntary basis with St Alfred's.' Rev Pru looked directly at Pearl. 'What an absolute tragedy.'

'Yes,' Pearl agreed.

The vicar then asked outright: 'So when you say that you're looking into all this, does that mean you'll be working in tandem with the police?'

Pearl hesitated before offering her reply, which she phrased very carefully. 'The best way forward, in my view, would be to pool resources – so if you have any thoughts about what happened that night, would you kindly let me know?'

'Of course,' said Rev Pru. 'But as I mentioned, I was rather distracted at the time because I had been chatting to Phyllis at the cake stall. She had baked a spectacular Hummingbird cake. Did you happen to try it?'

'Afraid not,' said Pearl, rather wishing she had, as Hummingbird cake was one of her favourites.

'Neither did I,' sighed the vicar. 'Though it looked superb. Three layers with walnuts and pecans, banana, mashed pineapple and a cream-cheese frosting. She said she would give me the recipe.' Rev Pru appeared bright at the thought then said more doubtfully, 'I can't quite remember why she said it was called Hummingbird.'

'Because it makes you hum with happiness,' said Pearl. 'And is said to be sweet enough for hummingbirds.'

'That's right!' said Rev Pru. 'Christmas is so full of culinary pleasures, isn't it? But I suppose we should all still bear in mind that gluttony is a sin.' The large grandfather clock by her desk suddenly chimed the hour. 'Four already.' Rev Pru tutted. 'I don't know where time goes.' She set down her empty cup and got to her feet. 'I have Christmas service cards to distribute all over town and I really must go and prepare the list of carols for tomorrow night.' She added guiltily, 'I suppose the season must go on in spite of Diana's death.'

Once they had left her study, the vicar turned again to Pearl, saying, 'Will you be all right seeing yourself out?'

'Yes, it's fine,' said Pearl.

Rev Pru duly took the stairs while Pearl headed

on towards the front door where she stopped and called: 'Rev Pru, do you know if Diana happened to try Hummingbird cake?'

Halfway up the stairs, the vicar stopped in her tracks to consider Pearl's question. 'I'm afraid I don't,' she admitted finally. 'Perhaps you might ask Phyllis?'

'I'll do that,' said Pearl.

Following the passage around to the front door, Pearl opened it and immediately pulled up the collar of her jacket against the cold wind. She had taken only a few steps when she spotted a familiar figure walking towards the church. Glancing back once towards the vicarage, Pearl decided to follow.

St Alfred's offered traditional Anglican worship and a relaxed and friendly atmosphere – helped considerably by Rev Pru's open style. Built in the mid-nineteenth century, the church seated almost five hundred people and was the heart of the community, both geographically and in relation to those it served, not solely for religious purposes and to commemorate births, deaths and marriages but also because it offered itself for public meetings on a variety of issues concerning the town. It had also provided a venue for many a classical candle-lit concert.

Pearl had expected to enter the church to find Martha taking off her winter coat to busy herself with some flower arranging or the stacking of hymn books. However, the old lady wasn't scurrying around in her usual fashion but was seated quietly in a front pew, head bent in prayer. Not wishing to intrude on this private moment, Pearl stood stock-still, noticing that she was, in fact, the only person, apart from Martha, in the old church.

The smell of damp hung in the air but St Alfred's remained relatively warm inside, since its squared ragstone block walls acted as adequate protection from the howling wind. A gallery had increased the seating capacity of the old church as well as housing the organ. The bench ends of the pews were numbered, harking back to a time when every parishioner had been allotted a seat. Finding the meditative atmosphere of St Alfred's a calming influence, Pearl took a seat at the rear of the church.

Pearl was not particularly religious and had never been a regular churchgoer, though as a child she had attended Sunday school and learned her Scriptures while feeling the presence of the church in the fabric of her life. St Alfred's held a special place in what had been principally, for so many years, a fishing town. Members of its parish had inevitably been lost at sea. Ministers had offered solace and a suitable memorial service.

Looking around at the stained-glass windows, Pearl viewed Biblical scenes familiar from her childhood: images of Christ preaching from a fishing boat on the Sea of Galilee – as though doing so to St Alfred's congregation. Pearl had attended weddings of friends and relatives in this church as well as funerals – including that of her father and the oyster fisherman, Vinnie Rowe, whose death last summer had first brought her into contact with McGuire.

Charlie had been christened here nearly two decades ago and although it was true that people

116

now seemed to prefer using their Sundays to worship at the altar of consumerism, with visits to supermarkets whose size matched those of some cathedrals, a parish church like St Alfred's still held significance in the lives of its community. Pearl was still reflecting on this when Martha rose from the front pew and headed directly towards the pulpit. Without turning to notice Pearl, she took a purse from her handbag and slipped a coin into a collection box. Choosing a tall slim candle, she lit the wick using the flame from a small tea light and placed it in a holder.

Watching the flame for a moment, Martha then replaced her purse in her bag, carefully closing its clasp before turning towards the central aisle. Seemingly distracted, it wasn't until she was nearing the exit that she recognised Pearl seated in the rear pew. She halted immediately, as though having been caught out in a guilty act.

Pearl spoke quickly. 'I'm sorry, Martha. I hope I haven't disturbed you.' Offering a smile, she continued with a single question: 'Would you like to join me for a cup of tea?'

Situated in Harbour Street, the Tudor Tea Rooms had resisted any pressure to modernise and remained, admirably in Pearl's opinion, that rare thing: an English tea shop within an authentic seventeenth-century building. Run as a family business for over thirty-two years, the Tudor, as it was known, opened every day, except Wednesday, and in the summer offered its customers a delightful courtyard garden, while in winter it became difficult to leave the comfort of its open fire. It now seemed the perfect place for Pearl to take Martha, away from the Christmas bustle of the High Street.

Sitting across a signature red gingham tablecloth, Pearl poured Earl Grey loose tea through a strainer. 'Milk?' she asked, to which Martha gave a quick nod of her head.

'I shan't be able to stay long,' said the old lady anxiously. 'I'll need to get back to Pilchard and Sprat.'

Pearl looked up from the milk she was pouring.

'My cats,' explained Martha. 'They're fed at five on the dot and I know they can tell the time because just before the clock strikes, they're always in the kitchen waiting.'

Pearl smiled and handed the cup and saucer to Martha before pushing across a china bowl containing brown sugar lumps.

'Have you had them long?'

'Nearly ten years,' said Martha proudly, dropping a number of sugar lumps into her tea. 'They were rescue cats. Brothers. In a house with a terrier who had an argument one day with Pilchard. He had to have his leg amputated.' She added glumly, 'Pilchard, not the terrier.'

'I'm sorry to hear that,' said Pearl.

'Oh, he's perfectly fine,' Martha told her. 'With the way he gets around, you'd almost never know. He's far more active than Sprat, who's becoming rather too partial to a snooze these days.'

She gave a small pinched smile before her attention was suddenly drawn to a plate that had been set before them by a pretty waitress. It contained two fruit scones.

'Please help yourself,' said Pearl.

Like a timid child, Martha picked up her knife and began buttering her scone, meticulously, thought Pearl, as though her life depended upon it. After a few moments Pearl began to wonder whether Martha was paying so much attention to the food in order to avoid eye contact – and the need to continue a conversation – so she herself took the initiative.

'Are you feeling better?' she asked.

The question was sufficiently general for Martha to have taken it a number of ways, but the old lady looked up, clearly keen for Pearl to be more specific. 'What do you mean?'

'Reverend Pru mentioned you hadn't been too well?'

Martha looked back again at her perfectly buttered scone and began to apply some lemon and ginger marmalade. 'I'm much better, thank you,' she replied guardedly, then, so as not to appear too secretive, she added, 'It wasn't anything very serious. Low blood pressure. But Dr Clayson was very thorough and ran lots of tests which were all negative. I'm quite well now on my medication.'

'I'm pleased to hear it,' smiled Pearl.

Martha took a small bite of her scone, munching with what Pearl assumed to be false teeth. Pearl had several questions to ask but didn't want to appear too insensitive or prying so instead she took a sip of tea, leaving the old lady to fill the gap in conversation, which Martha duly did, enlivened, it seemed, by the marmalade.

'I coped perfectly well with Miss Marshall's cleaning, you know.' The non sequitur took Pearl by surprise but Martha continued, 'There was really no need for me to give up working for my other employers. Dr Clayson mentioned that I might take it a little easier but there's really nothing wrong with me. It's just my age.'

Pearl nodded and decided the best approach might be to give Martha her head in the conversation. After another brief pause, Martha announced: 'I'll be seventy next birthday, you know, but that doesn't mean I can't keep a clean house.'

'I'm sure,' Pearl agreed. Martha took a sip of tea and Pearl recognised that as another person's tongue might be loosened by alcohol, sugar seemed to do the trick for Martha.

'I gave up quite a few of my jobs, or rather my employers gave up on me. I had five in all, one for every day of the working week, but now I have only Dr and Mrs Clayson.' She added ruefully, 'I've cleaned Miss Marshall's silver for the very last time.' She took out a lace-edged handkerchief from her pocket and blew her nose, producing a sound like a muted trumpet.

'You did more than simply polish the silver.'

'That's true,' Martha said proudly. 'I did everything bar the windows and she always said, "no one can get a shine on my silver like you, Martha".'

'I'm sure she was right,' Pearl said kindly. 'And Wednesday was your last visit?'

Martha nodded and took another small nibble of scone – this time from the other side as if to balance things out.

'Did you happen to dust the bottles on the drinks cabinet?'

'Of course,' said Martha, sounding defensive.

'You see, while I was there that evening,' recalled Pearl, 'Diana happened to open a distinctive bottle of Jenever. I remember it had a boat on the label – a Dutch barge with deep red sails a little like the *Greta* in the harbour. I think it was the same bottle she brought with her to the fundraiser. Did you happen to notice it in the church-hall kitchen? It was on the counter by the door.' She paused. 'I think it may have been called Skipper.'

Martha shook her head. '*Schipper*. It's Dutch,' she told Pearl. 'That was her favourite gin but I don't remember seeing it in the kitchen that night. Admittedly, I wasn't looking.'

Pearl took this in. 'And did you speak to her that evening?'

'Only about the couple from Mr Sullivan's house. She was upset about them. About the tree house.'

'Yes, she certainly was,' murmured Pearl.

Martha said thoughtfully, 'We were standing together near the raffle-prize table when I saw Miss Marshall look across the hall, and her face completely darkened – like the sky when a storm's blowing in.'

'What did you say?'

'Nothing. It wasn't my place to, but her eyes narrowed and she said they'd be the death of her.'

'She actually used those words?' Pearl frowned.

Martha nodded slowly. '"Those two will be the death of me",' she repeated.

A log shifted on the open fire and Martha popped the final piece of her scone into her mouth, chomping away as Pearl continued to digest what she had just heard. After a moment, she had an idea. 'Martha, would you be able or willing to lend a hand at my cottage before Christmas? I'm rather behind with things and I really could do with some help, so...'

Martha broke in quickly before Pearl had a chance to finish. 'I charge eight pounds an hour. If that's acceptable?'

Pearl smiled her agreement.

Resisting the lights of the Christmas gift shops in Harbour Street, Pearl convinced herself that she could still catch up with all her Christmas shopping. She was determined to find something special for Charlie, and now that she had recruited Martha's help with some light cleaning at Seaspray Cottage, she felt she had gained more time to do so.

A local agency took efficient care of all cleaning duties at The Whitstable Pearl, after attempts to hand the task to individuals had failed due to a variety of causes including bad timekeeping, sloppy work or personal problems in the lives of the cleaner concerned. Pearl had to keep things strictly professional with the restaurant, but her home was another matter and she felt sure that a few hours in Martha's capable hands would see Seaspray Cottage back in order as well as providing the old lady with a little extra income before the Christmas holidays.

Instead of heading home after the Tudor Tea Rooms, Pearl decided to stop by at Dolly's. Having checked her mobile she had found several invitations from friends to gatherings over the

Christmas period, but was surprised that Dolly had neither called nor texted for further news all day. The shops either side of her mother's were painted in fashionably dull shades of putty and grey, while the frontage of Dolly's Pots remained, in stark contrast, a striking pink. Pearl arrived to find a newly fashioned Christmas decoration attached to the front door, made from evergreen foliage secured with a tartan ribbon. She pressed the bell and waited for a response, but when none came she tried Dolly's mobile number. The call went straight to voicemail.

At that moment, a gust of cold wind blew up from the harbour, whistling its way across the triangular piece of green at Starvation Point, its name echoing a time when hungry seamen, desperate for work, would congregate there in the hope of being hired for a sea voyage. A shiver ran through Pearl and instead of giving up and heading home, she searched her bag for her mother's spare key. She slipped it in the lock and entered, but no sooner had she set foot in the hallway, than she heard Dolly's piercing scream. With her heart pounding in her chest, Pearl lunged forward and threw open the living-room door, totally unprepared for the sight that confronted her.

Dolly sat, gasping for breath as she laughed with someone beside her. It was Cassie who was giggling along with Dolly until she caught her landlady's gaze and followed it, to see Pearl looking on from the door. Both women had wine glasses poised in their hands.

'Pearl!' said Dolly. 'What a surprise.'

'Didn't you hear the bell?' asked Pearl, pointing

back to the door.

Dolly turned innocently to Cassie. 'Did you?'

'Not a thing,' said Cassie, smiling before she took a sip of her wine.

'The battery's probably gone again,' said Dolly. 'Here. Sit down and have a glass with us. Cassie bought some excellent sparkling rosé.'

Curiously, Pearl now felt like an intruder in her mother's home. 'No, thanks. I only stopped by to see how you were.'

'Shall we tell her?' grinned Dolly, turning to Cassie.

'Why not?' The girl shrugged and gave her own mischievous smile.

'Cassie here has been doing some test shots for my portrait,' explained Dolly proudly. Pearl was suitably silenced by the news but her mother went on: 'A photographic portrait, of course,' she explained.

'I thought your mum would make an excellent subject,' Cassie told Pearl.

Dolly beamed. She was no stranger to a little narcissism – another harmless part of her eccentricity. Cassie picked up a camera and selected a frame which she offered to Pearl for an opinion. As Dolly looked on, Pearl slipped on her glasses and checked a number of test shots in the camera, showing Dolly posed in a silk kimono by the window with Mojo reluctantly captured in her arms.

'What d'you think?' asked Dolly expectantly.

'Excellent,' said Pearl in all sincerity. 'But Cassie, I thought you were a landscape photographer?' She handed the camera back to the girl who began viewing the frames herself. 'I am, mainly. But some people are too fascinating not to record.' She turned to Dolly and promised, 'I'll do the next shots with lighting and then experiment with more colour in the printing process.'

'Good idea,' said Dolly, as she topped up Cassie's glass. 'Sure you won't have one, Pearl?'

'Another time, I'd better get back.' Feeling a little extraneous, Pearl turned for the door but before she had reached it, Cassie piped up.

'Any more news about the woman who was poisoned?'

Pearl turned to see the girl looking quizzically back at her. 'Afraid not,' she found herself replying, rather stiffly.

Outside on the pavement, Pearl pulled on her leather gloves, feeling disgruntled. She had intended to give Dolly an update and glean her mother's views, but for some reason she had been unwilling to divulge any news with Cassie present. Why that should be, Pearl wasn't at all sure, and she reflected on this during her short walk home. In no time, she had reached Seaspray Cottage – to find her answerphone blinking with numerous messages. It was the first voice that instantly raised her spirits.

'Mum,' began Charlie. 'Listen, I just wanted you to know that I'm feeling much better, OK? I know you must have been worried but please don't be. Just a few more days and I'll be there wishing you a Merry Christmas. I'll call again soon. Love to you and Gran.'

Pearl took a deep breath and enjoyed a warm glow of satisfaction. Soon Charlie would be home and Christmas would arrive at last. Just then, her mobile beeped and she wondered whether her son was trying to reach her again. Finding the phone, she read the text that had just appeared. *I'm here, where are you?*

Pearl looked up, and wondered how on earth she could possibly have forgotten McGuire.

Chapter Ten

Sunday 19 December, 7.30 p.m.

McGuire had been waiting at the Hotel Continental for almost half an hour. Having ordered an oyster stout he had spent a good while just staring through the window out to sea, hoping he didn't look either too lonely, or stood up, to the couples who sat at other tables. He had also studied the menu from cover to cover, aware that he could sample some 'natives' but he chose not to.

In the height of summer, during the town's annual Oyster Festival, he had admitted to Pearl that he was allergic to shellfish. It had not been an easy admission since over the years McGuire had begun to view this as a form of weakness. He had hoped that Pearl would give up trying to tempt him with oysters prepared in a variety of different ways: with a Mignonette sauce of chopped shallot, white peppercorns and wine or cooked up as some exotic fritter. But he should have known that Pearl was not a woman to give up easily with anything so, instead, she had offered up the possibility of a faulty diagnosis, suggesting that McGuire might be allergic only to crustaceans and not molluscs – something that a colleague at a staff dinner had irritatingly confirmed to be quite likely. McGuire wasn't keen on finding out, as he didn't much like the thought of oysters, even the Whitstable native, which he had learned was generally smaller than the Pacific and encased in a flat brown shell rather than the frillier grey version of its relative.

A waitress moved off with McGuire's empty bottle and as she did so, the detective now had a clear view of the door opening. Pearl entered, wearing her scarlet coat, and made her way directly across to him. She was also wearing her black Cossack hat, which was glistening with fine rain. She took it off and laid it on the wide window ledge, shaking out her long dark curls.

'Sorry I'm late.' Taking off her coat, she took a seat beside him while the waitress quickly returned to take Pearl's order of a pot of tea.

'Sure you wouldn't like something stronger?' asked McGuire.

'I need to keep a clear head.'

'For what?'

'For this case, of course.'

McGuire suddenly had to remind himself that this meeting had been his suggestion though it came as no surprise that Pearl was giving the impression that she was the one in control. She took out a small reporter's notebook and flipped open its cover.

'Right,' she began. 'On the positive side, we know the exact time and location of death and the last people to have seen Diana alive.'

'Agreed,' said McGuire.

The waitress returned with a pot of tea and Pearl poured herself a cup before going on, 'We also know the cause of death. Poison. And the means of administration.'

McGuire spoke now. 'The bottle was found.'

'I know,' said Pearl, taking the wind from his sails. McGuire felt vaguely irritated now as she flicked another page of her notebook, telling him, 'I'm pretty sure traces of ethylene glycol will be found in both the bottle of Jenever and the glass – that's if the broken pieces have been found? If they haven't, you might give the heads up to the investigating officer that they could have been left in the dustpan. That's what we do at the restaurant if the rubbish is full and someone's likely to cut themselves.'

McGuire took this in. 'The bottle's brand was called...'

'*Schipper.*' Pearl smiled. 'I remembered – with a little help.'

McGuire realised that the copy of the report that had been burning a hole in his pocket was now little more than a damp squib. He had spent some time before this meeting genning up on ethylene glycol, which he had learned had been discovered by a French scientist some time in the nineteenth century. As with ordinary ethylene, the primary alcohol in any drinkable spirits, it was moderately neurotoxic with slurring and stumbling providing the classic signs of ethylene glycol intoxication. But the main danger came from the way the body metabolised it with specific damage being caused

128

to a number of organs – especially the kidneys. The interesting part for McGuire had come from something Pearl had mentioned earlier about the taste. She had been correct that in its pure solution, ethylene glycol was indeed colourless and odourless – but McGuire had also learned that from a poisoner's point of view, it offered another advantage: since it was also sweet it could be used to lace any number of drinks or be lost in the flavour of desserts. It seemed reasonable now to McGuire that Pearl had also been correct in assuming that the sweet taste complained about by Diana Marshall after she had eaten the pastries and cakes on offer at the fundraiser had, in fact, been due to the poisoned Jenever.

'The idea of anyone pouring antifreeze by accident into Diana's drink has surely got to be discounted,' Pearl was saying now. 'As has suicide.'

'Why?' asked McGuire.

'Because Diana wasn't the type.'

'You'd be surprised how often that's said in suicide cases.'

'Perhaps,' Pearl conceded. 'But if I'm wrong, and Diana had any reason to take her own life, I'm sure she would have chosen an easier way. She had firearms and a licence to use them.'

McGuire considered this as Pearl continued: 'This investigating officer, DI Shipley...'

'How d'you know his name?' asked McGuire quickly.

'Giles told me – Diana's nephew. Is he up to the job?'

'Why d'you ask?'

'Because I promised Giles I would help.'

'Shipley won't want any interference in his case.'

'Even if I solve it?'

'Especially if you solve it.' McGuire picked up his glass of oyster stout and was about to take a sip of what was left when Pearl spoke.

'I can do it,' she insisted. 'I know I can find out who killed Diana Marshall.'

McGuire met her gaze. 'I'm sure you can,' he nodded, offering her a smile.

'And you're pleased about that?' asked Pearl, surprised, before she suddenly returned McGuire's smile. 'Ah, I get it. You don't like Shipley.'

'Let's say he's *not* up to the job.'

'OK,' Pearl agreed. 'Then how about you and I work together in a spirit of co-operation?'

'Co-operation – or competition?'

Pearl noted that the waitress was now bringing a tray of food to a nearby table. 'If you were a cook,' said Pearl to McGuire, 'you'd know that ingredients must always complement each other – never compete.'

'You're not working for Giles Marshall, are you?'

'Why?'

'Because it wouldn't be wise for you to be reporting back to a murder suspect.'

Pearl's eyes opened wide. '*Giles* is a suspect?'

'He's next-of-kin to the victim so there could be a financial motive. But I shouldn't need to remind you that...'

'...That a high percentage of murder victims are killed by members of their own family? No,' Pearl said sombrely. 'I don't need reminding of that.' She paused to take a sip of tea. 'But even if Giles were to inherit from Diana's death, I can't see him having killed her. She was always very generous to him and bailed him out on numerous occasions. If he had murdered her, why on earth would he have wanted to employ me to find him out?'

'You'd be reporting back to him as a client, so he could always remain one step ahead of you?'

Pearl considered this. 'Well, he's not my client and even if he were, Giles really isn't that savvy. Although Stephanie is,' she put in.

'His wife?'

Pearl nodded. 'But I swore I wouldn't take on a case before Christmas and I won't.'

'You are determined to find the murderer though?' asked McGuire while already knowing the answer.

Pearl had opened her mouth to respond but now closed it and clammed up.

'Pearl?'

Still she said nothing as she ignored McGuire, staring beyond him in a rather unfocused way.

'What is it?' he asked, concerned.

'I have to go,' she said unexpectedly, gathering up her coat and hat.

'But why? You've only just got here.' McGuire had allowed himself to think she might join him for supper – but instead she was now hurrying to the door.

'Pearl!'

As a response, Pearl offered only a quick wave before disappearing, leaving McGuire staring down at her unfinished tea. He turned in his seat, trying to see what it was that had so captured her attention, but noticed only a striking mural depicting the hotel with a stretch of beach before it. In a corner by the window, a large Christmas tree stood with a box beside it. Wrapped in scarlet crepe paper it had a gap in the front of it – rather like a post-box.

Chapter Eleven

Monday 20 December, 9 a.m.

The Leather Bottle pub didn't open its doors until 10.30 a.m. so Pearl had staged a meeting there for 8.15, which left plenty of time for those who had to get to work afterwards.

Everyone Pearl had invited had come along, even Adam Castle who she thought might have cried off, citing a full diary. He had taken his place at the table in the saloon bar with the other recipients of the poison-pen Christmas cards, including Phyllis, Jimmy, Charmaine and Nathan. One vacant seat remained as though pointing up the noticeable absence of Diana, but in fact, the chair had been occupied by Jimmy's wife, Val, who had vacated it only to head off to make some tea and coffee for guests. She now returned with a tray.

Pearl had explained to everyone present that while she was not in the process of investigating the cards, in the light of Diana's death and the fact that Diana had also received one, she felt it might be useful if there was some pooling of information. To this end, everyone had been as helpful as possible, bringing along both cards and envelopes, and though Jimmy had been hazy about the time of day his card had actually arrived, Val filled in a few gaps for him – as she seemed able to do on almost every aspect of her husband's life since he had surrendered it up to his wife.

'Does anyone have any questions?' Pearl asked.

In languid fashion, Nathan, who loathed organised meetings from his time spent in advertising, raised a finger for Pearl's attention. 'I'm presuming you're trying to find some connection between all of us here – and Diana, of course,' he added. 'Though I must admit, I fail to see one, other than the fact that a person, or persons unknown, had felt that we all deserved an insulting Christmas card.'

He lowered his hand and folded his arms across his chest as Pearl took his point. Looking around the table, it seemed that the assembled individuals had little in common, in personality, appearance or outlook.

Jostling for space at Jimmy's elbow sat Adam, a driven entrepreneur with perhaps more money than intelligence, while beside him sat Charmaine; superficial, sulky and synthetic. On Jimmy's other side sat Phyllis Rusk with her baby-fine platinum hair, her innocent expression and her dimpled knuckles. If Diana had been added to the mix – a proud, suburban Boadicea and doyenne of the golf course and Rotary Club – the group would certainly have seemed as diverse as one could possibly imagine.

Adam was next to speak. 'I'm not quite sure what your interest is in all this, Pearl,' he said truculently. 'You just told us you weren't investigating.'

'Not the cards specifically,' Pearl confirmed. 'But I am reconsidering them in the light of Diana's death.'

Phyllis frowned. 'What do you mean?'

Adam looked at Pearl. 'She means that both things could be related – the cards and Diana's murder.'

'Murder!' exclaimed Val. 'Who said Diana was murdered?'

Before Pearl could respond, Adam spoke again. 'She was poisoned.'

'Oh my God!' said Phyllis, putting her hand to her mouth.

'Is that true?' asked Jimmy.

'Yes,' Pearl confessed, before she turned to Adam to ask, 'How did you find out?'

Adam saw that all eyes were now trained on him, and suddenly guffawed. 'Oh, come on, this is Whitstable. Nothing stays secret here for long.' He paused. 'If you must know, I was told by a client.'

'Who?' asked Nathan.

Adam gave him a disdainful look. 'I really don't think I need to answer that. We're hardly dealing with the police here, are we?'

He looked back pointedly at Pearl. 'In fact, I'd say we owe you no more explanations, Pearl.'

He held her gaze for a moment but before she could respond, Phyllis asked fearfully, 'You don't think we could go the same way, do you?'

'What do you mean?' Val was terse.

Phyllis looked perplexed as she tried to organ-

134

ise her thoughts, gazing around at each person sitting at the table. 'Six of us received the cards,' she said breathlessly, 'but now Diana's dead so ... there's only five of us left.' She paused, her lip quivering like that of a frightened child. 'Perhaps soon there'll only be four.'

'Oh my God,' drawled Nathan. 'This really is like a bad play.'

'Agreed,' snapped Adam. 'It's all nonsense. Someone was just playing games with these cards.'

'I don't think we should let this upset anyone more than it has already,' said Jimmy. He poured a cup of coffee from Val's tray, dropping three heaped teaspoons of sugar into it before pushing it considerately towards Phyllis beside him.

'No,' said Pearl softly, as something just occurred to her. 'I think you're absolutely right, Jimmy.'

The meeting disbanded with all those who had attended heading off to their respective work duties. Pearl helped Val stack coffee cups then went off herself, to find Nathan waiting for her outside.

'Still avoiding your deadline?' she teased.

Nathan pulled up his collar against the wind and, ignoring Pearl's question, he surveyed her with a fair degree of curiosity. 'Did you get what you wanted from that?' he asked.

Pearl considered his question and finally replied, 'Actually, I think I got rather more.'

'Meaning?'

'Never you mind. Go home and finish that article,' Pearl said enigmatically before she set off down Squeeze Gut Alley – leaving her neighbour lost for words.

At fifty feet long by fifteen feet wide, the hut in front of Pearl was almost as large as the houses on the residential street that flanked it on either side. It was painted dark blue and backed onto an area of wasteland on which Pearl knew that a small bonfire wouldn't prove too troublesome for neighbours. A sign hung above the door so that no one could mistake it as anything other than the local Scout Hall.

Owen Davies was there to meet Pearl, not dressed in his signature khaki and woggle but this time wearing a fawn sweater and brown corduroy trousers. With his fair hair having been whipped up into a swirl by the cold wind, he looked to Pearl rather like a human cappuccino. Even in his 'civvy' clothes there was still something of the Boy Scout about him, with a keen vitality and willingness to help.

'Come in. Come in,' he welcomed her, ushering Pearl out of the cold into the hut.

The first thing Pearl noticed as she stepped inside was how warm it was, in spite of only a few ancient radiators pinned to the walls, and draughty windows from which some cobwebs floated wide. Owen seemed to read her thoughts.

'It's a little old-fashioned here but cosy,' he said. 'We're due to move to a new building in February.' He looked rather wistful.

'Good news?'

'Mixed feelings,' Owen said honestly, with a pinched look. 'We'll miss the land out the back.

It's been perfect for camping.'

'And bonfire skills?'

'Exactly,' said Owen. 'A few jacket potatoes thrown in at the end of a meeting? Nothing nicer.' He smiled politely. 'You had something to ask me?'

'About these.' Pearl took four envelopes from her bag and handed them to Owen, who checked there was nothing inside them before staring at her blankly. She explained, 'It was the stamps I was interested in.'

'Stamps?' echoed Owen, slightly confused. He looked down again at the envelopes and turned them over in his hands. 'This year's Scout Post,' he confirmed, as if she should have known better.

'Yes,' said Pearl. 'I happened to see the postbox in the Hotel Continental last night and it jogged my memory.'

'Ah, I see. The Conti's one of a dozen places that offered to take a box for us this year,' he said proudly. 'Great demand,' he informed Pearl. 'That's why we've done so well. Best year ever, in fact. No fewer than ten thousand cards. All sorted. Almost all delivered.'

'That's amazing,' said Pearl, genuinely impressed. 'Ten thousand? Delivered since when?'

'November the twenty-second,' beamed Owen. 'No time at all really. Superb effort by the boys. All within the local postal-code area, of course. Cards and letters posted using our special stamps.' He held aloft one of Pearl's envelopes, tapping the stamp with his fingertip. 'This year we've used the World Scout Emblem, symbol of the World Organisation of the Scout Movement.'

137

Indicating a large poster on the wall, which showed a variety of different emblems, he continued. 'Our founder, Lord Baden-Powell, first began awarding a brass badge, shaped like a fleur-de-lis arrowhead, to the Army scouts he trained out in India. Later he gave a copper fleur-de-lis badge to all who took part in his camp at Brownsea Island. The design for a badge in his book, *Scouting for Boys,* was a simple fleur-de-lis with the motto *Be Prepared.* The thing was, the fleur-de-lis was often used as the symbol for north on maps, so it was always felt to be very important that a Boy Scout should show the way in doing his duty and helping others.'

Owen paused for a moment, seemingly in reverence of the significance of the emblems on the poster. 'These plumes of the fleur-de-lis represent Service to Others, Duty to God, and Obedience to the Scout Law – the three principles of our Scout Promise which every new Scout makes when he joins our movement. Later, the fleur-de-lis became two five-pointed stars, which symbolise knowledge and truth. These are all tied together on the design of our stamp this year to emphasise the bond of our family of Scouts.' Owen's smile seemed to serve as a punctuation mark to his explanation.

'Fascinating,' said Pearl, wishing that Charlie hadn't developed such an obsession for skateboarding. His fire-lighting skills left a lot to be desired. 'So, anyone wanting to send a letter or card locally could buy a special Scout stamp...'

'From any of our outlets,' nodded Owen.

'And then use the special Scout post-boxes, like

the one at the Continental?'

'Exactly,' said Owen. 'They are then picked up, brought here for sorting – and delivered to the relevant addresses. Scouts, Beavers and Cubs are all involved, as well as the friends and family who escort the younger boys on their rounds. We wouldn't want them trudging out alone in the dark.'

'And the proceeds?'

'Some of the money goes to Scouting funds and the rest to charity,' Owen told her. 'Job done – almost.' Adding, 'We still have a few more deliveries to make.'

'And do the boys have specific rounds – just like a postman?'

Owen gave a nod. 'Oh yes, we try to match the Scouts up to an area near their homes, although it's not always possible.'

Pearl pointed to the envelopes still in Owen's hand. 'How about these?'

Owen put on a pair of tortoiseshell glasses and sifted through them. 'All Harbour area.'

'And a Joy Lane address?'

Owen frowned for a second before he worked it out. 'That would be a different round.'

'So two boys would be involved in the deliveries?'

'Yes. I'm pretty sure that would be Cameron McKenzie and Louis Morgan.' He did a double-take as he handed her back the envelopes. 'Nothing wrong with their deliveries, was there?'

'Nothing at all,' said Pearl. 'The cards arrived just fine.'

Owen beamed at this news. 'Jolly good. That's

what we like to hear. A Scout is always at the very heart of his community – that's why we decided on the world emblem this year. You see the rope that encircles the fleur-de-lis? That symbolises the family of our World Scout Movement, with the knot signifying our unity. I always tell the boys that there's unity in community.' He grinned before deciding to put forward an idea. 'Perhaps you might like to house a Scout box in your restaurant next year?'

Pearl looked down at the stamps on the envelopes, remembering the hours she had spent with her oyster fisherman father as he had taught her to tie a bowline knot for securing the line on his boat, not by the usual method of making loops through which the end of the rope was passed like a 'rabbit going down a hole', but instead by never once taking her hand from either end of the line so that she could tie the knot behind her back, without sight, should she ever need to do so on a dark and stormy night. She looked back at the Scoutmaster.

'I'd like that very much, Owen.'

An hour later, Pearl was sitting on the sofa across from Alice in the Claysons' home. Alice looked as pale as ever, wearing a white high-necked lace blouse, threaded with black velvet at the throat, wide-legged black velvet trousers and black pumps which gave the impression of mourning dress. Her mane of copper-coloured hair was pulled back and secured with a silver clasp, and the sorrowful expression on her face only reinforced her likeness to a Pre-Raphaelite beauty.

'Are you sure you're feeling better?' asked Pearl.

Alice nodded and summoned a weak smile. 'I'm fine,' she said. 'Really I am.' She raised a glass beaker to her lips which contained some pale mint tea and Pearl noticed how Alice's hand trembled slightly, perhaps from nerves under her gaze.

'I simply cannot believe that Diana isn't with us any more,' Alice continued. 'That ... I'll never see her again.' For a moment, she seemed to stare beyond Pearl to the window and beyond that towards Diana's home on the other side of the street. Her eyelids flickered before she gave her attention back to Pearl. 'The last time she was here, she was sitting just where you are now.' She set down her tea.

'And that would have been Thursday night?' Alice looked up quickly at Pearl's question. 'The night before the fundraiser,' Pearl reminded her. 'I was with Diana, going through my accounts, and she mentioned having to see Richard.'

Alice frowned as she tried to remember. 'Yes, that's right,' she agreed.

'Was she here long?'

Alice shook her head slowly. 'I'm not sure. I was upstairs when she arrived. I had a headache – I've been suffering from them for some time – and so I'd taken some painkillers and managed to get to sleep. I didn't hear the doorbell but I did hear voices. I'm not sure what time she arrived but I was on the landing when I recognised that it was Diana downstairs. Her voice was unmistakable, wasn't it?' She paused for a moment, aware that her references to Diana were now in the past tense. 'I got dressed and came down.'

141

'And did she stay much longer?'

'No. We had a drink and talked about her plans for Christmas. Giles and Stephanie were due the next day and Diana said she was finally ready, having done all she needed to do.' Alice suddenly raised a hand to her face, as though shielding her eyes. 'I'm sorry, Pearl, but I can still see the look on her face as she said that to us. She gave a sort of serene smile as though she felt relieved about something and said she would look forward to seeing us both at the fundraiser next evening. She said that very genuinely, Pearl, as if she really was expecting to enjoy it. And look what happened.' Alice's hand lowered and she took a deep breath. 'I so wish I had spent more time with her at the fundraiser but we hardly spoke – apart from simply to say hello.'

'And how did she seem to you?'

Alice gave a small shrug. 'Merry?' She looked at Pearl. 'That's a good euphemism, I suppose.'

'She had been drinking,' said Pearl.

Alice took Pearl's statement for a question and nodded. 'Quite evidently. But Diana could handle her drink. I mean, she may have got a little loud, a little strident? But she could drink most men, including Richard, under the table. I've seen her do it, at bridge parties and at the golf club. She could hold her own with any man – and in most things.' She added wryly, 'Actually she was a real man's woman, wasn't she?'

'I suppose she was,' agreed Pearl. 'But she never married.'

'That's true, but I think she would've liked to. I know she regretted not having children. We spoke

142

about it once. She was very sympathetic after my IVF failed.' She hastily went on, not wishing to say more about this, 'You know, for all that hard exterior, Diana was really a warm and passionate woman. Not the sort one might discuss fashion or home furnishings with – I didn't even discuss my paintings with her – but she told me once...' she broke off suddenly.

'Told you what?' asked Pearl.

Alice bit her lip as though torn, before deciding to continue. 'She told me that she knew she was considered an old maid in town but,' she stopped to search for exactly the right words, 'she also told me that she did understand the meaning of true love.'

'And what prompted her to say that?' asked Pearl, curious.

Alice looked troubled. 'I'm not sure. Perhaps she was just being honest. She told me there had been someone she was very close to at one time. Many years ago. I think she said that he had been a soldier.' She sighed. 'I really don't know any more.'

Alice then looked directly at Pearl and, as though fearing that she had said too much, she set down her mint tea and got to her feet. 'It was very nice of you to stop by, Pearl.'

The words served as a clear end to the meeting and Pearl stood up too, gazing beyond Alice as she noticed rain beginning to fall on the surface of the swimming pool outside.

'I really must get the cover on the pool,' Alice said, abstracted. 'The garden looks so bare now that all the leaves are gone. It will be months before it comes alive again.' She was staring at the tall poplar tree outside as though reminded of something she seemed to fear. She gave a sudden shiver and moved quickly away, heading to the door, and Pearl followed.

As Pearl took her hat and coat from Alice, she asked, 'Did Diana ever happen to mention Bonita Sullivan to you?'

'All the time,' Alice replied. 'The girl was making Diana's life a misery, all that business with the tree house. It had got under Diana's skin having someone like Bonita living so close.'

'Have you met her?'

'Not properly. We haven't been introduced but I've seen her around, and on that last night at the fundraiser, of course. She's a pretty girl but clearly thoughtless or perhaps she wouldn't have behaved so inconsiderately to Diana.'

'Perhaps,' echoed Pearl, determined now to find out for herself.

The rain had turned to a cold sleet by the time Pearl had reached the alley which ran alongside the boundary wall of The Grange. Across it sailed the faint strains of music. At first Pearl assumed it might be a tune sounding from a radio but as she grew near she could hear that it was in fact someone playing the piano. The piece of music wasn't familiar but the plaintive melody was carried on the cold evening air from the drawing room which faced the garden.

Pearl walked on towards the front of the property, the tree house now visible in the old oak tree, a continuing symbol of antipathy between warring neighbours. Pearl wondered if Diana had also been bothered by music from the new residents in Francis Sullivan's old home, although the piano-playing sounded proficient, performed by someone with obvious talent. Nevertheless, to Diana it could well have been yet another annoyance – more evidence of the old order intimidated by the new.

Pearl turned at the end of the alley and headed up the driveway to The Grange. The wind caught the chimes in the garden, and as though they had alerted those inside to her arrival, the front door opened before she had time to press the doorbell.

Simon stood facing her, his face implacable. 'Yes?'

'We met briefly in Diana Marshall's garden,' Pearl explained. 'I wondered if I might have a word with Bonita?'

Simon called straight back into the hall: 'Bonnie?'

The piano-playing stopped and a door opened from beyond the hall. Bonita approached and Pearl was about to introduce herself when a spark of recognition lit up the girl's beautiful blue eyes. 'You're the Whitstable Pearl!'

'Yes,' she replied with a smile. 'I just happened to be in Joy Lane and wondered if we could have a quick chat.'

'Of course,' Bonita said warmly. Her mood seemed to have a calming effect on Simon, who now offered a welcoming smile.

'Come through,' he said, leading the way to-wards another room off the hallway.

Pearl followed to find herself in a large kitchen. The room was a curious mix of two distinct styles, with latticed windows framed by Op Art curtains, and an old pine table surrounded by mismatched brightly painted chairs. Alongside Francis Sullivan's fine crystal and brandy bowls sat some 1950s tumblers studded with red spots. Pearl noticed one of Dolly's white oyster bowls in which lay some grapes and avocados.

Bonita moved to the kettle. 'Herbal or breakfast tea?' she asked breezily.

'Do you have any jasmine?'

Bonita opened a cupboard to reveal numerous packets and blends, amongst which she searched until she found what she was looking for. 'Here we are.' She dropped a tea-bag into a mug as she replaced the other packets.

'That's quite a selection,' Pearl commented.

'Bought mostly from the High Street. We're so lucky to have a herbalist in town, aren't we?'

'My mother would agree with that,' said Pearl. Bonita turned, suddenly curious.

'Dolly Nolan,' Pearl told her. 'She made this oyster plate.'

Bonita's eyes shifted to it and she said, 'Of course! I met her when I bought this. Dolly's Pots in Harbour Street. What a wonderful character she is.'

Pearl recognised this as a common description of her mother, suggesting something halfway between eccentric and crackpot. While most people became more conservative as they grew older, Dolly was an exception as she had become more subversive with each passing year.

'Here,' said Simon, offering a red painted chair for Pearl to sit on. Bonita brought a tray to the

146

table containing three mugs. Pearl noticed that one bore the words *Drama Queen,* while another was ringed with blue stripes and the third showed the astrological symbol for *Pisces.* Simon chose the striped vessel, Bonita opted for Pisces while Pearl, rather ruefully, picked up the mug marked *Drama Queen.*

'Have you heard the news about your neighbour?' asked Pearl.

'Diana, you mean?' Bonita looked vaguely puzzled as she sipped her tea. 'She was taken ill. We were there the other night, remember?'

'Has ... something happened?' asked Simon, noting Pearl's silence.

'Diana's dead,' Pearl announced starkly. 'It seems she was poisoned.'

'Poisoned?' echoed Bonita.

Pearl nodded. 'The police are investigating.'

Bonita exchanged a look with Simon. 'Are you saying she was murdered?'

'It appears likely she was poisoned at the fundraiser,' Pearl said carefully.

Bonita's jaw dropped open but it was Simon who spoke. 'And we're considered suspects, are we?'

'Simon,' chided Bonita.

'Well, it's true, isn't it?' He turned his attention to Pearl. 'Why else are you here? You saw for yourself how much she disliked us, and to be honest the feeling was mutual. She behaved as if she owned the whole area, as if she was part of some ruling elite. But we challenged her. Peacefully and in our own way. You saw how she was the other day. You were there in the garden with her when

147

she came barking orders about the fox Bonnie saved.'

'Saved?' queried Pearl.

'It had mange,' Bonita explained. 'When it first appeared, it was in a really bad way. It came right up close to us as though asking for help. So I contacted a wildlife charity and they gave me a homeopathic remedy. A few drops on some jam sandwiches every day.' She paused before adding, 'It had to be jam, they said, or it would be eaten by the birds. In no time Foxy was back to health and with a beautiful coat.' She smiled. 'After that, he seemed to trust us and came to visit regularly, but whenever Diana saw him crossing her precious lawn she would see red and start hollering at us.'

'She always threatened to shoot him,' Simon said fiercely. 'You heard her the other day.'

'Yes,' agreed Pearl. 'But if she'd done so, you warned her she would deserve to go the same way.'

'And I meant it,' Simon said boldly. 'But I wouldn't have had to kill her.'

'What do you mean?' asked Pearl.

'There is such a thing as karma,' he continued, calmly holding Pearl's gaze for a moment.

Bonita finally spoke. 'Look, Diana didn't shoot Foxy and we didn't poison Diana.'

At that moment, Pearl heard something at the window and recognised the large fox she had seen on Diana's garden, now sitting on the patio outside like a pet dog waiting to be fed.

'Why are you here, Pearl?' asked Bonita, suspicious too, now.

'I just thought I would introduce myself,' Pearl

said. 'You see, I happen to run a detective agency as well as the restaurant.'

Simon and Bonita shared a look. 'And I'm quite sure you know far more about all this than we do,' said Bonita. 'All we can tell you about the other night is that Diana bustled up to me and made very little sense. I thought she'd finally lost the plot when she took that Christmas card from her bag and started going on about it.'

'Can you remember what she said?'

Bonita shook her head. 'Not really. Something about ... having been pushed too far? The usual thing. Then Simon saw me with her and came over. Not long after that, she began shouting and attracting everyone's attention to the card.'

'Which you didn't send?'

'Absolutely not,' said Bonita emphatically.

Simon snorted. 'Diana Marshall would have been the very last person on our Christmas list.'

Pearl took a moment to absorb this. Then she said: 'The card had a message written inside it: *Lose your temper and you lose everything.*'

'True enough in her case,' agreed Simon. 'But it had nothing to do with us. We actually believe that in any conflict situation it is best to turn your opponent's aggression in on itself. It's the principle behind most martial arts.'

'Simon is a Black Belt karate student,' Bonita said proudly. 'I practise yoga and we both meditate. We don't lose our temper. Even where Diana was concerned we always believed that passive resistance was the right approach.'

'Gandhi said of his enemies, "First they ignore you, then they laugh at you, then they fight you",'

149

Simon stated.

'"Then you win",' Bonnie finished, smiling serenely.

As she did so, Pearl reasoned that such an attitude would only have served to frustrate Diana even more. She looked towards the garden, beyond the fox now lying on the patio. 'The tree house has been up for some months now, hasn't it? Do you use it much?'

Bonita followed Pearl's gaze. 'Not in this weather. But when it's warmer and not so windy I like to go up there and meditate.'

'Did you ever happen to see anything out of the ordinary from it? In Diana's garden?'

'If you mean did we use the tree house to spy on our neighbour, the answer is no.' Simon was emphatic.

'Look,' said Bonita, 'we realise we're new to the area and probably a little too progressive for most of the people around here, especially Diana, but we actually seek only harmony. We're really trying to fit in with the community. We make a point of shopping locally and we're delivering carol-service cards for the church tomorrow.' She sipped her tea. 'Here,' she said suddenly, before she got up and moved to a cupboard. Opening the door, she took from it a bottle and handed it to Pearl. 'Please accept this from us.' The liquid inside was a deep claret colour and the label showed a picture of The Grange and its garden, complete with the tree house and a fox stretched out on the lawn. Below it were the words: *Château Bonita*.

'It's elderberry wine,' the young woman explained to Pearl. 'A gift for you. For Christmas.'

Pearl looked up from the bottle, a single question in her mind, but Simon quickly answered it for her.

'And it isn't poisoned.'

Chapter Twelve

Tuesday 21 December, 8.15 a.m.

Martha wasn't due at Seaspray Cottage until 9 a.m. but Pearl had woken early and after showering, she had scooted around her home, wondering why she felt the need to tidy up before her new cleaning help arrived. She busied herself putting magazines into racks, laundry into baskets and clean clothes back in her wardrobe.

Opening the door to Charlie's room, she experienced the same pang she always felt since her son had left home for college over a year ago. The time had sped by, broken into manageable term-sized chunks, but in spite of all the myriad occasions she had commanded him to tidy his room, Pearl now longed to see Charlie's clothes strewn around as evidence of him in her life once again.

Over the years, the same bedroom walls had shifted from baby-blue transfers to cartoon characters, overlaid with toddler scribbles, covered yet again by film-star posters and, finally, images of Beyoncé. Pearl remembered the evening she had returned home after a hard day at The Whitstable Pearl to find that Charlie had actually painted the walls matt black and hung upon them various pieces of reproduction art – some Mondrian, Klee and Bridget Riley. It was a final assertion of independence and an indication of the direction his future studies were to take, because only a few years later, he had been accepted at university in Canterbury to study for a three-year degree course in History of Art. Four months ago, however, he had changed course after his world turned upside down when a summer romance had ended in tragedy. Pearl had worried about her son but had finally been relieved to see him bounce back with the resilience of youth. She now hoped that after a gap year to find his feet he would be back at uni, this time enjoying his new degree course, studying Graphics.

Pearl straightened the clean pillows on Charlie's bed and smiled to herself. She would spoil him throughout the Christmas holidays, allowing him to sleep late and to leave his clothes abandoned on what she always disparagingly called his 'floordrobe'. Closing the door on his room, she padded downstairs and thought to light the open fire for Martha – before deciding against it. The wind had subsided and the cottage felt warm and sufficiently cosy with only the central heating. Instead she filled the kettle and decided to make tea.

No sooner had it brewed than the doorbell sounded and Martha arrived exactly as the clock struck 9 a.m. She was wearing a large hat, not a beret nor a tam-o'-shanter but something in between the two, like a pale grey mushroom with a stalk on the top. She bustled inside, her neck craned forward as though she was trying to cross the finishing line of a race.

'Right on time,' said Pearl as she greeted her.

Martha nodded curtly, slipping efficiently out of the shapeless grey bouclé coat she was wearing. As Pearl took it from her, along with the mushroom hat, Martha smoothed down a few stray silver hairs at her temple. 'I have always set great store by punctuality,' she asserted. 'It shows due respect for others. Miss Marshall always said she could set her watch by me.'

'I'm sure,' Pearl agreed, not wishing to admit to the many instances of bad timekeeping she was guilty of herself.

Martha remained rooted to the spot, casting a long look around the living room with a searching eye while Pearl suddenly noticed the dust on the photo frames that sat on a low table by the window. They were mainly family snapshots, one showing Charlie as a toddler on the beach during an Oyster Festival while another featured Dolly with Pearl's father, Tommy, looking happy and relaxed at a beach bar in Spain. Yet another showed Pearl outside The Whitstable Pearl on the very first day she had opened, so many years ago, looking proud but somewhat apprehensive.

Usually, Pearl took these images for granted, much like the books upon her shelves that included cloth-bound copies of Dickens, Austen and Trollope alongside cookery books from all over the world: tomes she hoped to lose herself in over the Christmas holidays. Now she allowed herself to view these things with fresh eyes – Martha's eyes. The other women had apparently led a sheltered life but in her role as a trusted cleaner, Pearl recognised how Martha must have entered many homes and become acquainted if not with their owners, then with the possessions with which those owners surrounded themselves.

'This must be your first time in Seaspray Cottage,' realised Pearl.

'I believe it is,' Martha replied politely.

'But not I hope the last,' Pearl told her. 'I always invite some friends and neighbours to an early-evening drinks party on Christmas Eve and it would be lovely if you could come along?'

'Thank you,' said Martha, a little embarrassed by the invitation. 'I'll certainly consider it.'

Pearl smiled. 'Good. Come through into the kitchen and I'll show you around.' Martha dutifully followed and Pearl took two cups from their hooks and moved towards the teapot.

'Not for me,' said Martha abruptly. 'I want to get cracking, but I take a tea break at ten, if that's all right with you?'

Taken aback by Martha's businesslike attitude, Pearl nodded. 'Of course. But do help yourself to anything. There's homemade bread for toast.' Martha seemed uninterested in this but Pearl quickly remembered. 'I have some delicious lime marmalade, if you'd like to try it?'

Martha's eyes lit up at the sight of the jar in Pearl's hand, with its paisley cloth top, secured by an elastic band.

'That's very kind of you,' she said happily.

Pearl indicated the cupboard beneath her sink. 'All the cleaning materials you'll need are here and I really am very grateful for your help,' she added sincerely, reaching for her scarlet coat and

Russian hat.

'Will you be at the restaurant?' Martha asked.

'No, we're closed most Wednesdays during the winter. Gives me a little time to catch up.'

'I'm sure,' said Martha as she cast a disapproving eye across some spillages on Pearl's cooker.

'I'll be back before you go, but if you need to speak to me, I'll leave my numbers for you.' Pearl scribbled them onto the back of a Whitstable Pearl business card which she handed to Martha.

'I shall be fine,' said Martha confidently, putting the card in her pocket.

'Thank you.' Pearl gave her a warm smile before she put on her coat and tucked her long dark hair into her hat. Stepping out into the day, she felt as though she had finally been liberated.

Pearl always enjoyed the bus journey into Canterbury, whatever the season, but today, after speeding along past the village of Blean, with fields either side of the winding road, the spires of the cathedral finally came into view, rising above a haze of mist which indicated that perhaps a welcome change of temperature was due.

Alighting at St Dunstan's, Pearl made directly for the old bridge over the Great Stour, where summer visitors were ferried by punt to observe the ancient priories or the wildlife upon the riverbank. At one time, this had included otters, kingfishers and even cormorants. Pausing to look down into the swollen river, she watched the ever-changing patterns of emerald-green weeds snaking with the fast-flowing current, then moved quickly on to the Westgate, the largest surviving

155

medieval city gate in England, its towers rising sixty feet high.

Pilgrims and visitors had entered the city through its arch since 1379 and Pearl now made her way immediately to a new store in Pound Lane. She was intent on finding the perfect gift for Charlie and in less than half an hour she had done so. A young man called Shane, who appeared to be no older than Charlie himself, capably demonstrated the myriad features of a stunning new Smartphone, most of which meant little to Pearl apart from being dust and water resistant while boasting a superfast network connection and a powerful camera. More importantly to Pearl, the item promised reliable communication with her son, so when Shane embarked on a lengthy presentation about something called a download booster, Pearl stopped him with a simple question. 'If someone were to buy you this phone for Christmas, which colour would you choose?' To which Shane replied, with a confident shrug, 'Electric blue, of course.'

And so it was that Pearl found herself walking along St Peter's Street with a spring in her step, a smile on her face and a gift that would allow regular face-to-face communication with Charlie even after he returned to Berlin. So pleased was she with her purchase that she decided to treat herself to a visit to one of her favourite shops that had been trading for over twenty-five years from the same premises: a veritable Aladdin's cave of evolving fashions and styles of handbags, jewellery, corsetry, gentlemen's bowlers and top hats and tails – relics from Carnaby Street's Swinging

Sixties vying for attention with staid hacking jackets, briefcases and deerstalkers.

Revivals was managed by a stylish owner whose brief was always to ensure that no one ever left empty-handed. Waving goodbye to some satisfied customers as Pearl entered, she sighed while commenting, 'It's amazing how many people don't realise they need a fez.' As a telephone rang at the back of the shop, she hurried off to answer it, leaving Pearl alone in the shop.

Entering Revivals always reminded Pearl of the many afternoons she had spent as a child, dressing up in her mother's eccentric clothes, teetering around in Dolly's stiletto heels that had long since been exchanged for flat pumps. As a teenager, Pearl had raided her mother's wardrobes once more, this time for items that had regained fashionable status, until finally she had found her own distinctive style with a rejection of brand names and a celebration of all things vintage. Glancing around the walls of Revivals, Pearl glimpsed Teddy Boy jackets and drainpipe trousers on display beside silk dressing gowns that would have required only a cravat to have satisfied Noel Coward. Fifty years ago, young men had fought one another on the beaches of Clacton and Margate, but now the Mod uniforms of parka jackets and mohair suits co-existed peacefully alongside Rocker gear of heavy studded leather jackets scalloped with chains. Beautiful brocade waistcoats and long satin dresses were the only remains of happy wedding days from long ago.

Among a section of military uniforms, a white US Navy officer's jacket immediately reminded

Pearl of one of Dolly's favourite Hollywood romances: *An Officer and a Gentleman*. Pearl had watched the film many times, never tiring of the ending where a handsome newly graduated US Navy pilot returns to rescue the factory girl he loves. There had been times over the years when Pearl herself had wished to be rescued from her steaming kitchen and carried off in the arms of a handsome young man, though he had proved elusive so far. Dolly always complained that when it came to men, her daughter was far too fussy, but the truth was that Pearl didn't suffer fools gladly and Charlie's father had been a hard act to follow. Blind dates organised by well-meaning friends had led nowhere other than to some quick thinking about how to extricate herself from them, proving ultimately that there had not yet been a man in Pearl's life to match her own intelligence and spirit – nor to promise the passion of a summer long gone. Until, perhaps, McGuire had arrived in Whitstable.

There was something about the detective that intrigued and attracted Pearl – although in so many ways they were opposites, even in appearance. The Nolan genes of spirited Celt had produced a daughter whose gypsy black hair and grey eyes reflected the colouring of the 'black Irish' – the descendants of the Spanish Armada sailors who had escaped death on the beaches of the west coast of Ireland to serve under rebel chieftains. McGuire's cool fair looks matched his reserved nature, and while Pearl acted on her instincts, the police detective relied instead upon procedure. Still, there was plenty to connect them – not least

158

a determination to leave no mystery unsolved. For a moment, in the quiet shop, Pearl tried to summon up a picture of McGuire wearing the white Navy officer's jacket, but the image was hazy and soon vanished with the sound of the shop owner finishing her call.

'Is there something in particular you're after?' she asked, returning from the back of the store. Pearl shook her head, uttering what were surely the most irritating words for any shopkeeper: that she was 'only looking'. In a perfectly timed moment, the woman smiled and moved off to greet new customers, and it was then that Pearl spotted the white dress, hanging at the end of a rail. It was crepe, with tiny glass beads that caught the light like falling snowflakes; its low neckline was lined with soft velvet ... the perfect Christmas dress, thought Pearl, if only it fitted...

Half an hour later, Pearl emerged from Revivals with several bags. They contained a black leather jacket for Charlie, a red tartan waistcoat for Nathan, a pale pink satin duster coat for Dolly and the white beaded dress, carefully wrapped in tissue paper. Time had flown and Pearl considered returning to St Dunstan's to catch the bus home, but instead decided to make one other visit along St Peter's Street. An increasing number of charity shops had sprung up alongside the chain restaurants, but a strong, independent spirit was still evident with shops like the old family bakers of A. E. Barrow & Sons, still advertised as purveyors of pies and pastries – confectioners whose 'celebration cakes' were smothered in traditional icing, decorated with butterflies and roses, and tied with colourful ribbon.

Passing the old Pilgrims Hospital and the Chapel of St Thomas, the building to which Pearl was headed now came into view on the opposite side of the street – the Beaney Royal Museum and Free Library. With funds bequeathed by its namesake, Dr J. G. Beaney, the distinctive Tudor Revival building had opened in 1899 but had recently undergone a £14 million makeover, during which the museum had been redesigned and extended with its original features restored, including the re-carving of one of the pair of griffins that guarded either side of the doorway. A distinctive landmark, Pearl's grandparents had relayed tales of a time when the Beaney's visitors had once patted the head of a stuffed lion and looked with awe at the hand that had been severed in a duel in the film, *A Canterbury Tale*, directed by Michael Powell.

Entering the hall, Pearl was enticed into the Front Room, a gallery where an exhibition from a local Whitstable artist, Andy Malone, featured not paintings but curious works made up of elements familiar to Pearl from her childhood. Tiny forms, cut from guidebooks to butterflies and birds, peeked out from a display of matchboxes. Old cigarette cards formed concertina books, and a spectacular work was comprised of no fewer than 365 matchboxes, one for each day of the year. Each was filled with nature's surprises – a feather, a wasp, a crab's claw – items prompting a moment of sweet nostalgia for Pearl for a time when Charlie had pored over boyhood collections of fossils such as tiny ammonites discovered on walks along the shoreline.

Across the imposing hallway, the Green Room housed paintings by the artist Thomas Sidney Cooper. *Sheep in the Snow,* a work which had been left unfinished on the artist's easel when he had died at the grand old age of ninety-nine, showed a canopy of pink-grey sky above a herd of sheep, huddled in a snowscape, prompting Pearl to hanker for a white Christmas to make the bitterly cold weather worthwhile.

The room was filled with other paintings that were well known to Pearl from her childhood, for Dolly had brought her daughter here on other winter days, and neither mother nor child had ever tired of the images on display. In time, Pearl had done the same with her son. As a toddler, Charlie had become fascinated with one of the large paintings which dominated the room because its subject, a prize Shortland bull, was also called Charlie.

Cooper's work was mainly landscape, studies of cattle and sheep, but one painting in particular now caught Pearl's attention. *The Stolen Horse* showed the animal wide-eyed with fear, galloping at full stretch with all four feet off the ground like a fairground horse on a merry-go-round while the thief on its back looked urgently across his shoulder for pursuers. Held forever in this guilty pose, the figure in the painting led Pearl suddenly to reflect on Diana's murderer, who would surely be looking back across his or her own shoulder, always needing to remain one step ahead.

Pearl wandered through the upper rooms of the Beaney that had been filled by global travellers,

161

including mercenaries and missionaries, with donations of finds and mementos. Antiquities from Egypt and Ancient Greece were displayed together with memorabilia from the Royal East Kent regiment, The Buffs, and Pearl tried to lose herself in the items, thinking back to seeing them for the very first time. Amongst the collection of stuffed creatures such as goldfinches and siskins, the sight of a fox couldn't help but remind Pearl of Diana's fury with her new neighbours. Trapped forever behind glass cases, each small piece of history contributed to unlocking its own door to the past just as it now fell to Pearl to reassemble the sequence of tragic events from all the clues that lay available to her.

In the final room, among various oils and studies of the murder of Thomas à Becket, hung Pearl's favourite painting. Harriet Halhed's 1910 work, *The Little Girl at the Door*, was dominated by a tall, beige door, in front of which stood a little girl, dressed in a black hat, winter coat and polished boots much like Pearl's own. The child's small hands were clenched around the brass doorknob while she looked back towards the viewer as though unsure quite what, or whom, she might find on the other side. Down through the years, the image had continued to intrigue Pearl not least because the door in the painting remained forever closed. Countless times throughout her childhood she had imagined what the little girl might have encountered if it were to open. Now, perhaps for the very first time, Pearl recognised how much she herself resembled the figure in Halhed's painting, forever wishing to open that door, forever needing to solve the unsolved mystery.

An hour later, Pearl left the Beaney, descending its steps to find herself back on busy St Peter's Street, but this time with the warm sun on her face. The mist had cleared, to be replaced with patches of blue sky, and the sight of the Boho café reminded her that she hadn't eaten since breakfast. With its blackboard menu, bright red tables and Art Nouveau lettering, the Boho had an old Parisian feel about it. Boldly today, and perhaps in celebration of some sunshine, two tables had been placed on the pavement. Pearl sat herself down at one and began to study the menu.

Chapter Thirteen

Tuesday 21 December, 2.15 p.m.

McGuire stepped out on to Best Lane and locked the wrought-iron gate behind him. On a clear day like this, it seemed a novelty to live so close to the river, though in some ways when the Stour was high it reminded him of Venice and his time there with Donna. He knew it was time to confront the past because he had spent so long trying to escape it. The immediate pain of grief had left him, but still he could be caught off-guard when a certain song came on the radio or wafted on the air from the bar across the road. Donna had fully assimi-lated herself into London life, but the trip to Venice had shown McGuire another side to her. That summer had been special: a learning time, a time for him to fully appreciate the woman he loved.

In London, they had circled one another, had come together and retreated, both finding excuses with their busy careers, but finally they had been drawn back together as though by gravitational force. They had conquered all hesitation and moved in together, celebrating that fact with the trip to Venice. If McGuire had ever feared that familiarity might breed contempt, his fears had been misplaced. Work kept them apart too much: long hours for Donna as a solicitor, the same for McGuire spent climbing the ranks to DCI. And then, out of the blue, she was gone.

McGuire slipped the keys to his new apartment into his jacket pocket and walked on. Avoiding the noisy bar which served a fine mojito when required after a long day, he glanced instead towards the dark triangle of the Marlowe Theatre's roof which rose incongruously above the ancient churchyard of All Saints Church. The area was now home to the Three Cities Garden, dedicated to the curious twinning of Canterbury with Bloomingdale in the USA and Vladimir in Russia. McGuire harboured the hope of sitting here one day, perhaps studying the headlines of a newspaper for once, instead of a police report. Today, the weather was simply too cold. Instead he moved on towards St Peter's Street, intent on getting himself a cappuccino in a little Italian place by the bridge. This was when he was stopped in his tracks, brought up short by the sight of the customer who was being served by a young waitress outside the café across the road.

For a moment, McGuire simply observed Pearl from a distance, noting that she looked relaxed compared to the anxious shoppers who were hurrying by. Her hair was loose and her Russian hat was sitting on top of her shoulder bag on the ground, black leather gloves lying on the table beside her as she cut into what appeared to be a slice of thick quiche. McGuire suddenly wondered if she was here to do more than shopping and crossed the road to find out.

Pearl's fork hovered before her mouth as McGuire approached.

'What a surprise,' she said. 'Are you stalking me?'

'I was about to ask the same of you,' said McGuire. 'This is my patch, remember?' Seating himself opposite her at the table, he leaned across and studied her plate. 'What've you got there?'

'Lemon meringue pie.'

'Good?'

'Excellent.'

Pearl popped a forkful into her mouth, savouring it as McGuire looked on. Raising his hand, he caught the attention of a passing waitress, indicating that he would like the same. The young girl smiled and moved off while Pearl eyed McGuire.

'Copycat.'

McGuire leaned back in his chair and considered her. 'Just following your opinion.'

'A first!' Pearl exclaimed triumphantly.

'You're a chef, Pearl. With a great taste for food.'

'A private detective,' she added pointedly. 'With

165

a good instinct for people.' She thought that McGuire, who was wearing a navy reefer jacket over a white shirt and jeans, looked well rested – for once.

The waitress returned with a cappuccino and an order of lemon meringue pie and, as she leaned forward to set both on the table, McGuire nodded his thanks. The girl smiled before straightening, giving Pearl the distinct impression that she was responding to McGuire's good looks. He waited until she had moved off before asking Pearl: 'What brings you to Canterbury?'

'The clues are all here,' she replied, indicating the shopping bags at her feet. 'I've finally managed to buy Charlie's Christmas present.' Relieved at the thought, she gave a small sigh, closing her eyes before tilting her face towards the pale wintry sun.

McGuire asked quietly, 'So, where did you disappear to?'

Pearl quickly re-opened her eyes.

'The other night,' he continued. 'At the Continental?'

'I had an idea,' she said enigmatically.

'And ... are you going to tell me what it is?'

Pearl hesitated, gathering her thoughts. 'Do you know if the envelope was found?'

'What envelope?'

'The one to the Christmas card Diana was brandishing before she collapsed. I'm assuming it had been delivered to her in an envelope and was from the same batch as the others. Her nephew, Giles, mentioned that the police had searched Grey Gables and taken away papers, together with Diana's computer. They must also have searched

166

St Alfred's Hall for the bottle of *Schipper*, so I'm wondering if they came across the envelope?'

McGuire frowned. 'How would they have recognised it?'

'Aside from having Diana's name on the front, it would have had glitter in it. Just like the others.' She reached into her bag and took out a clear plastic folder. Inside it, Diana's Christmas card was clearly visible. Showing a snowman in the front garden of an Edwardian home, much like Grey Gables, it nestled on a small pile of glitter that lay gathered in the bottom of the folder.

'I picked it up that night,' Pearl told McGuire. 'The message inside had also been cut out in newsprint: *Lose your temper and you lose everything.*'

'Including your life,' noted McGuire, reflecting on this. He took the folder, but Pearl now offered him something else.

'Here,' she said. 'You'd better give the rest of them to Shipley. I've had them in my handbag since I went to see Owen.'

'Owen?'

'Owen Davies, the local Scout-master. I wanted to establish if they were all delivered by Scout post.'

Pearl could see this meant nothing to McGuire as he chased down a mouthful of pie with a gulp of coffee.

'It's a charity postal service run by the Scouts,' she explained. 'I'd have liked the chance to compare Diana's envelope with the others, but I'm betting it was delivered the same way.' She paused, thoughtful. 'At least we have the card. And the message would suggest that whoever sent it knew

167

all about Diana's temper.'

'Like the girl who was at the sharp end of it that night?'

'Bonita,' mused Pearl. 'Yes, it's true Diana blamed her, but she and her boyfriend, Simon, strongly deny sending it.'

'Would you expect them to do otherwise?'

'No,' acknowledged Pearl. 'And they certainly had cause to dislike Diana since she was threatening to sue them about a tree house.'

'A what?'

'In their garden. It overlooked Diana's property.'

'Hardly cause for murder.'

'Territorial disputes have been known to lead to it.' Pearl looked thoughtful.

'What are you thinking?'

Pearl shook her head. 'Nothing.' Keen to change the subject, she glanced towards Best Lane. 'Is your new home nearby?'

'Yes.' He gave an awkward shrug. 'And I'd invite you to come and see it, but...'

He was about to explain that he had yet to finish unpacking his belongings that had spent so long in storage, but Pearl recognised his hesitation and quickly broke in. 'Another time. I really must get back now.'

She stood up and began gathering her things while McGuire took some money from his wallet and set it down beneath the bill, saying, 'I'll walk you to your car.'

'I came on the bus,' Pearl said, picking up her hat. 'Parking's so difficult at this time of year.'

McGuire wasn't about to lose her so quickly. 'Then I'll give you a lift.' He gestured for the bags in her hand. Pearl allowed him to take them.

'Thanks,' she said, and smiled gratefully.

The journey back to Whitstable was short but instructive for McGuire as Pearl explained fully about the Scout Post scheme.

'If Diana's card had also been delivered by the Scouts, it would have been during a separate round from the others. Those addresses were all based in the Harbour area.'

McGuire took this in as he rounded a tight bend on the Blean road while Pearl observed his strong hands on the wheel. 'Were you ever a Boy Scout?' she asked, vaguely amused at the thought.

McGuire gave her a slightly admonishing look. 'Nope.'

'Cubs? Boys' Brigade?'

McGuire shook his head.

'So what did you do for fun?'

The detective remained silent. A few spots of rain had begun to splash across his windscreen and he switched on the wipers.

'Come on. You must've been into something?'

McGuire sighed and said, 'If you must know, I made model boats.'

'Really?' asked Pearl with some surprise. 'What kind?'

'Aircraft carriers, German and Japanese flying boats. From kits mainly.' He glanced at her for her reaction, but saw she was still trying to assimilate this. 'Let's just say it was a phase I went through,' he said.

'And you've moved to Canterbury when you could have opted for a sea view?'

They had just reached the top of Borstal Hill

169

and the estuary waters lay spread beneath them like a grey metal plate in the cold rain. 'These days I'm happier in the city.'

McGuire had expected this might put an end to Pearl's line of questioning but in her usual persistent way, she continued. 'In Whitstable you'd be closer to it than you think. Haven't you heard the story of how the devil created my town?'

'No. But I'm sure you'll tell me.' He smiled.

Pearl leaned closer, keen to offer an animated account. 'The devil had his eye on Canterbury,' she began. 'But the pilgrims kept it safe with regular prayers until, one night, the chaplains at the tomb of St Thomas went to sleep before saying their prayers. The devil saw his chance. He flew down and tried to pick up the city in his arms but his talons were too long to keep hold of it. He tried several times, swooping down with huge strokes of his black wings along this road, dropping armfuls of the city into the sea until there was very little of it left. Then, just in time, one of the friars woke up and rushed into the church, to sound the great bell. As the devil reached this spot, he heard it ringing and dropped the last houses in his arms. They tumbled all the way down Borstal Hill, finally creating that spit of land called the Street that runs out to sea from Tankerton Slopes.' She looked out of the window at the white clapboard cottages that lined Borstal Hill before the entrance to town. 'Charlie used to love that story when he was little.'

McGuire saw that she was still staring out of the rain-spattered window, toying with the locket that sat at her throat, while the windscreen wipers seemed to sound a message to him. *Go on. Go on.*

'There's a restaurant out on the Slopes, right?' he said.

'Jo Jo's,' said Pearl, turning to him.

'Could we get a table there tonight?'

'Without a reservation? You'll be lucky. Their calamari rivals mine.'

'Can we try?'

Pearl looked back at him now and saw that he was serious. 'OK,' she replied, 'but you might have to flash your ID.'

McGuire returned the smile she offered him, caught in her look for just a moment before he put his foot once more on the accelerator at the roundabout.

'Oh God!' exclaimed Pearl suddenly.

'What is it?' he asked, unsettled.

'I forgot to leave money for the cleaning lady this morning.'

'Is that all?' McGuire was relieved.

'You don't understand. Martha's elderly and it was her first day. I remembered the marmalade, the biscuits, the freshly baked bread – and I forgot her money. Stupid.' Pearl broke off and turned to McGuire, to ask charmingly, 'Would you mind very much doing a detour?'

Five minutes later, McGuire had parked his car in an unadopted road on the border of Whitstable and Tankerton. Martha's cottage was set back from its neighbours and fronted by a small garden with borders of shrubs and mallow that looked equally sad in the rain. 'I won't be long,' promised Pearl.

171

Opening Martha's wooden gate, she hurried up the crazy-paving pathway to a small glass porch containing a few succulent pot plants and circulars. A local newspaper, pushed halfway through the letterbox, was getting wet in the rain and Pearl was just about to post it through when the porch door opened under her hand. Standing at the front door, she pressed Martha's bell which sounded a merry tune, but there was no reply, only the sound of mewing on the other side. A moment later, a cat joined Pearl in the porch – then another. Remembering Martha's tale about a lost fight with a terrier, Pearl was able to identify Pilchard due to his missing leg but still he deftly wound his body around Pearl's ankles as Dolly's own cat, Mojo, was apt to do when he wanted feeding. Checking her watch, Pearl saw that it was almost 6 p.m., too early for the evening church service but certainly long past feeding time for Pilchard and Sprat. At that moment, Sprat ducked quickly out of the porch as though spooked by something and Pearl followed to see the animal darting towards the back of the house.

Pilchard quickly took the same route through a cat flap carved into the kitchen door. Pearl approached and looked through the door's glass pane before knocking on it.

'Martha?' Pearl tried the handle and found the door unlocked. Once inside the kitchen, the two cats began purring.

'Anyone home?' Pearl called out. No answer. She moved on from Martha's ordered kitchen, with its Formica table and a smell of floral disinfectant, through into the hallway, passing the open

172

door of a downstairs bathroom with an ancient avocado-coloured suite. The door to the living room was closed so Pearl tapped lightly on it, not wanting to scare Martha should she be taking a nap. There was no response so Pearl opened the door and entered.

A television set provided the only light in the small room and Martha was seated in front of it in a comfortable armchair with its back positioned to the door. As Pearl approached, she saw that the old lady had nodded off, her head tilted to one side, her mouth slightly open, but in the half-light Pearl noticed a tiny trail of saliva bleeding from the corner of Martha's lined mouth. Beside her lay a tray with an empty cup, a small plate and a knife close to what appeared to be an empty jam jar. A postcard with a line drawing of St Alfred's Church on its front advertised a list of Christmas services available throughout the season.

Leaning forward, Pearl gently laid a hand on the old lady's shoulder, whispering her name. 'Martha, it's Pearl...'

The woman responded by slumping sideways in her chair, a dead weight beneath Pearl's hand, with her arm flung wide from the chair as though indicating something on the floor: a Christmas-card design that was all too familiar – a Victorian carriage speeding against a snowy landscape studded with glitter. The card lay close to a pair of scissors and a scattering of tiny words that appeared to have been cut from the pile of newspapers stacked against the wall. The television continued to screen a programme about baking cakes, offering a banal backdrop as Pearl took a pen from her handbag and with a trembling hand, pushed open the card to read the message inside it.

I know what I did was wrong.

Chapter Fourteen

Tuesday 21 December, 9.15 p.m.

'How dare they arrest you!' said Dolly. 'How incompetent can the police be, to think you had anything to do with Martha's death? I've got a mind to sue that Flat Foot.'

'I wasn't arrested,' Pearl said patiently. 'It was routine questioning. They had to speak to McGuire too.'

'Good,' said Dolly. 'He'll have got a taste of his own medicine for once.' She smouldered for a moment then eyed Pearl suspiciously. 'What were you doing with him in the first place?'

Knowing Dolly's antipathy towards the police, Pearl decided against explaining about the dinner invitation to Jo Jo's. 'I happened to bump into him in Canterbury,' she replied. 'He offered to give me a lift home. It was raining.'

Pearl was sitting on her mother's sofa, nursing a glass of Scotch while she gently stroked Mojo. He was not the friendliest cat but seemed to know when a member of his family required some comfort and had crept on to Pearl's lap as soon as she had been delivered back to Dolly's by two police constables. Though she may not have

174

admitted it to Pearl, Dolly had been relieved to discover that McGuire had been on hand to take care of her daughter after she had stumbled upon the dead body of Martha Newcombe.

Two deaths, occurring in such a short space of time, and linked by Martha's association to Diana, was certainly sufficient cause for suspicion from the police, so Pearl had co-operated fully at the police station in Canterbury. There, she had witnessed the froideur between McGuire and Shipley – a young man whose self-important manner seemed to Pearl to be over-compensation for some inadequacy. She now understood McGuire's reservations about DI Shipley having been placed in charge of a case which was becoming more complex with each passing day.

Hours had dragged by at the station, spent clock-watching for the most part as procedure was observed, but having given her statement and answered all questions, Pearl had finally been allowed home, while McGuire remained behind.

'Do you think she was murdered?' Dolly asked, baldly.

'It's possible,' Pearl conceded, aware that the contents of the jam jar found beside Martha's body had been sent for analysis. Only the results might provide a final answer. 'Everything points to Martha having sent the spiteful Christmas cards,' she went on, 'though something about that last message...' She trailed off.

'In the card you found near her body, you mean?'

Pearl nodded. *'I know what I did was wrong.'*

Dolly looked confused. 'Like what?'

'No,' said Pearl. 'That was the message in the card.' She continued to stroke Mojo whose loud purr filled the room as Pearl waited for her mother to respond.

'An admission of guilt?' asked Dolly finally.

'Perhaps.'

'Or a suicide message?'

Pearl frowned at this. 'If it was, why would Martha go to the trouble of cutting it out in newsprint and placing it in another Christmas card?'

Dolly gave a small shrug. 'Perhaps to make it clear that she was the sender of the cards?'

When Pearl failed to respond, Dolly said, 'Well, surely that seems more likely than someone having murdered the old girl for sending a few poison-pen messages.'

'You're right,' her daughter agreed.

Spurred on by this response, Dolly added, 'If you think about it, of all the people who received a card, only Diana was likely to blow a gasket.' She paused for a moment. 'And she's dead so she has the perfect alibi.'

Pearl looked down at Mojo on her lap and thought of Martha's cats. Pilchard and Sprat had been delivered by the police to a local cat sanctuary and Pearl hoped they would remain together if they were ever re-homed.

'You're tired,' said Dolly suddenly. 'Finish your drink and I'll make up the sofa bed.'

'No,' said Pearl quickly. 'I'd rather go home.'

'Don't be silly, you've had a terrible shock.'

'It's OK. The walk will do me good.' As she reached for her bag, Mojo scooted from her lap, recognising that his comfort services were no longer required.

'Then at least let me drive you,' said Dolly in frustration. 'For heaven's sake, Pearl, there's a murderer out there somewhere!'

Too exhausted to argue, Pearl gave in to her mother's concern and accepted Dolly's offer of a lift home.

A short while later, Pearl was fastening her seat belt, for which she was always grateful when Dolly was driving. Lights in the Harbour Street shops shone brightly and a variety of children's stores showed displays filled with traditional toys such as rocking horses and teddy bears. Strewn with old-fashioned garlands of holly, they offered Pearl the impression that she had gone back in time – until a group of tipsy young kids wearing festive space-boppers on their heads stepped out in the road, only to duck quickly out of the way as Dolly's Morris Minor raced towards them, making for Terry's Lane. Aware that life had been going on elsewhere regardless of Martha's death, Pearl suddenly asked of Dolly, 'So what did you do today?'

'The photo session with Cassie,' Dolly replied, as if Pearl should have remembered.

'Did it go well?'

'Great fun. We had a spot of lunch afterwards and a few beakers. That girl is great company, you know.'

'So ... you were with her for most of the day?'

'Until about four thirty,' said Dolly, looking out for more reckless pedestrians before she headed across the junction at Sea Street.

'Did she have to go somewhere?'

177

'No. I did,' said Dolly. 'I needed a nap.' She drew up outside Seaspray Cottage and stared at the icy wind blowing the bare trees in the gardens of Island Wall. 'Are you sure you wouldn't rather stay with me?' she asked.

'I'll be fine.' Pearl leaned forward and kissed her mother's cheek, remembering to take her Christmas shopping bags from the back seat. As she walked to her door, Dolly waited then blew a kiss to her daughter before finally waving good-bye. 'See you tomorrow!' she called.

With the sound of Dolly's car retreating in the background, Pearl entered to find Seaspray Cottage transformed. Her Christmas-tree lights were flashing and the smell of spiced pot pourri lingered on the air. Cushions had been plumped, surfaces polished, photograph frames dusted and books arranged so that they now stood to attention rather than lying slumped on shelves. Martha had made Seaspray Cottage a home once more and Pearl remembered, with a dreadful wave of regret, that she had failed to pay the woman for all her hard work.

Burying her head in her hands, she allowed herself to weep for Martha Newcombe, who would never see another Christmas. At that moment, her mobile phone quickly shattered the silence and she saw the caller was McGuire.

'Are you OK?' His tone, both curt and formal, told Pearl that he was still at the police station.

'I'm fine, what is it?'

'I can't speak too loudly because I'm not meant to know this, but the toxicology report's come through.'

'The jar that was found beside Martha's body?'

'Right. It contained marmalade – laced with plenty of mistletoe.'

Before he could continue, Pearl responded quickly, with: 'Poisonous.'

'Not always fatal,' said McGuire, 'but in someone elderly...'

'Like Martha.'

McGuire paused. 'I understand toxicity is dependent on the person who ingests it. It can cause a dangerous fall in blood pressure.'

'Martha suffered from low blood pressure.'

'Are you sure?' asked McGuire.

'She was put on medication after a recent illness. Tell me more about the marmalade. Presumably it was home-made?'

'No,' said McGuire. 'Store bought, but added to with berries and extract of mistletoe. All cooked up with enough sugar to mask the taste.'

Pearl remained silent as she absorbed this.

'What are you thinking, Pearl?'

'That Martha had a sweet tooth.' In her mind's eye, Pearl was seeing the old lady's face lighting up at the prospect of lime marmalade. 'What does DI Shipley have to say?'

'He's not sharing anything with me.'

'Well, someone clearly is.'

'I've had to pull in a few favours to get this much,' McGuire explained.

'And the cards?' Pearl asked. 'Is there any news about them yet – including the one found by Martha's body?'

'Don't hold your breath. Forensics aren't hopeful as the scene was contaminated.'

Pearl reflected on this. 'But you could use the print from the pile of newspapers for a comparison with what was glued into the cards? That could provide a source for the print – and possibly a sender.'

'Possibly.'

'Martha may have been poisoned by someone who arranged everything to make it appear as though she sent the cards.'

'Along with a suicide message,' added McGuire.

'Yes,' Pearl agreed. 'Except something about that message bothers me.'

'Like what?'

'I'm not sure,' she admitted honestly. 'I need to think about it more.'

McGuire sensed her frustration. 'OK. Get some rest,' he ordered. 'We can talk tomorrow.'

Pearl was about to end the call when she heard his voice again. This time his tone was softer.

'Pearl?'

'Yes?'

'I promised you supper.'

'And I'll hold you to it.'

'Tomorrow night?'

Pearl smiled to herself. 'Why not? Meet me outside St Alfred's Church at six p.m. I'll be there for the carol concert.'

'The what?'

'It's OK – Rev Pru won't call upon you to sing.'

'How can I be sure?'

'Because I'll rescue you if she does.'

McGuire was warmed by the thought. 'I'll be there.'

Ending the call, Pearl moved to the kitchen and

switched on the light. The room was spotless. Stains had vanished from the cooker, and jars of herbs and spices were stacked in orderly rows. She checked inside her fridge and noted how everything looked fresh and sanitised. A half-eaten jar of lime marmalade sat on the upper shelf, a poignant reminder of Martha's guilty pleasure. The latter's sweet tooth had been her downfall and Pearl now recognised that someone had counted on that.

Closing the fridge, Pearl noticed that her stainless steel kettle had been polished so well it now offered back her reflection. Propped against the side of it was an envelope and Pearl's name was on the front. Opening it with trembling hands, she almost expected that glitter might fall upon the clean kitchen top, but instead she took out a small peach-coloured notelet. Its short message had not been cut from newsprint but written in thin, spidery handwriting. It read:

Thank you for your kind invitation. I will look forward to seeing you on Christmas Eve. I remain, Martha Newcombe.

Chapter Fifteen

Wednesday 22 December, 10.15 a.m.

'Poor Martha,' said Rev Pru, perplexed. 'And you say the evidence points to her having sent all those Christmas cards – even the one Diana accused Bonita of sending before she collapsed?'

'It would appear so from a message that was left,' Pearl replied, cautiously.

Rev Pru frowned before slowly shaking her head. 'I suppose she must have been overcome with guilt.' She looked up at Pearl. 'She had a profound sense of conscience.'

'Christian conscience,' said Pearl pointedly. 'So I was wondering if you thought someone as devout as Martha could possibly have taken her own life?'

'The Church view, you mean? Well...' the vicar said thoughtfully, 'those who suffer such despair as to consider taking their own lives are perhaps not always influenced by the Church's views on suicide. What is the phrase that's used in inquests? "When the balance of the mind is disturbed"?' She paused before remembering something. 'I once had a friend who worked as a chaplain, counselling people who had attempted suicide. She told me that in her experience, there *was* no typical suicide case. In fact, I understand that the majority of people who do try to take their own lives suffer from depression, either reactive – the result of an event like a marriage break-up or a bereavement – or biological, as with the result of a chemical deficiency in the brain. Sometimes it might even be delusional – due to drugs, prescribed or otherwise, or a severe mental illness.' Rev Pru sighed. 'Martha did give the impression of being a lonely soul but she was rather self-contained and I wouldn't have said she was depressed. She was, after all, a charitable woman so I can't imagine why she would have felt the need to send these messages.'

'Unless the balance of her mind really was disturbed?' mused Pearl. 'I admit I didn't know her well, but she came to help me with some cleaning only yesterday. She'd mentioned that she had lost work due to her illness, but that she had worked for five clients at one point – one for every day of the working week.' Pearl broke off for a moment. 'I know that you were one of those clients.'

'Yes,' nodded Rev Pru, 'but I let Martha go because I felt the work here at St Alfred's was getting too much for her. She did so much for the church in all sorts of ways. She was practically an unpaid verger. Oh dear,' she fretted, 'do you think losing her clients could have possibly tipped her over the edge?'

'Suicide, you mean?'

'That *is* what we're talking about, isn't it? I know she never married and had no family to speak of, just those two cats of hers. She thought the world of them. I remember on one occasion, Martha called me, in rather a panic because she'd left her pills at home, and asked if I could drop by in the car and collect them for her. I did so, of course, but when I opened the back door, there were Pilchard and Sprat sitting in the kitchen, looking back at me, and I got into quite a state. I'm allergic to cat hair, you see, and Martha always let them have the run of the house. I couldn't get out of there fast enough.'

'Did she ever mention her other clients?'

Rev Pru struggled to think. 'Well, there was Diana, of course. Martha remained working for her until her death, I believe. Then there was Dr and Alice Clayson. I seem to recall Martha cleaned for them too.'

'Anyone else?'

Rev Pru wracked her brains for a moment longer then shook her head. 'I'm afraid that if I ever did know, I've forgotten.'

'If you do remember, would you please let me know?'

'Of course,' said Rev Pru. 'Two deaths,' she reflected gloomily, 'and just before Christmas. What a tragedy.' She waited for Pearl to gather her bag before she sprang to the door to see her out. 'Do you think we should go ahead?' she asked suddenly, an earnest look on her face. 'With tonight's carol service?'

'Yes,' Pearl said confidently. 'I think it's what Martha would have wanted, don't you?' She paused suddenly as something occurred to her. 'That day you just mentioned, when you went to Martha's to collect her pills – why did you enter through the back door and not the front?'

'I didn't have the keys,' Rev Pru replied. 'But Martha explained that she'd left the back door unlocked. She used to do it all the time during the day. I told her she should be more careful, but she always said, "I've nothing left to steal".' Rev Pru smiled sadly as Pearl reflected on what she had just heard.

Half an hour later, Pearl was sitting at a table in the Leather Bottle pub as Valerie told her: 'Well, if it really was the old girl who sent that poisonous card to my Jim, I can tell you now that neither of us would have wanted to see her dead.'

'I'm sure you wouldn't.' Pearl cast a glance around the empty pub. It was a dark place with hunting prints on the walls and a few darts trophies lining heavy shelves. An old Rockola jukebox stood against the wall, one of Jimmy's prized possessions, and in spite of Val's presence in his life, the place still lacked a woman's touch. 'What time are you expecting him back?' she asked.

'Oh, he'll be a few more hours yet,' said Val. 'Traffic's so bad these days, especially at the end of the week, so he always goes to the Cash and Carry on a Wednesday. The one out near Sturry?' Pearl nodded and Val continued, 'I know we're meant to shop local and keep the town traders going, but we've got to make a living, right?' She picked up her cup and took a sip of coffee.

'Martha worked for many years as a local cleaner. Did she ever clean for you?' Pearl asked.

'Here, you mean?' Val looked suitably shocked by the suggestion. 'I can't imagine that Martha Newcombe had ever set foot in a pub.'

'Or at home in your flat upstairs?'

Val gave a derisive snort. 'To tell you the truth, I have two Polish girls, Ewa and Celina. They whip through this place like greased lightning but they're as thorough as anything. You know yourself, you can't take chances in catering or licensing. Last time me and Jim went out for Sunday lunch it was to a lovely place in the country, but it was in that much need of a good clean, my elbows stuck to the table.' She gave a shudder and then checked her watch. It was almost ten-thirty and clearly she needed to get on.

'I won't keep you,' Pearl said. She was quickly finishing her tea when her attention was suddenly drawn to the sugar bowl on the table.

'What's up?' asked Val immediately. 'Not dirty, is it?'

Pearl hesitated. 'No. I ... just remembered something, that's all. Perhaps I'll pop in later when Jim's back?'

Val shook her head. 'He always has Wednesday nights off,' she explained. 'He'll be playing darts down the Labour Club or at the British Legion, followed by a stop at the kebab house on the way home. I warn him every time about his cholesterol. In fact, I made him go to see the doctor a while back and it gave him a right scare when he was put on statins – but he now thinks he can eat what he likes.'

'Was that Dr Clayson?'

Val nodded. 'I see Dr Leigh, because I prefer a woman GP but Jim's always been with Clayson. Not that he's a very good advertisement.'

'For?'

'Health,' Val said. 'That wife of his looks terrible these days, doesn't she? As if she's fading away. I'm sure if she turned sideways you wouldn't see her.' She paused. 'Think there might be something wrong with her?'

'I'm sure I don't know,' replied Pearl, draining her tea cup.

As she got to her feet, Val spoke once more. 'Well, thanks for telling me about poor old Martha. It's sad news, but at least it's solved a mystery about those cards. When something like that happens, you even start doubting your neighbour, eh?'

'I suppose you do,' agreed Pearl.

'Can't help feeling sorry for her though. Nothing much in her life apart from two old moggies and the church.' She looked at Pearl. 'Must've been lonely, eh?'

'Yes,' said Pearl, thinking much the same of Val as she left her in the empty pub.

It was no more than a five-minute walk to Phyllis Rusk's store, Herbicus, and Pearl took the High Street route, passing a Salvation Army brass band stationed outside the Library. The musicians were playing 'Once in Royal David's City' and the horns sounded suitably mournful as though in respect of another death in the town. Pearl deposited some loose change in their collection box and moved on quickly to Herbicus to take refuge from a fine drizzle of rain. Entering, she saw that Bonita was there, dressed in a mohair duffel coat with its hood down. A moment's awkward silence followed, broken by Phyllis.

'Terrible news about Martha.'

Pearl stepped up to the counter. 'How did you hear?'

'The vicar,' said Bonita, indicating the mobile phone in her hand. 'I just called about the carol service and she told me you had broken the news.'

Phyllis tutted. 'Poor old Martha. If she felt guilty about what she'd done, she could've just come and told us. Whatever it was that led her to send those cards, I'm sure we'd have understood. I've always been brought up to speak ill of the sin, not the sinner.'

'As a Catholic, you mean?' asked Pearl.

'Cradle Catholic,' Phyllis clarified. 'Somewhat lapsed. But I certainly would have forgiven a poor old lady with not enough to keep her occupied.'

'I didn't really know her,' admitted Bonita. 'Did you?' She had directed the question at Pearl, who shook her head.

'I was hoping to get to know her,' she said ruefully. 'She used to clean for a few people in town – Diana, St Alfred's and the Claysons. Do you happen to know of anyone else?'

Phyllis shrugged then suddenly reacted. 'The estate agent, Adam – I think she may have worked for him recently.'

'Really?' asked Pearl, surprised.

Phyllis nodded. 'I'm sure Diana mentioned it the last time she came in. She said she'd recommended Martha to him as he was looking for someone local. Oh my Lord!' she suddenly exclaimed. 'If Martha sent all those poison-pen cards, d'you think she could have actually poisoned Diana too?'

'Why would she?' asked Pearl.

'I don't know,' said Phyllis. 'You're the detective.'

Pearl noted that Bonita was quietly taking everything in. 'Will you be around later if I need to speak to you?'

Phyllis looked apologetic. 'I'm afraid not. I have to go out after the concert tonight but I'll be here tomorrow.'

'Fine, I'll catch you then.' She moved to the door then paused for a moment. 'I almost forgot. Do you happen to stock something for high cholesterol?'

'I do indeed.' Phyllis turned to the shelf behind her, from which she plucked a small box. 'Red Yeast Rice,' she said proudly. 'Nature's statin.'

'Thanks,' smiled Pearl. 'I'll be back tomorrow.'
Offering a smile to both women, Pearl left the
shop.

Just before eleven o'clock, Pearl was sitting in
Adam Castle's office, waiting patiently as he
listened to someone on his phone. Finally he
wound up the call. 'OK, we'll do that on Monday
and I'll get the details up with our photographer.
I'm sure we'll swing a buyer for the dump.
Thanks for putting this my way.'

He set down the receiver and eyed Pearl, clearly
unapologetic for his tone. 'I did tell you I was
busy.' He gave his attention to an e-mail alert on
his computer screen.

'Would you prefer it if I came back another
time?' she asked.

'Not really,' Adam said bluntly. 'I'm always
busy.' He finished tapping out a response to his
e-mail then saw that Pearl was going nowhere.
He slumped back in his chair and stared at her
before making a decision. 'All right. Five minutes
then. What is it you want to know?'

'I hear Diana recommended Martha to you as
a cleaning help.'

Adam frowned. 'What if she did?'

'Had Martha actually started work with you?'

'You've got the wrong end of the stick,' Adam
said impatiently. 'I already have someone who
cleans my place. I just happened to mention to
Diana that it comes in handy to have someone I
can call on before a viewing – for a quick polish
and freshen up. The properties I usually deal in
are high end of the market and I like things to be

just so. First impressions are important.'

'And Diana suggested Martha?'

Adam gave a shrug. 'She gave me the old girl's number. It's here somewhere.' He opened a drawer of his desk but his phone rang again and he quickly reached for the receiver. 'Adam Castle.' His keen expression suddenly lost all interest. 'One moment, please.' Placing a hand over the receiver, he called out, 'Paula?'

From another office, she dutifully called back, 'Yes, Adam?'

'Take this call, will you?' Adam replaced his receiver and looked back at Pearl. 'Where were we?'

'Diana gave you Martha's number.'

'That's right. She said the old girl was reliable and did a good job.'

'And when was this?'

'Last week. I noticed how immaculate her own place was.'

'Diana's.'

Adam gave a quick nod.

'Why you were there, Adam?'

'Why do you think?' He leaned back and held Pearl's gaze as though weighing up some options. 'You're really not much of a detective, are you?' He gave a smug smile. 'I was there to value the place, of course.'

'Diana was planning to sell Grey Gables?' Pearl was shocked.

Before Adam could respond, his phone rang once more but his eyes remained on Pearl as he let it ring. 'Why else would she want it valued?' He signalled that the meeting was over by finally taking his call, leaving Pearl to reflect on what she had just heard.

Half an hour later, Pearl stood at the reception of Whitstabelle.

'Do take a seat and Charmaine will be with you in a moment.'

Pearl did as she was told by the young receptionist, whose heavy eyeliner, false lashes and thick foundation made her appear considerably older.

Muzak was playing, a version of something vaguely oriental to match the incense sticks and water feature which consisted of a fibreglass wall that was doused perpetually with a running fountain – all of which, Pearl supposed, was intended to put the salon's customers in a state of meditative calm.

She had to admit that after a busy day, Whitstabelle did seem a haven of sorts though she herself wasn't here for relaxation. It was interesting, nonetheless, to observe the salon from inside since she had passed it so many times without ever having crossed its threshold. As far as pampering was concerned, a visit to the same hairdresser on Harbour Street was as far as Pearl ever got, and even then, only three or four times a year – though she felt she might have to consider more regular visits after having found the odd silver hair lately. Visiting a beauty salon had never been part of Pearl's routine, though Dolly sometimes treated herself to a massage to ease an old back problem acquired on the dance floor of a local pub some thirty years ago. Winning a raffle prize, however, had offered Pearl the opportunity to extract some information from Charmaine – but should it come with any improvement to her general appearance, all the better.

A buzzer sounded suddenly, interrupting the Zen calm of Whitstabelle. The young receptionist tore her attention away from Facebook to announce: 'Charmaine is ready for you now. In the Lotus Room.'

Pearl passed two doors in the hallway, marked *Saffron* and *Nirvana*, before she found Charmaine waiting for her. Whitstabelle's owner was wearing a crisp white tunic and trousers which Pearl assumed was intended to convey some clinical authority, but the uniform was at odds with Charmaine's make up and scooped-up hair. In fact, she looked about as authentic as a glamorous actress in a television hospital drama.

'Very wise of you to use your voucher appointment so quickly,' Charmaine advised as she closed the door after Pearl. 'We wouldn't have been able to fit you in any closer to Christmas.'

'That busy?'

'Inundated,' said Charmaine, gesturing for Pearl to take up position on a large treatment bed. 'Make yourself comfortable.'

Pearl took off her boots and lay down upon the bed. A heavy scent of essential oil of lavender hung on the air while Charmaine, in a few swift and efficient moves, popped a soft pink towel across Pearl's chest and a bandeau about her head to keep her hair back from her face.

Dimming the overhead lights, she now switched on a bright Anglepoise lamp, more suitable to

192

interrogation than relaxation, and moved closer, carefully investigating Pearl's features before finally asking, 'And when was the last time you had a facial?'

Something in Charmaine's tone made Pearl feel instantly guilty. Rather than admitting the simple truth – that she had never experienced any such thing – she murmured, 'I ... can't quite remember.'

Charmaine gave an admonishing 'tut' before selecting some moist cloths and a variety of lotions. 'You really should make an appointment at least once a season,' she counselled. 'A few visits during summer and winter are essential due to the extremes of temperature. You have a few spider veins peeking through.'

'Have I?' asked Pearl, perplexed.

'Don't frown!' ordered Charmaine. 'Unless you want to encourage more furrows.'

'What furrows?' asked Pearl helplessly.

'You've a few settled in on your forehead, and your complexion will only be made worse by heat or wind. You might start thinking of a good barrier cream when you're out on that boat.'

Pearl gave a slight nod, aware that it had been months since she had been out on her little dinghy, and that many more would pass before she felt the sun on her face again at sea.

'Now, close your eyes and let's see what I can do.'

Pearl obeyed, trying to relax as Charmaine's long, slender fingers began smoothing her skin in upward strokes as though trying to coax any drooping flesh back into position. It wasn't an unpleasant experience apart from Charmaine's proximity: her sweet breath was just a little too close for comfort and her cloying perfume, with its musky base note, clashed with the existing smell of lavender.

'Shocking news about Martha,' said Charmaine in a soft tone.

'Yes,' agreed Pearl, unable to elaborate as Charmaine's fingertips teased the skin around her mouth.

'I'm going to start with a mask,' the beautician stated. 'Cleansing and firming.'

Pearl felt a cold unguent being deftly applied to her face as Charmaine returned to the subject of Martha Newcombe. 'Is it true you found her?'

Pearl gave a nod and Charmaine reflected on the news. 'Poor woman must've lost her mind, don't you think?'

Sounding much like an amateur ventriloquist, Pearl tried to respond without moving her lips. 'Why do you say that?' she managed finally.

'Well, from what I've heard, it was Martha who sent the cards to us all. The guilt must have got to her – about Diana's murder?'

'There's no evidence that she killed Diana,' mumbled Pearl. Charmaine prevented further comment as her fingertips pressed Pearl's lips shut.

'She left a note, didn't she?'

'A card.'

'With a message?'

'*I know what I did was wrong,*' said Pearl, adding: 'That was the message cut out inside.'

Charmaine said nothing until she finished applying the mask. 'Seems to say it all, doesn't it?'

'Does it?' asked Pearl. 'Why would Martha have murdered Diana? She was one of her few remaining employers.'

Charmaine gave an elegant shrug. 'Maybe she'd had enough of Diana. Maybe she was going senile and lost the plot. Who knows?'

Pearl observed Charmaine as she wiped her hands with a tissue. 'When was the last time you saw Diana – apart from the fundraiser, I mean?'

Charmaine dropped the tissue into a pink litter bin. 'About a week ago. Saturday, I think it was. She came in for a full treatment – facial, manicure, pedicure.'

'Diana?' Pearl was surprised.

'She'd been coming regularly for a few months.'

'But not before?'

'She said she was taking herself in hand. You must have noticed she'd had her hair coloured?'

'Yes,' admitted Pearl, remembering how feminine Diana had looked on the last evening at Grey Gables. 'Why do you think she chose to do all that now?'

'It happens,' said Charmaine. 'A woman reaches a certain age and decides she doesn't want to let herself go. I'm all for that,' she continued. 'And not just because it's good for my business...' she smiled '...but because every woman deserves to look her best. Besides, Diana had almost everything: a beautiful home like Grey Gables? That's worthy of some house envy.'

Charmaine turned back with a look that was slightly too pointed for Pearl's liking. Pearl found it difficult to open her mouth since her skin was

195

tightening from the mask that had just been applied but she managed to ask, 'Were you here at the salon yesterday?'

'Until lunchtime,' replied Charmaine. 'Then I went to do some Christmas shopping.' Seeing Pearl was about to respond, she quickly ordered, 'Not another word. That mask has set and needs a good ten minutes to work its magic.' She got to her feet and moved to the door. 'I'll be back in a while.'

Pearl heard the door softly click after Charmaine's exit.

It wasn't until forty minutes later that Pearl finally left Whitstabelle. She felt as though she had been put under some form of anaesthetic but the cold wind soon brought her to her senses. Staring down at her fingernails, she saw they were now a blushing pink with white crescents at their tips – a French polish thrown in by Charmaine as an extra treat. Warily now, she took a small mirror from her bag and raised it to her face, instantly wishing she hadn't agreed to Charmaine's suggestion of a special eyebrow treatment. The threading technique, which used something resembling a 'cat's cradle', had left Pearl with two thin arches where her dark eyebrows usually framed her moonstone eyes. She exhaled a long sigh, hoping nobody would notice – least of all McGuire.

Chapter Sixteen

Wednesday 22 December, 6 p.m.

'What on earth have you done to your eyebrows?' asked Nathan.

'If you must know, they've been threaded,' said Pearl in response.

Nathan winced. 'Ouch.'

'You know about it?' Pearl was surprised that Nathan's look showed he not only knew about threading but had no doubt experienced the brutal, if thankfully brief technique himself. 'Let's just hope they grow back, sweetie.'

'That bad?' asked Pearl glumly.

Nathan examined Charmaine's handiwork. 'Executed by a jealous woman, I shouldn't wonder.'

Nathan's remark suddenly resonated for Pearl. Though she had never sensed that Charmaine might be jealous of her personally, there seemed always to be a general air of covetousness about Whitstabelle's owner, articulated in the phrase she had used only today concerning Grey Gables: 'house envy'.

It was envy that motivated Charmaine, a general dissatisfaction for not possessing all that she wanted or felt she rightly deserved.

A click sounded as Nathan locked his vintage Volkswagen with the key in his hand. He had just driven back to Whitstable from London, where he had been doing some Christmas shopping as a distraction from getting on with his article, and had called Pearl to explain that he was running late and would meet her at St Alfred's. The small car park was packed, promising a good turnout for the carol service, and the rain that had been forecast had mercifully held off. Even the northerly wind had dropped as though in respect of the occasion. In fact, the air seemed strangely still as it does sometimes before snow, making Pearl wonder if it might prove to be a white Christmas, after all. She took Nathan's arm and walked on with him.

Having texted McGuire to remind him of the start time, when he had failed to respond, she had texted once again, this time making sure he was in no doubt as to both the time and venue. Now, as she rounded the corner of St Alfred's with Nathan, her eyes scanned the crowd already assembled around the church Christmas tree. Festive lights shone from its boughs, their glow illuminating a number of familiar faces. Rev Pru, somewhat swamped in a white chasuble emblazoned with gold brocade, stood on the church steps with members of the choir, who wore a more casual uniform of red and black.

A cross-section of the community had turned out for the event and Pearl quickly spotted Phyllis, wearing a furry white pixie hat as she stood close to Bonita and Simon. The Claysons were a short distance away, Alice shivering slightly until Richard placed a protective arm around her. Val, wearing glasses, looked uncharacteristically studious as she perused the carol sheet in her hand. Was Jim finally managing the bar of the Leather Bottle on his own for once, wondered Pearl – until she remembered that Wednesday was his night off. Charmaine was somewhat over-dressed for the occasion in a figure-hugging outfit of a purple velvet jacket and black knee-high boots over ski pants. She gave Pearl a self-satisfied smile and moved closer to the choir while Pearl recognised a familiar finger-rippling wave as Dolly's face bobbed up above the heads of an elderly couple.

Pearl returned her mother's smile but found it hard to keep the smile in place as she noticed that the person standing beside her was Cassie. The girl's kohl-rimmed eyes sparkled though her lips remained tightly fixed in their usual pout, contributing to a rather smug, if not triumphant, expression. Triumphant about what? Pearl began to consider whether any misgivings she might have harboured about the girl were simply down to resentment of the amount of time Cassie seemed to be spending with Dolly. Sensing that something was wrong, Nathan asked, 'What is it?'

'Nothing,' replied Pearl quickly, stifling any negative feelings about Cassie as she saw Rev Pru open her arms wide in an all-embracing gesture towards those assembled.

'Welcome,' said the vicar. 'And thank you, one and all, for coming to this short carol service this evening.' She paused to look up at the tree before continuing. 'Christmas is a time for coming together, as we have done on so many occasions, and we do so now to celebrate the birth of Christ, but also to share our recent loss of two much-loved members of our community, Diana Marshall and Martha Newcombe.'

Rev Pru paused again and only now did Pearl notice Stephanie and her son, Nicholas, beside Giles who looked pale and diminished as he fished for something in his pocket, finally withdrawing a white handkerchief with which he wiped his eyes.

Rev Pru went on gently, 'We grieve with their families and friends, especially at this time, but we remember that we stand united in our grief, in our compassion and in our togetherness, symbolised by our singing this evening.'

She bowed her head, and as if on cue, the choir behind her began singing, 'O Little Town of Bethlehem'. Each person present, young and old, joined in, including Pearl and Nathan who shared a look as the final lines of the verse rang out: 'Yet in thy dark streets shineth The everlasting light, The hopes and fears of all the years Are met in Thee tonight.'

After a short prayer from Rev Pru, a shriek of inappropriate laughter rang out, causing heads to whip round. Adam Castle, dressed in a black cashmere overcoat, was passing by with his secretary, Paula, when he suddenly saw all eyes were upon him. His arm had been wrapped tightly around the girl but it immediately dropped as the two shared a guilty look. They quickly tried to move on but Rev Pru was quicker and called out pointedly: 'All are welcome!'

Looking suitably trapped, Adam and Paula approached like a pair of naughty children. As they joined the carol singers, Rev Pru finally smiled and announced: '"The Holly and the Ivy".' Once again, the choir led the singing but throughout the carol, Pearl kept glancing around, seeking out McGuire. It became painfully obvious that the detective had not come and, as time had moved on, he was not about to. Reaching for her mobile phone, Pearl recognised to her disappointment that he had ignored both of her messages.

With the service finally over, Nathan eyed Pearl as they returned to St Alfred's car park. 'Something's up,' he said. 'What is it?'

'Nothing,' Pearl said flatly. 'Really.'

Nathan was forced to accept that the subject was off-limits. He took out his car keys, about to open the Volkswagen, when Pearl laid a hand on his. Her quick look silenced any further questions as she stared across at another parked car. A light shone within it, allowing Pearl to identify Phyllis Rusk at the wheel. She was looking into a vanity mirror on the back of her sun visor, carefully applying some lipstick before tossing her pixie hat onto the back seat. She spruced her hair and a moment later, the light in the car went off and the engine started up.

As Phyllis accelerated out of the car park, Pearl made a decision and grabbed Nathan's car keys to unlock the Volkswagen. Taking the passenger seat, she secured her belt, looking back at him as he peered into his own car.

'Well?' she said. 'What are you waiting for?' She handed the keys back to him and ordered: 'Follow that car.'

It seemed an eternity before Phyllis finally turned

off the small country road on which Nathan had been doggedly pursuing her. As the woman's car was crossing a small bridge, Pearl's outstretched hand issued a warning to Nathan as he turned to follow. 'Wait.'

Nathan rolled his eyes. 'But you've been on to me not to lose her ever since we left Whitstable!'

'It's important she doesn't see you,' argued Pearl. 'She's turning into the car park of that pub. Do you know where we are?'

'Haven't a clue,' Nathan said sincerely. 'How would I? I've had my eye on the bumper of Phyllis's car for the last half-hour.'

'Fordwich,' said Pearl. 'The smallest town in England.'

Nathan looked at her with interest. 'Really?'

Pearl nodded and explained. 'There are fewer than four hundred people living here, but Fordwich officially qualifies as a town – with its own council.'

Nathan looked suitably impressed. 'You don't say.'

A sucker for history, he peered out of the driver's window at the half-timbered buildings in the distance, but Pearl interrupted him with, 'Don't relax. I want you to go and see what she's up to.'

'Me?' Nathan looked suitably shocked.

'Yes, you,' Pearl insisted. 'Believe it or not, you're far less conspicuous than I am.' She looked down at her scarlet coat then reached onto the back seat for Nathan's scarf and a black corduroy Gatsby cap that he was rather partial to wearing in wet weather. As she handed them to him, Nathan knew better than to argue.

A few moments later, once they had parked at the rear of the old pub, Nathan headed off, but he had taken only a few steps before he returned, whispering urgently, 'What do I do if she sees me?'

'Make sure she doesn't.'

Nathan took a deep breath, pulled his cap down over his eyes and, rounding the building towards its entrance, he disappeared from sight. Pearl was left in suspense for far longer than she had expected. A full moon was due but as yet there was no sign of it. The sky was black and streaked with smoky cloud. Pearl checked her phone once more but still there was no message from McGuire. Her heart began to harden a little; she felt ashamed and angry in equal measure at the thought that McGuire could stand her up without a suitable explanation. She tried to summon the courage to call him, but a hand on the car door suddenly caused her to gasp in shock. Nathan jumped into the driver's seat.

'Well?' she asked, relieved.

Nathan turned to her, still wearing his hat. 'You'd have been proud of me,' he replied with a smile. 'I pretended I was French.'

Pearl frowned. 'To whom?'

'*L'homme à la porte,*' he said airily. 'The guy at the entrance. It's a private function. A curry night special for a supper club.' He handed Pearl a leaflet. 'You have to join and then members are notified of future culinary events by e-mail.' Nathan grinned in a manner that was both victorious – and mischievous. He leaned closer to Pearl, confiding: 'Phyllis just met up with someone. Gave him a great big kiss.'

'Jim?'

The wind was suddenly taken from his sails. 'How on earth did you know?'

'That would be telling,' Pearl teased. 'OK. Let's get out of here.'

As Nathan put the car into gear, Pearl's mobile phone sounded. The caller was McGuire. For a moment she considered ignoring the call but curiosity got the better of her.

'Hi,' she responded tersely.

'I'm sorry,' McGuire said immediately, having noted her clipped tone. 'Something came up and I just couldn't make it in time.'

'Clearly,' Pearl replied, aware that Nathan was listening.

'There *is* a murder investigation going on, Pearl.'

'Which you are not in charge of,' she reminded him. 'Didn't it occur to you that the murderer might very well have been among the people at the carol service this evening?'

McGuire sounded suspicious as he asked, 'Did ... anything happen tonight?'

'Yes,' Pearl told him. 'As a matter of fact, I've just discovered something rather important.'

'Where are you?' asked McGuire, concerned.

'Leaving Fordwich.'

'Where?'

'It's a little village...' Pearl broke off and corrected herself. 'Town. On the River Stour. A couple of miles from Canterbury.'

'Stay where you are. I'll meet you,' instructed McGuire.

'*No.*'

McGuire became increasingly frustrated by her

clipped tone and cryptic remarks. 'Why not?'

'Because there's no need. I'm here with a friend,' she announced. 'He's driving me home.'

McGuire felt suddenly winded. 'OK.'

'I'll talk to you tomorrow,' she added quickly before ending the call.

A moment later, Nathan opened his mouth to speak but Pearl raised her finger.

'Don't say a word,' she commanded.

Having taken a more direct route home, Nathan pulled up outside Seaspray Cottage twenty minutes later. Pearl turned to him: 'You did well tonight.'

Nathan preened. 'Yes, I did rather, didn't I? Feel free to call on my services again, sweetie. It was so much more fun than struggling with my article.' He leaned in to kiss her but Pearl's look reminded him that he was still wearing his cap, so he took it off before giving her a peck on the cheek. 'I can see why you enjoy this detective business. But wouldn't you rather be playing cops with your inspector?' He gave her a knowing look. 'That was him on the phone, wasn't it?'

Pearl's look was all the reply Nathan required. 'I think you have it bad, sweetie.'

'Good night, Nathan,' said Pearl pointedly.

Pearl got out of the Volkswagen while Nathan waited until she had reached her front door. He offered a mock salute then drove down the narrow little road to his garage on the other side of Island Wall. Pearl watched his car headlights fade before she turned back to Seaspray Cottage, fumbling for her door keys in her bag before she noticed the heavy pebble that lay positioned on her front doorstep. Beneath it was a piece of paper. Picking it up, Pearl saw that in neat, controlled handwriting its message read: *Please come to the Battery ASAP. And come alone. C.*

Chapter Seventeen

Wednesday 22 December, 9.30 p.m.

Deciding against asking Nathan to drive her in his car, Pearl took the beach route to the Battery – alone. She was taking a risk but a calculated one, for in her pocket was a meat skewer she had plucked from her kitchen drawer for some protection, though she sensed the only real danger she faced would be in scaring off her informant by taking someone along with her.

Before leaving Seaside Cottage, she had changed out of her boots and into a pair of flat canvas shoes, which made little sound on the pebbles underfoot. Her mobile was in her pocket, ready to dial for help if required. The moon had risen: swollen in the cloudy sky, sending a silvery light across Sheppey which lay stretched out on the western coast, lights blinking on its own shore. Waves thundered up on the high tide, white foam crashing and dissolving on the beach, lighting a path for her to follow.

Pearl reflected on the note and the way in which the sender had signed off with the single letter 'C'.

Arriving so soon after her salon appointment at Whitstabelle, Pearl's first thought was that it had been left by Charmaine, but as she passed the huts at West Beach, another thought suddenly came to her: the memory of a young girl asking her way to the Battery just a few days earlier. Cassie had been on her way to take photos on the morning that news of Diana's poisoning had come through from McGuire. Alice's collapse at the beach hut that day had put an end to the girl's visit to the Battery, but Pearl now considered it might be Cassie who was summoning her, though why the girl had not left her complete name remained a mystery.

Having passed a stretch of beach homes, deserted now for Christmas, the unmistakable silhouette of the Battery became visible on the shore, looking out to sea as it had done for over a hundred years.

The solid rectangular building served as a punctuation mark to all further beach residences on the western shore, since nothing followed after it but a grassy slope that had long become home to wild rabbits. A single dim light within the building signalled someone's presence.

Pearl heard nothing but the waves upon the shore as she approached. Looking back, she saw the beach was deserted as she climbed the few wooden steps to the door. She rang the bell and waited but there was no response. Raising her arm, she knocked this time, considering that she had perhaps been summoned to this remote place to ensure she was suitably out of the way. But why? Pearl knocked again, this time moving to a window through which she could see nothing but the glow of light behind heavy lace curtains. Frustrated to have been sent on such a fool's errand, Pearl was about to move off when she felt the hand upon her shoulder.

Hearing her own sharp intake of breath, she turned to see the man towering behind her. His imposing frame was silhouetted against the moonlight, his eyes pale like those of a wolf, while his thick dark hair was streaked with grey, adding to his lupine appearance.

'Who are you?' gasped Pearl as she tried to calculate from which direction he had appeared.

The man replied in a sombre voice, 'Please come inside and I'll explain.' He opened the door and gestured for Pearl to step inside. As soon as she had done so, Pearl noted that the glowing light she had seen outside came from the Battery's huge wood-burning stove, famously known as The Beast. The click of the door behind her sent a shiver of fear through Pearl until the man switched on a light.

'I was just in the garden,' he explained. 'I waited so long, I wasn't sure you would come.'

'I was at a carol service in town.'

'I know.'

'You were there?'

The man nodded slowly and moved towards some bottles that were crowded together on a side table. 'Can I get you a drink?'

Pearl shook her head but the stranger poured a generous measure for himself, and in the light of The Beast it took on the colour of warm honey. Pearl recognised it to be a good malt whisky. She sat down on a sofa which was lined with a soft tartan throw.

'Who are you?' she asked.

'My name is Christopher Hadley.'

'You're Scottish,' she said, noting the hint of an accent.

The man looked surprised for a moment. 'Correct. I was born in Leith near Edinburgh.'

'On the coast,' Pearl remembered. Then: 'Why didn't you come and introduce yourself to me at the carol service instead of leaving a note for me?'

'You were with someone.' The man shrugged. 'I needed to take stock.'

'To spy on me, you mean?' Pearl said accusingly.

Christopher Hadley fixed her with a gaze of his pale amber eyes. 'To recognise who I can trust.' He paused. 'I've been watching you. You're a detective.' As he sat down in an armchair, his eyes remained trained on her. 'Who are you working for?'

Pearl failed to reply and Christopher Hadley offered up a suggestion. 'Giles Marshall?'

'And what if I were?' she asked.

Christopher shook his head slowly. 'He can't be trusted.'

'Why do you say that?'

'Because she was going to cut him off and he knew it.'

'Diana?' Pearl struggled with the thought. 'Why on earth should I believe you? A complete stranger...'

'Not to Diana.' He swallowed hard, as though trying to hold back a weight of emotion. 'I was her fiancé.'

The words settled, creating a silence broken only by the sound of the waves on the shore outside. As if summoned by this, the man got to his feet and moved across to the window. Parting the lace curtains with his hand, he looked out, motionless, for a moment before finally letting the curtains fall. His gaze remained fixed, however, as though staring at an after-image. 'I fell in love with her,' he said, softly. 'Almost from the very first moment we met.'

He looked back at Pearl who asked warily, 'And ... that was many years ago?' She remembered a conversation with Alice Clayson. 'You were a soldier.'

'Yes,' he replied. 'In the Guards. Diana was at university.'

'In Edinburgh.'

Christopher nodded. 'We met at a shooting party. Diana was a kindred spirit, my...' He broke off suddenly, as though ashamed to continue, but finally he summoned up courage and found the word he was searching for. 'Soulmate.'

As he uttered the word, he appeared in that single moment both exposed and defenceless. Pearl felt for him – a strong man diminished by loss.

'It's become rather a cliché, hasn't it?' he asked. 'But I can think of no better description of Diana.'

Pearl felt stung by the sorrow in his pale eyes. 'What happened?'

'Life,' he said simply, before he knocked back the last of his Scotch and moved to refill his glass. His hands began to shake as he did so but he managed to carry on. 'I was sent to the Falklands in 1980.' Strangely, he said nothing more as though this in itself had been sufficient explanation.

'But you returned. The war was won.'

'Yes,' he agreed. 'But some of us lost.' He looked down at the glass in his hand. 'I promised Diana I would return – and I did – but not as the man she knew.'

'What do you mean?' frowned Pearl.

Knocking back his drink, Christopher wiped his hand across his mouth. 'We were part of the final advance towards Stanley – land forces. But it was tougher than any of us expected. I was twenty-two years old but the Argentine soldiers were much younger. We clashed during a night battle with a marine company on the lower slopes of a mountain. One of our tanks was taken out by a booby trap but we held fast until a heavy fire-fight broke out. For hours. Until we finally secured our position.' He refilled his glass. 'Some time before midnight, we took cover.'

Pearl noted how Christopher's hand clenched and unclenched in a reflex action as he continued with his story.

'We had to abandon our dead,' he said in a low voice. 'We lost more men because the area was mined and the explosions alerted an Argentine mortar platoon. It would have been worse for us if the mortar bombs hadn't landed on the soft peat, which absorbed most of the explosions. But we fought through the night and gained the high ground before continuing with the attack. By that time, we'd taken scores of prisoners, and ... just as many had died. But still the enemy were in position. Only the intervention of an Argentine Colonel brought the fighting to an end. At last they retreated. We were victorious.'

His eyes closed as he remembered. 'From somewhere at the top of the mountain I heard a piper playing a march.' He tilted his head slightly as if he were hearing it again. 'Then everything went black.'

Pearl said nothing but Christopher finally answered her enquiring look. 'A sniper's bullet had passed through my skull. I was airlifted to a makeshift operating theatre. Much later, they told me that I had been the last to be operated on because my chances of survival were so slim.'

He set down his glass. 'Then came the difficult part. They warned me I would never walk again.' He looked Pearl in the eyes. 'Life was cancelled.'

'And so you broke off your engagement to Diana?'

'A bullet did that,' said Christopher firmly. 'I couldn't expect her to wait for me. I spent over a year in a wheelchair...'

'But you recovered,' Pearl said. 'You did walk again and you're here to tell your story.'

'Now that it's too late.' Christopher turned to Pearl. 'How could I possibly know?' he asked helplessly. 'I had to set her free, do you see? There were no guarantees. I thought that she would find someone. Another soulmate. I thought she would marry and go on to have a family...'

'But she never did.' In the silence that followed, Pearl's words seemed to echo.

Christopher said nothing but his head was bowed.

'And you?' Pearl asked softly.

'I ... married, briefly, for all the wrong reasons.

212

And just when I'd grown accustomed to being alone, I went to see a play. In Chichester. Something I had once seen with Diana many years ago – *A Woman of No Importance.*' He passed a hand over his brow. 'And suddenly there she was. In the same theatre – as though we'd never left it. It was the strangest thing. We tried to make sense of what had happened, but there *is* no sense to it. We couldn't waste any more time so ... I proposed and Diana accepted. She said that we would enter the third act of our lives – together.' The ghost of a smile appeared on his lips.

'And you ... kept this a secret?'

He nodded. 'Nobody knew. Diana planned to make an announcement at Christmas. That's why I'm here. She booked this place for me – said that I would love it here, by the sea. She planned it all, booked a flight for me to arrive after she had told her nephew. She wanted to do that, face to face, on Friday. Then she would telephone me at my home. It was all arranged.'

'So ... she planned to tell Giles on the night of her death,' realised Pearl.

'Yes,' Christopher said. 'I didn't know what had happened ... I didn't receive her call. I left several messages for her at the weekend, but they all went unanswered so I took the flight as arranged and arrived here yesterday.'

'Giles and his family have been staying at the house,' Pearl told him.

'I know. His wife explained everything to me today when I called again.'

'Stephanie knows about you?' asked Pearl.

Christopher looked away, as if unsure of what

213

to say.

'You haven't explained to them, have you?' Pearl realised. 'Haven't told them who you are.'

'Diana has been murdered. I told you, I don't know who I can trust.'

'But Giles and Stephanie are her family!' And then the light dawned on Pearl. 'She was planning to sell Grey Gables – and start a new life with you.' Pearl made an effort to collect her thoughts. 'But if what you say is true, if she really was going to cut Giles loose...' She registered the message in Christopher's dark look. 'You can't possibly think that *he* murdered her. Giles was bereft at her death. He *adored* Diana!'

'So did I,' said Christopher fiercely.

Suddenly, it seemed as though Pearl was viewing Christopher Hadley through the wrong end of a telescope, as though he was somehow receding from her into the distance of the vast sitting room. The Battery had served as a refuge for wounded servicemen to convalesce and it now appeared clear to her that it was doing so yet again – this time for an old soldier's grief.

Christopher Hadley's pale eyes began to darken as the glow of The Beast subsided, leaving Pearl in no doubt that, with Diana's death, the small flame that had burned in two hearts, the hope for a new future with an old love, had been effectively and forever extinguished.

Chapter Eighteen

Thursday 23 December, 4 p.m.

McGuire's anger was born of frustration. 'What on earth were you thinking of by going to that house alone? Why didn't you call me?'

'Why didn't *you* come to the carol service?' countered Pearl.

McGuire had been trying to keep up with Pearl as she marched along Island Wall towards the High Street, but now she stopped in her tracks and eyed him accusingly, clearly smarting that McGuire had stood her up the night before.

'I told you...' he began. But he got no further as he suddenly broke off, distracted.

'What is it?' asked Pearl.

McGuire raised his forefinger and circled it vaguely around her face. 'There's ... something different about you,' he said. 'What is it?'

Pearl's hand went quickly and self-consciously to her forehead. 'Nothing,' she lied. Choosing not to attract any more attention to her newly arched eyebrows, she neatly changed the subject. 'The important thing is that Christopher Hadley has willingly come forward to give a statement to the police. He's done that, hasn't he?'

'Yes,' confirmed McGuire.

'Well, I very much doubt that he'll have given Shipley anything more than he told me last night

– but it's clear that Giles certainly has a motive for murder if Diana really was planning to cut off further financial support.' Having just entered Keams Yard car park, she now looked pointedly back at McGuire. 'Only the police can possibly tell me how much debt he is in.'

'Perhaps now you'll understand why I couldn't make it to your concert last night,' said McGuire.

Pearl frowned. 'What d'you mean?'

'I needed further information.'

'Another ... "favour", is that it?'

'Believe it or not, I'm owed quite a few.'

Pearl leaned back against her Fiat and considered him. 'And what did you find out?'

McGuire shot a quick glance around the empty car park before continuing. 'Firstly, the cards. They were all from the same batch – a box set – and the glue used for the cut-out newsprint messages was a light paper adhesive that was found in Martha Newcombe's home.'

'So ... everything points to Martha having sent the cards?'

'Apart from one slight anomaly.'

'Like what?'

'She used mainly newsprint from the local *Courier.*'

'The newspapers that were stacked in the living room?'

McGuire nodded.

Pearl thought about this. 'What do you mean by "mainly"?'

'I mean with the exception of a few words.'

'Which ones?'

216

'"I" and "was wrong" on the message in the last card that you found by her body.'

Pearl cast her mind back. 'And the full message inside that card was ... *I know what I did was wrong?*'

'Correct.'

'So why would she use a different newspaper?'

McGuire shook his head. 'I don't know. It would seem likely that she'd have found those words easily enough in the pile of *Couriers*...'

'Precisely,' agreed Pearl thoughtfully. 'Is it known which paper they *did* come from?'

McGuire looked at her. 'This is Canterbury, not Hollywood.' He took a sheet of paperwork from his inside pocket and gave it some attention. 'What may be more significant is the fact that Diana Marshall had made quite a bit of money from the sale of her accountancy business. She managed only a few accounts...'

'One of which was mine,' offered Pearl.

'And the Claysons,' nodded McGuire. 'Phyllis Rusk, Adam Castle, Charmaine Hillcroft...'

'Jim and Valerie Herbert?' asked Pearl, trying to find a pattern.

'No,' said McGuire. "The only other clients were her nephew, Giles Marshall, and Francis Sullivan, now deceased.'

'Bonita's grandfather,' said Pearl. 'She inherited The Grange from him.'

'All those accounts have now been studied.'

'Including mine?'

'Yes. There don't seem to be any obvious irregularities.'

'Then I suppose I should feel relieved,' mused

Pearl. 'What kind of irregularities were looked for?'

'Undeclared earnings, savings, sudden windfalls – the usual thing.'

'I am very honest,' smiled Pearl.

'As opposed to many others,' McGuire replied. 'I'm trusting you with this, Pearl, but it appears Whitstabelle and Castle Estates are on the up and Dr Clayson's surgery is on an even keel ... with a few large cash withdrawals last summer.'

'How large?'

'Ten thousand pounds in total.'

'Wow.'

'Spread over a few weeks.'

'Attributed to?'

'Not declared as a deductible expense so it was treated as personal spending money.'

'Oh.'

'What're you thinking?'

'Alice Clayson had an affair with a young artist. Perhaps she had plans for them to run off somewhere.'

'No sign that they ever did.'

'No,' agreed Pearl. 'But she and Richard took a holiday in Italy when it was all over. Venice, I think.' She smiled wistfully. 'I've never been. Have you?'

'Once upon a time,' McGuire answered sparely. 'The most significant fact in all this is that Giles Marshall seems to be a dead man walking – financially speaking. He's been in debt for years and forever living beyond his means.'

'With regular bail-outs from Diana?'

McGuire's look confirmed this but Pearl

remained pensive for a moment.

'Generally speaking,' she said, 'depending on the bequests of her will, if Diana *had* gone on to marry Christopher, her estate would have naturally passed to her new husband, though I can't see she would ever have left Giles penniless. She may have been irritated by his reckless attitude to money but he was her only family – and she cared about him. Perhaps she was intending to clear whatever debts he might have had while sending him an unequivocal message that things would be changing from now on.'

She suddenly recalled something. 'The night I saw Diana about my own accounts, she spoke about lessons having to be learned – that she couldn't keep throwing good money after bad. "We must all keep to a budget," she said. "Though I'm not sure Stephanie knows the meaning of the word". Yes, that's what she said to me that night. So perhaps it was Stephanie who was the drain on her resources?'

Pearl looked at McGuire. 'Remember at the fundraiser when Diana came into the kitchen? She was in a strange mood so it's possible that she was bracing herself to talk to Giles and Stephanie – which would back up everything Christopher said about her intention to break the news of her impending marriage.'

'Except she didn't get to do that,' McGuire said heavily.

'Because somebody got to her first.'

McGuire said nothing more but appeared to be eyeing Pearl with some suspicion. For one awful moment she imagined he might be about to broach the subject of her eyebrows, but instead, he asked, 'Who were you with in Fordwich last night?'

Pearl hesitated. 'I told you – a friend.' She kept her silence, preferring to appear enigmatic, before going on, 'What's important is what we discovered.'

'Which was?' asked McGuire, irritated that she had dodged his original question.

'It looks as though Jimmy Herbert and Phyllis Rusk might be having a secret affair. They were seen together last night – although they don't know that. We followed them.'

'You and your ... "friend"?'

'That's right,' said Pearl. 'The other morning, I invited everyone who had received a poison-pen Christmas card to a meeting at the Leather Bottle. I had no reason to believe that any of these people knew one another very well, if at all, but I noticed Jimmy put three spoonfuls of sugar into a cup of coffee.'

'And what's that got to do with anything?' asked McGuire, confused.

'He passed it to Phyllis straight afterwards. No one seemed to notice but me – but this proved to me that he knew Phyllis rather better than I thought.'

McGuire looked unimpressed. 'And if they *are* having an affair, what's the significance?'

'I'm not sure yet,' Pearl told him. 'Other than the fact they're both capable of being dishonest.' She looked back at McGuire then up suddenly, her attention caught by something in the sky. 'Oh – look at that!'

McGuire followed her gaze to see a flock of birds swarming in the sky, circling before settling on a rowan tree in the car park.

'Sparrows?'

Pearl shook her head. 'No. These birds are larger. Look at the yellow in their wings and tails. I think they may be waxwings.'

Seeing this meant nothing to McGuire, she explained, 'They usually winter in Scandinavia and Siberia, but if the weather's very harsh they head south to find food. Hundreds came a few years ago. They flew right across the North Sea and made a beeline for a tree in a supermarket that happened to be full of berries.'

She stared up again at the tree that was now full of waxwings. Pulling her mobile from her pocket, she took a couple of shots of the birds, the results of which clearly didn't satisfy her.

'I wish I had a proper camera with me,' she said, then bit her lip suddenly as a thought came to her. 'Of course,' she said slowly, looking at McGuire as she admitted, 'I've been stupid. Why on earth didn't I think of it before?'

'Think of what?'

To McGuire's intense frustration, Pearl failed to explain; instead she quickly jumped into her car. 'I have to go,' she called as she hurriedly started up the engine, leaving McGuire tapping urgently on the driver's window.

'Where to?' he asked, but Pearl was concentrating on reversing out of her parking space and then drove off.

Abandoned, McGuire looked up at the birds in the rowan tree, stumped if he knew what inspiration they had just offered to Pearl.

Less than an hour later, and after a request put in to Cassie from her mobile phone, Pearl was sitting in the living room of Grey Gables watching Giles Marshall pour himself a drink. 'We got a lot of calls after Aunt Diana's death,' he explained.

Pearl watched him as he set down a crystal decanter on Diana's silver tray. In contrast to Pearl's last visit, he was now smartly dressed in a pale pink shirt and grey trousers. His hair was neatly combed to one side but he still looked pale and his expression was tense with what appeared to be repressed emotion.

Pearl clarified. 'I'm talking about one person in particular. His name is Christopher Hadley. He told me he left several messages...'

'I spoke to him.'

It was Stephanie who said these words. She was standing at the open door, wearing a black dress with a string of fine crystal beads at her throat. She came forward, closing the door behind her. 'He left some messages for Diana but I couldn't call him back as I didn't have his number. I happened to answer the phone when he rang again yesterday morning and I broke the news to him then.' She glanced across at Giles then back again to Pearl. 'Why?'

Pearl waited a second before asking, 'Did he explain to you exactly who he is?'

Stephanie shrugged and sat down close to Giles but said nothing.

'What's going on?' Giles wanted to know.

'Nothing,' said Stephanie airily. 'I believe he's

just an old friend of Diana's.'

Giles turned to Pearl for an explanation but something in Stephanie's look warned Pearl to choose her words carefully.

'I believe they had recently become re-acquainted,' she said. 'Mr Hadley gave a full statement to the police today.'

Giles looked puzzled. 'About what?'

'About the fact that he was ... expecting to meet up with Diana over Christmas.'

'Then he'll be disappointed,' Giles said dejectedly. After taking another sip of his drink he stared at the glass in his hand and then at Pearl. 'Is it at all possible that Martha could have murdered my aunt?'

'I don't believe so,' she said.

'But she left a note,' argued Stephanie, stiffly.

'A message in a card,' Pearl clarified. 'Ambiguous at that. There's little evidence that Martha may have done anything other than send some upsetting Christmas cards around town.'

'Like the one she sent to Diana?' asked Stephanie.

'Yes. But I don't believe she killed her.'

'Then who did?' Giles said urgently. 'You promised that you would help – but we're no closer to the truth, are we?' His look was plaintive as he repeated sadly, 'Are we?'

Knocking back the last of his drink, he slammed down his empty glass and marched from the room.

Stephanie stared after him, clearly anxious about her husband, but after a few moments, she gave her attention again to Pearl. 'They were more than

223

friends, weren't they, this man Hadley and Diana? He was upset on the phone. I knew there had to be more to it.'

'I understand that they'd once been engaged,' Pearl said quietly.

'Diana?' Stephanie looked suitably shocked.

Pearl nodded slowly. Giles's wife put a hand to her brow. 'Could *he* have had something to do with her death?'

'I don't think so,' said Pearl. 'He only arrived in Whitstable yesterday and I think they were very much in love. Did she never mention this to you?'

'Never,' Stephanie insisted. 'I can hardly believe it. Diana always seemed so...' She paused, searching for the right words '...very self-contained – very much a single woman. Giles mustn't know,' she announced firmly. 'Not yet. He's so affected by Diana's death I don't want him to be upset any further. Do you understand?'

Pearl hesitated a little before replying. 'Yes, I do.'

'Thank you,' said Stephanie curtly. She moved to the door as though signalling that the meeting was over. Opening the door, she waited for Pearl to join her but was unprepared for the advice she was about to receive.

'The truth will come out, Stephanie,' Pearl told her. 'Sooner or later, it always does.' She fixed the woman with a look – and then took her leave.

Heading away from Grey Gables, Pearl passed Stephanie's silver Mercedes sports car in the driveway. Its personalised number read STE9H. Stephanie was continuing to observe her from the window, but once Pearl had stepped beyond the Victorian streetlamp in the front garden, a large oak tree obscured the frontage of Grey Gables. She had taken just a few steps down Joy Lane when she saw Richard Clayson across the road, taking his jacket from the back seat of his car as Alice got out of the passenger's side. Richard saw Pearl and waited for her.

'Just finished at the surgery?' Pearl asked.

'That's right,' he nodded. Looking across the road, he tipped his head towards Grey Gables. 'How are they bearing up?'

'Giles seems a little better,' said Pearl.

'Richard and I were thinking of inviting them to join us on Christmas Day,' Alice said. 'We were planning to go to the Hyde Hotel in Canterbury, but everything changes from day to day.'

Her husband slipped a comforting arm around her.

'Have the police been in touch?' asked Pearl.

'About?' queried Richard.

'Martha mentioned that you were her doctor – and while I know you can't discuss her condition with me, surely you can confirm that her chances of surviving mistletoe poisoning would have been poor?'

'True, as Martha's GP, I'm bound by confidentiality – but I'm ready to help the police as much as I can, as soon as they contact me.'

Pearl glimpsed in his pale blue eyes a certain softness and sympathy, something of the regular care he might offer to all his patients. He was a quiet, self-effacing man, deeply in love with his wife and no doubt worried about the sadness

225

Alice carried around with her like a burden.

'Of course,' said Pearl.

Richard had turned towards the house when he became distracted by something. Following his gaze, Pearl saw that Bonita and Simon had just emerged from the alley that led from The Grange on to Joy Lane. Laughing together, they were immediately silenced on noticing Pearl with the Claysons. Having stopped in their tracks, they appeared to assess the situation before deciding to approach.

Any tension was broken by the smile Alice Clayson offered to the couple.

'Hi,' said Bonita, relieved. 'I really want to thank you for the wonderful watercolour. It looks amazing in our dining room so I hope you'll come over soon to see it in place. For drinks or supper?'

Alice looked at her husband who responded politely, 'That would be nice.'

'Has there been any news about the old lady?' asked Bonita.

Pearl shook her head. 'I'm afraid not.' She looked between the young couple and the Claysons, aware that she was acting as a bridge.

Bonita took a step forward and held out her hand to the Claysons. 'I am so very sorry for your loss.'

'Ditto,' said Simon. 'We may not have seen eye to eye with Diana, but we know you were friends and ... we are genuinely sorry she's gone.'

Richard Clayson nodded appreciatively, taking Bonita's hand before finally issuing an acknowledgement of this détente. 'Me too.'

Bonita and Simon were just about to move off

226

in the direction of town when a squeak of cycle brakes was heard. A young girl wearing a fur-trimmed anorak and tight blue jeans had just stopped outside the house on a rented bicycle marked *Whitstable Bikes*. She pulled back her hood, revealing that it was Cassie.

'Well, well,' she smiled. 'Fancy seeing you all together like this. Not interrupting anything, am I?'

Pearl recognised that once again Cassie had managed to arrive on the scene at an awkward time and with an inappropriate manner. 'No,' she replied. 'Have you been out taking photos?'

'Yup. Down in Seasalter by the old oyster racks,' Cassie said brightly. 'But the tide and the weather got the better of me so I'm off for a cup of hot chocolate at the Conti.' She smiled. Remarkably, the girl was sounding increasingly like a native but for her northern accent. 'Is everyone OK?' she asked.

Bonita smiled back. 'Fine, thanks.'

Simon gave a nod of his head but Richard remained quiet and his wife appeared self-conscious.

Cassie turned to Pearl. 'Well, I ... just wanted to say that I got your message and popped what you asked for through your door, OK?'

'Thanks,' said Pearl.

Cassie prepared to cycle on then suddenly hesitated. 'I really hope it helps, because ... well, this is such a lovely place with lots of kind people – and the very least that should go to those who've lost someone they love is the truth, don't you think?'

'Of course,' Pearl replied. Cassie then jumped back on to her saddle and pedalled off, giving a small wave before she disappeared amongst the traffic moving back into town along Joy Lane.

'We'd better go inside,' ventured Alice.

'Same here,' decided Bonita, slipping her arm through Simon's.

Pearl stared after the couple as they headed down the road – buoyant, young and in love – then she looked back and saw the front door closing on Richard and Alice Clayson.

Chapter Nineteen

Thursday 23 December, 7.30 p.m.

McGuire had no wish to get on Pearl's wrong side again so he made sure he arrived at Seaspray Cottage five minutes early and brought with him a good bottle of Chablis together with a bunch of white roses he had bought from a flower-seller's stall in Palace Street, Canterbury.

Pearl was warm and welcoming, as was her cottage with its open log fire roaring in the grate and lights flashing on the Christmas tree, below which now lay wrapped presents, tied with gold and silver ribbon. McGuire found her dressed casually, wearing faded blue jeans and a black roll-neck sweater, her hair gathered up in a ponytail, exposing her fine cheekbones and slender neck. She had put together a tray of Kalamata olives,

228

charcoal biscuits and English cheeses bought from an independent store in Harbour Street: a fine selection that included Somerset Brie, Cornish Yarg, Shropshire Blue and Sage Derby.

After ferrying the food into the living room together with McGuire's wine, she offered him a seat beside her on the sofa.

'So what's all this about?' he asked with a fair degree of curiosity as Pearl inserted a memory stick into the laptop that sat before them on her coffee table.

'The fundraiser,' she replied. 'I really don't know why I didn't think of it before. Or why you didn't?' She looked at him challengingly. 'Perhaps you were too preoccupied at the time?'

'What do you mean?' he asked crisply.

'While you were choosing raffle tickets and handing out prizes, someone was actually recording the event.' She clicked an option on her laptop. 'It was only when I tried to photograph those waxwings yesterday that I remembered that Cassie had been taking photographs throughout the evening. I asked if I could see them and she made copies and dropped this memory stick off to me today. I've already looked at them and made notes.'

Picking up an embroidered notebook from the table, Pearl opened it as a gallery of images appeared on her laptop screen.

'Some of the early shots don't feature any guests at all,' she told McGuire. 'These, for instance, show the prizes before they were moved up onto the stage for you to hand out to the winners.' She cued some further images. 'This seems to be the first shot of a guest.'

She turned the laptop towards McGuire as the screen filled with a photo of Dolly, looking suitably festive in her Christmas-tree earrings, a glass in her hand and a broad smile on her face, cheeks as flushed as the festive red Santa suit worn by Jimmy in the background.

'That was taken at precisely 7.12 p.m.,' Pearl said. 'It's shown on the data on the photo and the time on the clock that's visible on the wall in the church hall.' She clicked on another image. 'This shot was taken next, just a couple of minutes later.'

'The doctor,' said McGuire.

'And his wife, Alice,' added Pearl. 'Richard Clayson is shown here talking to Rev Pru while Alice appears to be straightening her watercolour on the prize table.' She brought up another image. 'A short while later, Cassie took this photograph of Adam Castle, the estate agent, with Charmaine, the owner of Whistabelle – the beauty salon in the High Street.'

'The place you won the voucher for.'

'That's right,' said Pearl, turning slightly away from him in case McGuire's interest settled on her scanty eyebrows. She pointed to the laptop. 'This next shot of the Scout stall is important.'

McGuire craned forward but saw only Owen Davies smiling proudly with members of his Scout troop.

'Take a look in the background,' said Pearl. 'There's a figure by the stage, turned so the face isn't visible but the clothes are exactly the same as Diana wore that night – remember the maroon dress? I'm pretty sure that's her – and it looks like

230

she's heading for the cloakroom at exactly 7.18.'

McGuire registered the point Pearl was trying to make. 'So, at that moment, the bottle of Jenever in the kitchen could have been left unattended for anyone to tamper with.'

'Exactly,' confirmed Pearl. 'And it would have taken only seconds to pour a sufficient amount down the sink and replace it with anti-freeze.'

'Brought along specially for the purpose.'

'And in sufficient quantity.' Pearl nodded. 'Perhaps in a couple of hip-flasks or even a small plastic water bottle, hidden in a bag or the inside pocket of a jacket or coat.' She looked again at the photograph and sighed. 'Neither this shot nor the following shows the entrance to the kitchen, so we have nothing to go on as to who may have been standing close by.' She clicked further. 'There are no other photographs until much later, possibly because Cassie was being introduced to other guests by my mother. The next are of the prize-winners. Here's Marty accepting his French perfume.' She gave a smile. 'The sweetest-smelling fruit and veg salesman in Whitstable.'

'The same guy who had the hots for you in the summer,' remembered McGuire.

'He's moved on,' Pearl informed him, without explaining that the main reason for Marty having done so was his resentment of the time Pearl had chosen to spend with McGuire during the summer.

'Here's Mum collecting her yoga prize,' she noted. 'And here you are awarding me the envelope containing the Whitstabelle token.'

McGuire leaned in, took a careful look at the

photo then back at Pearl in a Eureka moment. 'That's it!'

'What?' asked Pearl.

'You did something to your eyebrows.' McGuire gently tipped her chin towards him. 'I'm right, aren't I?'

Caught in his gaze, Pearl replied softly, 'Yes, you're right. But can we now get back to the photographs?' She clicked on the next image. 'Here you are, throwing yourself into your prize-awarding role.' She indicated a close-up showing the detective kissing Bonita's cheek. 'She's a very pretty girl,' Pearl said pointedly.

'Stunning,' agreed McGuire, unabashed, taking a sip of his wine as he continued to study the photograph.

Pearl bit into a black olive. 'Quite.' She replaced the shot with another while McGuire casually helped himself to some Shropshire Blue cheese. 'Here's a photo of Martha looking towards Bonita as she shows Simon her prize of the watercolour. Giles and Stephanie are close by. Martha seems to be standing next to someone. Do you see the glass there in that person's hand? Unfortunately, it's not possible to make out who it is.' Pearl sighed in frustration. 'There are several other photos of children's paintings, the ones that lined the walls of the church hall. And then there's this shot, which shows Giles talking to Adam Castle. I remember seeing them together much earlier in the evening because I wondered what they could possibly be talking about.'

She turned the laptop towards McGuire. 'Do you remember this?' The next image showed

Pearl blindfolded, the makeshift 'donkey's tail' in her hand and McGuire's palms resting on her shoulders.

He smiled. 'You didn't do too well.'

'You're right,' she murmured. The next image that filled the screen showed Pearl and McGuire standing close together in the crowded hall, frozen in time, in a moment of expectation as Cassie had also captured the mistletoe above them. Pearl looked back now at McGuire. 'If you remember...' She broke off, noticing the reflection of firelight dancing in his blue eyes.

'Remember what?' he asked softly.

Pearl hesitated, then collected her thoughts and gave her attention once more to the laptop. 'It was just at this time that Diana's voice called out – the outburst that happened before she collapsed.'

'So this was the last photo Cassie took – the one of us together?' asked McGuire.

Pearl nodded. 'If you look at the background, everyone seems to be there. That's Alice Clayson looking on.'

'Sad-faced woman.'

'Yes,' said Pearl. 'It appears that last summer she fell in love with a young man who seems to have left her heartbroken. Diana mentioned to me that Alice had a breakdown of some sort, but Richard has been very understanding and trying all he can to help her to move on. Hence the extravagant holiday in Venice, no doubt.' She frowned in thought. 'My mother says Alice has the look of Ophelia about her – the Pre-Raphaelite painting by Millais. Do you know the one I mean? It's a striking image of a young woman lying drowned in a lake with her hands upturned as she holds a garland of flowers.'

McGuire shrugged. Fine art was not a strong point. 'Not sure that I do.'

'I have a book on the Pre-Raphaelites here somewhere.'

Pearl got up from the sofa and moved to her bookshelves to search for a reference but she stopped in her tracks and McGuire caught the look on her face. 'What is it?'

'Martha straightened all these books,' Pearl recalled. 'I never got the chance even to pay her for everything she did that day.'

'You couldn't possibly have known that she was about to be murdered.'

'No,' Pearl said, but her expression began to darken.

Concerned by her silence, McGuire moved across to join her and saw that she was now taking a small hardback book from a shelf. She opened it and stared thoughtfully down at the index page. 'I haven't opened this for years,' she confessed. 'But Martha must have moved it. It's a book of Tennyson's poetry. I studied it at school.' She continued to look at the page.

'Does it have anything to do with the murders?' asked McGuire.

'Perhaps,' she said enigmatically. 'Tennyson wrote several poems based on Arthurian legend...'

'And?'

'And the Pre-Raphaelites used subjects from that same period: paintings of King Arthur, Guinevere and Galahad...'

'I'm not sure of the relevance of all this,' said McGuire.

'Nor am I,' she said simply, and McGuire remembered how infuriating she could be in taking him down these blind alleys – though the smile she always gave him at the end was worth it. She turned her head inquisitively to one side. 'Will you still be working at Christmas now that Shipley's been made Investigating Officer?'

'I'm not sure,' responded McGuire in all honesty.

'Well ... do you have any plans for Christmas, if you're *not* working?'

McGuire paused and shook his head very slowly, still held captive by the gaze of her beautiful grey eyes. 'How about you?' he asked softly.

'We'll be here,' Pearl replied as though he should have known better. 'Charlie's coming home, remember?'

'Of course.'

Pearl continued tentatively, 'But you're quite welcome to join us for lunch ... if you'd like to?'

McGuire wished he had time to form a more considered response but instead he found himself asking, 'What about Charlie's father? You mentioned once that ... he's no longer around?'

Pearl hesitated for a moment, unused to giving up information about Carl but feeling somehow that it was time for McGuire to know. 'He hasn't been around for a very long time,' she stated finally.

McGuire took this in and nodded slowly.

'How about you?' asked Pearl. 'Is there ... someone?'

McGuire answered truthfully, 'There was. But not any more.'

In the next instant, with the sound of the wood fire crackling in the grate, McGuire moved towards Pearl ... but the telephone suddenly rang out, startling Pearl, who almost dropped the book in her hands. Caught in an awkward moment, she and McGuire listened to the phone ring three more times before the answerphone finally clicked on. A voice sounded in the room.

'Mum, are you there?'

Pearl immediately picked up the receiver and said, 'Charlie, I'm sorry. I didn't realise I had left the machine on. How are you?' She glanced back at McGuire before giving her attention fully to her son.

'I'm doing fine,' said Charlie in a croaky voice. 'But the weather here's still pretty lousy and it's more than likely that my flight's going to be delayed.'

'They won't cancel it, will they?' asked Pearl, panicked by the thought.

'I don't think so. The snow's easing but there are plenty of flights stacked up. I just thought I'd warn you. Will you still be able to meet me?'

'Of course,' she promised.

'Great.' Charlie coughed slightly before asking, 'So, what's been happening?'

'I'll tell you when you arrive,' Pearl said.

Charlie registered her change of tone. 'You and Gran are OK, aren't you?'

'Absolutely fine,' she replied. 'And we can't wait to see you.'

'Same here,' said Charlie. 'I've got the corn

schnapps you asked for and some marzipan from a great shop in Charlottenburg.'

'Wonderful,' smiled Pearl. 'I'll refund you once you're home.'

'No problem,' he replied. 'I'm in the money. We sold a whole load of T-shirts in a Christmas sale.'

'Really?'

'Really.' Then Charlie said: 'Look, I'd better go, but I'll see you soon.'

Before Pearl could wish her son a proper good-bye, the line went dead in her hand and she stared at the receiver before setting it down. For a few moments in her mind's eye she imagined her son wearing a festive T-shirt in the freezing Berlin weather, then she came out of her reverie and remembered McGuire.

'Sorry about that...' She turned to see that he was no longer there. Moving to the kitchen, she found him settling his glass near the sink.

'Would you like some more wine?'

McGuire shook his head. 'No, thanks. I'm driving.'

She sighed, recognising that the special moment between them had been broken by Charlie's call.

'Is everything all right?' McGuire asked.

Pearl managed a smile. 'Yes. Charlie's fine, but...' She broke off, staring towards the window as a powerful gust of wind rattled the pane. The branches of the old apple tree clawed at the glass as though trying to enter. 'What is it?' he asked. Pearl had been thinking about the weather in Berlin, and though the strong gusts outside her window now began to subside, she suddenly felt chilled to the marrow. 'Nothing,' she said. 'Maybe

I'm coming down with something.'

McGuire came to a decision. 'I should go,' he said, 'and let you get an early night for once.' He went into the sitting room and picked up his coat as Pearl quickly followed.

'McGuire?'

'What is it?' he asked.

Pearl hesitated. 'Nothing,' she lied, dismissing all apprehension.

'OK,' said McGuire. 'But if you need anything, just call me.' He gave her an understanding smile then turned for the door and walked out of Seaspray Cottage.

An hour after the detective had left, Pearl put away the last of her washed crockery while her thoughts returned to the night of the fundraiser. In hindsight it now seemed very likely that Diana's spiky mood had been due to the fact that she had been bracing herself to tell Giles and Stephanie about her secret engagement – at least, if Christopher Hadley was to be believed.

Pearl glanced once more out of her kitchen window, noting that the cold north wind was now quietened, offering the possibility that an earlier forecast for heavy rain might have been somewhat premature. Perhaps the bad weather might hold off until morning. Seizing the opportunity, she put on a warm jacket and headed out of the back door and on to the beach. At sea, a sprinkling of red and green navigation lights showed the path of some fishing craft heading back into harbor, but Pearl took a westerly direction towards Seasalter. The night air was strangely still, a possible lull before a storm, and West Beach was deserted. Only the waves of a rising tide accompanied her on the shoreline.

It wasn't long before she found herself at the Battery – but this time, no lights glowed at the windows. Instead the building was as dark as the clouds which masked the usual canopy of stars. Pearl ran lightly up the wooden stairs to the front door and listened for a moment before rapping hard upon it. There was no response apart from the creaking of an old swing chair in the Battery's terraced garden.

'Is anyone there?' Pearl moved closer to the garden gate and called into the darkness but her question remained unanswered as the swing chair creaked into silence. Ready to give up, she was about to move back on to the beach when a car engine broke the silence. In an access road, be-yond the property's landside boundary, headlights suddenly flashed on. Pearl craned her neck to get a better view but it was impossible to identify the driver of the vehicle which began speeding away in the direction of town. Nevertheless, Pearl was sure that she had recognised part of the car's distinctive number plate – which read STE9H.

That night, Pearl found it difficult to sleep. The weather forecast had proved to be accurate, with the wind strengthening, bringing with it a torrent of rain that lashed against the leaded panes of her bedroom windows. It was not until after midnight that the storm began to abate but the wind con-tinued to howl mournfully, and Pearl drifted back to a fitful sleep that was haunted by strange dreams. Dolly would have sworn that they had been brought on by eating blue cheese before bedtime but, in fact, they were prompted by long-buried memories of lines from an old book of poems.

Pearl's dreams summoned images from Tennyson's poem called 'Mariana'. A woman waiting for a lover who is never to return, Mariana remains trapped in her loneliness, observing the minutiae of her bleak and isolated surroundings, and when night falls, she fails to sleep but instead grieves for the lover who will never come again: *'With blackest moss the flower-plots were thickly crusted, one and all: the rusted nails fell from the knots that held the pear to the gable-wall. The broken sheds look'd sad and strange: Uplifted was the clinking latch; weeded and worn the ancient thatch upon the lonely moated grange...'*

In her mind's eye, Pearl saw a figure lying like Ophelia in shallow water, buoyed by the skirts of her dress, as she continued to hear the lines of the poem about Mariana: *'But when the moon was very low and wild winds bound within their cell, the shadow of the poplar fell upon her den across her brow. She only said, "the night is dreary, he cometh not," she said. She said "I am a weary a weary, I would that I dead ... were dead..."'*

The image transformed into one of Alice Clayson, staring unsettled towards the poplar tree in her own garden by the swimming pool ... and swiftly vanished as an unearthly scream woke Pearl. Breathless, she sat bolt upright to see the bedroom curtains lifted by the cold draught at her window. The scream faded with the dawn light, segueing into the high-pitched sirens of emergency vehicles approaching, and passing, until they fell silent in the near distance.

Pearl threw on some warm clothes then made her way hurriedly along the beach, passing some early-morning walkers who were comforting a woman seated on a timber groyne as a small terrier ran in a circle, seemingly distressed for its owner. The tide was approaching and Pearl hastened on to where police officers were holding back a small group of onlookers.

A paramedic team surrounded a figure lying on the shoreline, a form almost impressed into the mudflat, elbows bent at the waist, forearms stretched back, hands upturned, grasping not a posy of flowers like Millais' Ophelia but a long strand of dark seaweed floating on the incoming tide. As in the painting, the woman was pale and lifeless but there the similarity ended. Her eyes bulged and a necklace of black bruises circled her throat while her hair floated back and forth with each wave that approached and retreated on the shore.

Moving closer, Pearl could see quite clearly that the body was not Alice Clayson but Cassie, her lips no longer pursed in their usual cupid's bow but stretched wide, mouth gaping as though issuing forth a final silent scream that would forever go unheard.

Chapter Twenty

Christmas Eve, 9 a.m.

'Ghastly *ghastly* detective,' wailed Dolly. She was rocking to and fro on her day bed, a handful of tissues pressed to her eyes, ineffectively stemming tears.

'Shipley, you mean?' Pearl moved closer to comfort her mother.

Dolly nodded, blowing her nose loudly with a sudden trumpeting noise that scared Mojo from his basket and sent him, with one balletic leap, to a safe hiding place on top of a tall dresser.

'The police have been swarming like blue-bottles all over the attic – constables, sergeants, family liaison officers ... why isn't *your* Flat Foot dealing with this?' Dolly demanded.

'I told you,' Pearl reminded her. 'McGuire can't lead the investigation as he was a witness at the fundraiser.'

'Rules, rules, rules,' Dolly exploded, 'are meant to be broken! They're for the guidance of wise men and the obedience of fools!' This was an axiom Dolly had drummed into Pearl throughout the years, and it had never seemed more apt than now. Pearl herself was quite sure that there would have been more answers provided if McGuire *had* been in charge of the case.

'I feel so helpless,' grieved Dolly, articulating

Pearl's own feelings. 'That poor girl came into my home...'

'It's not your fault.'

'Isn't it?' barked Dolly. 'She was under my roof, in my care.'

'You can't be held responsible for her death.'

'Her *murder*,' corrected Dolly. 'They say she was strangled.'

'They can't know for certain. Not until there's been a post-mortem.'

'You saw her,' Dolly wailed. 'So did others. She was strangled and left out there in the cold mud. If that woman hadn't been walking her dog and found her body, she could have been taken off with the tide – no doubt what the demon who murdered poor Cassie intended.'

Pearl found it difficult to disagree with anything Dolly had just said. Instead, she asked, 'What did the police tell you?'

Dolly wiped her nose and stuffed the tissues up her sleeve. 'That they needed to make a full search of the attic,' she replied. 'To go through her things – photographs, everything. They'll have to notify her relatives. Why on earth would somebody murder that poor young girl? She had so much life about her, didn't she?'

'Yes. I saw her only yesterday afternoon, cycling home from Seasalter along Joy Lane. She'd been out taking photographs.' Pearl thought for a moment of the old rusting oyster racks at Seasalter which, at low tide, looked much like a skeleton on the mudflats. The thought sent yet another shiver through her, reminding her of Cassie's lifeless body lying on the cold Whitstable shoreline. She looked at Dolly, bereft about the girl's loss.

'I'll cancel going in to the restaurant,' Pearl decided.

'You'll do no such thing,' Dolly said immediately. 'The staff will need paying and they're due their Christmas bonuses.'

'I know, but...'

'No "buts",' said Dolly firmly. 'I'll be all right. It's just been a terrible shock. But we can't give in to this monster, Pearl, so you carry on.' She blew her nose again and this time, Mojo leaped from the dresser and bolted into the conservatory where the cat flap was heard to swing shut after his swift exit.

'In that case, I will,' said Pearl, capitulating. 'As long as you're sure.' She leaned in and gave Dolly a warm hug then moved to the door where she suddenly turned back and asked, 'By the way, do you happen to remember the name of the young man Alice was in love with?'

Dolly frowned. 'Does it really matter?' she asked dully. But seeing her daughter's enquiring look, she endeavoured to collect her thoughts.

'Michael,' she recalled. 'Michael ... now what was it? Oh dear, I can't remember his surname.' Then it came to her. 'Arthur!' she suddenly recalled. 'That's it – Michael Arthur. Why d'you want to know?'

'Curiosity,' said Pearl truthfully.

The Whitstable Pearl always closed early on Christmas Eve. A glass or two of champagne was enjoyed by the staff – the first that young Ruby said she had ever tasted. Pearl handed out wages

244

and a bonus that represented a share of the restaurant's profits. A two-week holiday would ensue, the longest all year round, and though it was usually one that everyone looked forward to, today it seemed marred by the recent tragic events. Nevertheless, spurred by Dolly's order to carry on, Pearl locked up the restaurant and went off to meet someone she had contacted that very morning. She found him standing outside a High Street bank, wearing a warm jacket but with a Scout woggle showing at his throat.

'Did you manage to find it?' asked Pearl.

Owen nodded. 'It was just as I told you, but I looked it up to make doubly sure. The last delivery of Scout Post was made on Friday.'

'The day of the fundraiser,' Pearl realised.

'That's right,' Owen confirmed.

'And no other cards were delivered after that?'

Owen shook his head. 'None.'

Pearl considered this for a moment then took out her purse and stuffed several notes into Owen's collection tin – at which he looked suitably taken aback.

'Well, I ... must say I'm extremely grateful.'

'So am I,' Pearl told him.

Moving on up the High Street, Pearl recognised a certain change in the atmosphere in town. Many of the offices had already closed and notices of New Year opening times were already going up in shop windows. There were fewer cars parked on the street, mainly belonging to the last-minute shoppers who were ferrying parcels or Christmas trees to their vehicles before escaping the attention of traffic wardens, but Pearl noticed that one car bore the name of a local company on its doors – *Castle Estates.*

As Pearl approached, she saw that Adam Castle was in the driver's seat talking to a passenger beside him. It wasn't his assistant, Paula, as Pearl had expected but instead, Whitstabelle's owner, Charmaine Hillcroft. Adam was handing her an A4-sized leaflet which she studied for only a moment before she offered the nearest expression Charmaine ever gave to enthusiasm: a mixture of vague curiosity stifled by some dissatisfaction. It proved sufficient for Adam to act upon and he turned the key in his ignition to drive with his passenger towards the lights of Harbour Street.

Pearl continued on down the High Street, stopping as she saw Rev Pru outside St Alfred's. Whitstable's vicar was rearranging the figures of the Magi that surrounded a crib on the front lawn close to the church's Christmas tree. On seeing Pearl, Rev Pru paused to have a word.

'A little advertisement for the crib service later,' she explained, then heaved a heavy sigh. 'I can't be sure people will come along. There's always the chance they'll prefer some last-night Christmas shopping.' She stopped and said more sombrely, 'I heard about the murdered girl. It appears we have a monster in our midst. I do so hope the police catch him.'

'Or her,' said Pearl.

'Of course,' agreed Rev Pru, looking slightly shaken.

A moment's silence passed until Pearl spoke again, glancing at the nativity scene on the lawn.

'I'm sure people will come along, Rev Pru.'

'Thank you,' the vicar replied. 'I do regret the consumerism of Christmas. People feel the need to spend so much money these days. If only we could return to a more simple and less material-istic life.'

'Money is the root of all evil?' asked Pearl, sud-denly reminded of the message that had been cut out and placed in Adam Castle's Christmas card.

'Perhaps,' the vicar agreed. 'Though the line is incorrect.'

'I'm sorry,' queried Pearl.

'Well, the exact reading is: "for the *love* of money is the root of all evil",' Rev Pru then continued with the passage: '"Which while some coveted after, they have erred from the faith, and pierced themselves through with many sorrows". One Timothy, verses six to ten.' She smiled at Pearl. 'It's often misquoted.'

'But not by Martha,' realised Pearl. 'That was the exact quotation in Adam's card. And Martha would have known her Bible.'

'Oh yes,' Rev Pru agreed. 'Chapter and verse.'

Pearl looked away for a moment towards St Alfred's Christmas tree.

'Are you all right, my dear?' asked Rev Pru.

'Yes,' Pearl replied. 'Yes, I'm absolutely fine. Thank you.'

Pearl had gone straight from St Alfred's to Nathan's cottage, and now sat across from him in his elegant conservatory. A general mood of calm and order usually exuded from her neighbour's home, but today his laptop was open and sheets

247

of paper were crumpled on the table. He gave a puzzled look to Pearl.

'You did say to call on your services again?' she reminded him.

'Detective work, you mean?'

'In a way.' She took out some cards from her pocket and explained: 'I just need you to write out some extra invitations to this evening's drinks and then deliver them by hand. All the guests are local.'

Nathan considered the cards as Pearl went on: 'It's short notice, I know, and you're struggling with your article...'

Nathan looked back at his computer screen for only a moment before closing it down. He held out his palm. 'Who do you want them delivered to?'

Pearl gave him a list and Nathan eyed the names carefully before looking up again at Pearl. 'Are you sure about this?' he asked, curious.

'Positive.'

An hour later, Pearl was settling a tray of food into the oven while talking to the mobile phone pressed to her ear.

'Well?' she said.

'You're throwing a party?' asked McGuire, confused.

'No,' Pearl replied. 'I'm just inviting a few guests around for Christmas drinks. I do it every year but I need you to be here too. Tonight at six o'clock sharp.'

McGuire quickly warmed to the idea, although his police instincts told him he should be wary.

'What's this about, Pearl?'

She wiped a hand across her hot brow. 'I left things too late,' she confessed.

'For what?'

'For Cassie,' she replied. 'I had a bad feeling about her, right from the start – but now the poor girl's dead.' She added, torn, 'I still think I was right to mistrust her.'

'Why?' asked McGuire, baffled.

'I'll explain when you get here. But first, I need you to do something for me. Urgently...'

Chapter Twenty-One

Christmas Eve, 6.15 p.m.

By the time the Crib Service had ended, Seaspray Cottage matched every other home on Island Wall for festive spirit – written in Pearl's own style. A beautiful evergreen garland hung on the front door with white ribbon, while candles flickered in the window and the smell of winter spice met Pearl's guests as they crossed her threshold.

Everyone who had received an invitation had come along, even the vicar – though she explained she had Midnight Mass to conduct later. Pearl had prepared a selection of simple but delicious canapés, and Nathan had contributed a beautifully iced cake from an Italian store in Faversham. Relaxed by alcohol, a glowing fire and the sense of Christmas at last, the guests seemed able to forget, for a few hours at least, the tragic deaths that had preceded it.

Phyllis stood by the tree with a glass of Prosecco in her hand, talking to Bonita, though Pearl noted how her gaze remained fixed on Jimmy across the room. He was standing sipping a glass of beer with Valerie beside him for once. She looked attractive, her slim figure encased in a stylish navy trouser suit, but she seemed under pressure as though unable to forget her many duties at the pub which she insisted she had to return to in just a short while. Bonita's boyfriend, Simon, was engaged in conversation with Alice Clayson while Richard had been captured by Dolly, who was trying to persuade him of the benefits of homoeopathy. The doctor was doing his best to give his full attention to the conversation but he kept an attentive eye on his wife. Alice, for once, looked animated and glowing, smiling at Simon as if she was reminded of another young man.

Giles and Stephanie had arrived late and stood close together – Stephanie behaving much as her husband's protector, fielding awkward questions about Christmas while their son, Nicholas, explored culinary delights in the kitchen, peeling and discarding the bacon from Pearl's 'pigs in blanket' to devour only the pork and sage chipolatas within. Adam Castle had come alone, without his young assistant, Paula, explaining that he had another 'date' to rush off to, which appeared to explain the girl's absence. He spent his time engaged in conversation with Charmaine at the fireside, and as Pearl passed by to refill glasses, she eavesdropped, catching phrases that pertained to property: 'sought-after location' and 'a bargain ripe for renovation'.

Christopher Hadley had been the last guest to arrive, and though Pearl had introduced him to McGuire, he stood apart from all the other guests, looking edgy and distracted beside Pearl's Christmas tree. Giles shot furtive glances towards him and there was clear animosity between the two men as well as a fair degree of suspicion, prompting Pearl to recognise that she must keep a careful eye on how events progressed. Her instincts told her that it was Christopher she should fear most, his quiet control belying a capacity for great violence, the force of which had surely been demonstrated when he had fought for his own life, some thirty years ago, on a cold and barren mountaintop in the South Atlantic. The Falklands War was long over, but somehow it still lived on within Hadley, and Pearl couldn't help wondering, as she watched him, separate and brooding in his grief, whether his one chance of finding true peace had been snatched from him with Diana Marshall's death.

When McGuire sidled across to Pearl and asked in a whisper, 'Are you ready?' she nodded and prefaced her announcement with a tap of a small spoon on her wine glass.

'I'm very grateful that you could all come tonight,' she began. 'It's become a bit of a tradition for me to invite friends into my home on Christmas Eve. Cassie and Martha should be here too. And Diana,' she added quietly. 'But now it's only right for us to remember them.' She glanced around the room at her guests and noted the bowed heads before she continued. 'As Rev Pru said at the carol service, Christmas is a time for us to recognise the significance of our relationships. I had been reading some poetry by Tennyson just the other evening and I remember how perfectly he captured a sense of loss and longing.' She cleared her throat. 'Diana knew how painful it could be to lose someone. She shared that experience with someone else who knew the pain of separation. But by a remarkable coincidence, she was to be reunited with that person.' She looked towards Christopher.

'What do you mean?' asked Alice, confused.

'I'll explain,' promised Pearl. 'But first – the cards.' She waited for a moment. 'I was very wisely advised not to take on a case before Christmas.' She eyed Dolly and Nathan. 'But still one arrived – the case of the poison-pen Christmas cards. I turned it down,' she explained, noting Charmaine Hillcroft giving a pointed sniff. 'Instead, I asked the police to investigate.' Pearl looked across now at McGuire. 'But Diana also received one of these cards, and when she was poisoned, Giles asked me to investigate her death.'

Giles and Stephanie shared a look at this.

'I couldn't do so,' Pearl informed everyone. 'Not as an assignment. Instead, I considered that solving Diana's murder was a responsibility I held towards someone we all respected – even if we didn't always see eye to eye.' She looked now to Bonita and Simon. 'For a time, I was distracted and went off on a wrong track. Martha had told me that at one time she had five clients, and because there had been five cards I thought that perhaps there could be a connection. But then, two things Rev Pru said to me caused me to think again.'

'Me?' asked the vicar innocently.

Pearl nodded. 'Yes. The first was when I met with you before the carol service and you happened to mention the subject of sin.'

'I can't say I remember,' fretted Rev Pru.

'We were talking about the excesses of Christmas and you reminded me that gluttony is a sin.'

'Ah yes.' The vicar smiled, nodded. 'And so it is.'

'That same night, I happened to follow Phyllis to Fordwich.'

'You did what?' asked Phyllis, alarmed.

'Where you met Jim,' Pearl said calmly. 'After the carol service.'

Val turned instantly to her husband. 'You met up with *her*?' Val's shock darkened into suspicion. 'But that was on Wednesday and you said you were—'

'I know,' said Jim quickly. 'I told you I was at the British Legion, but I was actually at the Foodies Club.'

'The what?'

'Phyllis is a member too,' he muttered. 'It's something we have in common.'

'What is?' Val demanded.

Jim paused guiltily before replying, 'Food.'

Val's jaw dropped open. With all eyes suddenly upon him, Jim spoke up defensively.

'That's all it is. I just happened to go into her shop one day and asked about cholesterol. I didn't want to start taking the doctor's pills so she gave

253

me something else and we got talking.'

'I bet you did,' said Val, shooting a look at Phyllis.

'About *food*,' Jim insisted. 'We both enjoy a nice meal, but – well, you don't even make time to sit down these days, Val.'

'How can I, with everything I have to do?' she protested.

'Well, that's the difference – because Phyllis finds time, for the things that matter. The little pleasures in life.'

'Stuffing your face, you mean?' asked Val, furious.

Jim continued calmly: 'Sitting down, once a week, to share something really delicious, and some conversation, with someone – someone who actually cares about you.'

Val's mouth remained agape as she stared from her husband to Phyllis, who looked down shamefacedly.

Pearl took advantage of the moment to continue, turning to Phyllis. 'The card Martha sent you was hurtful. Its message said...'

'"Greedy pig"!' broke in Val. 'And that's right enough, for sure.'

'Stop it, Val,' ordered Jim.

'Why should I? I've been working in that pub night after night while you've been creeping off with her every Wednesday. I'd like to know what else the pair of you've been up to!'

'Nothing,' Phyllis faced her down bravely. 'It's just like Jim said. It's about food. We enjoy it.'

'Anyone can see that,' Val said spitefully.

Pearl took up her thread. 'The message in Jim's

card was different.'

'"Lazy slob",' Val cried. 'That's right enough too.'

Pearl went on doggedly 'Nathan's attacked his sense of...'

'Style,' hissed Nathan. 'Do you *have* to remind me?'

'Actually,' said Pearl, 'it was your pride that came under attack.'

Nathan looked surprised but Pearl enlightened him: 'You have pride in your sense of style.'

Nathan considered this for a moment and then agreed, 'Absolutely right.'

'And it was Rev Pru correcting me today that made me realise that there was a biblical significance to all the messages. Most of us would say: "money is the root of all evil", but Rev Pru was quite right in pointing out to me that the exact quotation from the Bible is "the *love of* money is the root of all evil." Those were the words that had been cut out in newsprint and glued inside the card that was sent to Adam.'

Adam shrugged. 'So?'

'So,' continued Pearl, 'this confirmed for me that Martha had sent the cards – but it also led me to suspect that there had been a greater message behind them all.'

'What *are* you talking about, Pearl?' asked Dolly, fearing that her daughter was losing the plot.

'Greed,' announced Pearl, looking apologetically at Phyllis. Her gaze shifted to Jimmy. 'Sloth.' Then she eyed Nathan: 'Pride. Ire, of course, was for Diana.' Then, looking now at Adam: 'Avarice.' Finally, her gaze settled on Charmaine. 'Envy.'

'The Seven Deadly Sins,' breathed the vicar.

Adam broke in. 'But there were only six cards.'

Pearl exchanged a look with McGuire. 'Martha had the seventh card,' she informed them. 'It was lying beside her dead body.'

Charmaine frowned. 'What did it say?'

McGuire now spoke. *'I know what I did was wrong.'*

'I don't understand,' said Richard Clayson. 'That doesn't actually refer to a specific sin, does it?'

Dolly piped up, 'But it does refer to the sending of the cards?'

'Or perhaps,' mused Rev Pru, 'Martha only ever intended to send six?'

'Maybe she was overcome with guilt before she sent the last,' suggested Stephanie. 'And poisoned herself.'

Pearl nodded. 'That would fit with all the evidence. But what most people may not have known is that on the day Martha died, she had actually helped out here, in Seaspray Cottage. She left a note for me, written in her own hand, explaining that she was looking forward to coming to this small party tonight, on Christmas Eve. That doesn't offer me the impression of someone who's planning to take their own life. So, if Martha did commit suicide, what could possibly have changed her mind and her mood so drastically and in only a matter of hours?'

Pearl's guests exchanged confused glances.

'Martha had a sweet tooth,' said Pearl. 'Anyone who knew her would have been aware of that. The marmalade that was found beside her body contained mistletoe. Seasonal – and poisonous,' she added darkly. 'To some.' She paused. 'Martha had a condition. Her blood pressure was low. Practically everyone knew this because she didn't keep it a secret. Her doctor, Richard, knew this. A herbalist might know?' Pearl looked towards Phyllis. 'Rev Pru certainly knew and anyone Martha had told may have spread the word because, as Adam said, all news travels fast in a small town.'

Pearl took up her story again. 'So how much effort would it have taken to poison a jar of marmalade with mistletoe berries and extract, then sweeten it further, making it appear to look like a home-made Christmas gift with a new label and a circle of cloth on its lid? I'm a cook but there are plenty of Christmas preserves on sale all over town right now which could be used as a simple base.' She took a sip of her wine and set down her glass.

'I discovered myself that Martha left her porch door unlocked. Rev Pru told me that she often did so, so it would have been easy for someone to have left the jar on her entrance porch shelf, as a Christmas surprise. On the day Martha died, a card listing St Alfred's Christmas services was delivered locally, and if the card had been propped against the jar, who would Martha be most likely to believe had left it? Surely the one person she saw more of than anyone else?' Pearl looked at Rev Pru.

'But I told you,' the vicar protested. 'The cards containing the list of services were delivered by church volunteers.'

Pearl persisted. 'And the volunteers for Martha's area were?'

Rev Pru looked at Bonita and Simon.

'Hold on there a minute,' said Simon. 'We didn't even know where this lady lived.'

For an instant, the sudden flash of anger in the young man's eyes took Pearl back to the last afternoon she had spent in Diana Marshall's garden – but then Bonita's voice cut through her thoughts.

'Simon's right,' she said. 'We delivered lots of cards to homes in Tankerton but they were random, unaddressed. And why on earth would *we* want to kill her?'

'Why would anyone?' asked Rev Pru, lost.

'We need to look at Diana's murder for that,' said Pearl. 'She had asked Adam to value Grey Gables.'

'*What?*' asked Giles, shocked.

Pearl reminded him, 'You were talking to Adam at the fundraiser. I wondered what about.'

Giles turned to the estate agent. 'He was asking me about property prices in Surrey.'

'Adam was close to selling the house for Diana,' said Pearl. 'In fact, you had a buyer lined up, didn't you, Adam?'

'Who?' barked Giles.

'Charmaine.' Pearl looked at her.

'And why shouldn't I have bought it?' she snapped. 'I've always wanted to live in Joy Lane – and now I can afford to.'

'That house belongs to Giles,' argued Stephanie.

'No,' said Pearl. 'Grey Gables was Diana's home and she had made a decision to sell up and move to Scotland.'

'What're you talking about?' yelled Giles, incredulous.

'I believe Diana was about to settle with you once and for all. One last payment to try to clear your debts,' said Pearl. 'Then she would have been free to sell Grey Gables and marry Christopher.'

All eyes now shifted to the quiet stranger who stood in silence close to Pearl's Christmas tree. He said nothing but his face was illuminated by the glow of the lights that flashed on and off like neon.

'If he's told you that, it's not true,' Giles objected.

Pearl ignored his anger and took up her story. 'She mentioned something about us all needing to stick to a budget. At the time I thought she was simply referring to Christmas, but perhaps what she meant was that it was time you stood on your own two feet, Giles.'

Giles's mouth dropped open. 'Me?' he asked, confounded.

'Yes,' Pearl told him, unabashed. 'The problem was that you'd got used to a certain standard of living – of being constantly rescued by Diana. Surely, it would have been a difficult future ahead if you had been cast adrift by the one person who had always rescued you?'

'This is all nonsense – sheer speculation,' Stephanie protested.

But another voice suddenly spoke up. 'It's true.' Christopher Hadley now stepped forward. 'Everything that Pearl has just said is true. Diana and I were going to marry and settle in Edinburgh. It's where we first met...'

'So *you* say,' Stephanie said boldly. 'But the truth is, we've never met you. You're a complete stranger.'

'Is that really so, Stephanie?' Pearl asked. 'I happened to see your car leaving the road behind the Battery only last night. What were you doing there?'

At a confused look from Giles, Stephanie looked pained. 'I ... wanted to talk to *him,*' she explained, glaring at Christopher Hadley. 'We only have this man's word for all this, and you've been through enough, Giles. I wasn't going to stand by and let some lowlife fortune-hunter make things worse for you by trying to lay claim to Diana's estate.' And noticing that all eyes were upon her, 'I'm telling the truth!' she cried. 'So I drove to the Battery last night to have things out with him. But he wasn't there. The place was all locked up. So I left.' She put a hand to her brow. 'I planned to go back and tackle him today, but this morning the news came out of that poor young girl's death and...' She broke off suddenly, frowning in frustration. 'Well, why aren't you asking *him* these questions? There's no evidence at all that he meant anything to Diana.'

A silence fell and before Pearl could respond, someone else spoke.

'I believe it's true she loved a soldier,' Alice Clayson said quietly. 'Diana told me that herself.'

'What are you talking about?' asked Giles.

When Alice failed to respond, Pearl continued for her: 'It's true,' she said. 'Christopher and Diana found one another after years of being apart. They met again at the theatre in Chichester. Inspector McGuire confirmed this today by their ticket payments. You see, even though Diana had lost her love many years ago, she reclaimed it. She knew that it was possible. That it was never too late.'

Giles stepped across to Christopher. 'Oh yes? So where were you, all these years, if you loved her so much?'

Christopher Hadley looked on impassively at Giles, who was trembling with rage, but kept his silence and simply allowed Pearl to continue. 'Martha told me that on the night of the Christmas fundraiser, when Diana had seen Bonita and Simon enter the hall, she had claimed to Martha that they would be the death of her.'

Everyone present now looked at the young couple as Pearl went on: 'I looked again at a photo taken that evening which showed Martha staring across at Bonita and Simon as someone stood beside her. The person isn't identifiable but I know that everyone had goblets for the mulled wine or tumblers for soft drinks – except Diana. I had given her a highball glass for her Jenever and that's the glass that is visible in the hand of the person standing next to Martha.'

Pearl lowered her voice. 'What is also quite clear in the photograph is that Bonita and Simon were in the same line of vision for Diana as another couple. What if Martha had misconstrued Diana's meaning and it was Giles and Stephanie she was referring to?'

Stephanie threw back her head. 'This is absurd.'

Pearl looked at Christopher Hadley. 'Sometimes life has a way of coming between us and the people we love.' She then turned to Alice. 'As it did for you.'

Alice Clayson looked hunted. 'I ... don't know

261

what you mean,' she said glancing at her husband for help.

Pearl explained. 'You told me that on the very last night that Diana had come to your home, you heard her downstairs with Richard. You were upstairs...'

'Yes,' Alice said quickly. 'I told you – I had a migraine.'

'And you had taken some painkillers for it. Perhaps you weren't thinking straight and misunderstood.'

'Misunderstood what?' asked Richard. 'What is it you're implying, Pearl?'

'I'm suggesting that Alice might have got the wrong impression from what she heard you discussing.' Pearl moved closer to Alice. 'Diana told me she was due at your home to give Richard some financial advice. If you had heard her telling your husband that he should be honest about something, what might you have assumed from that?'

Alice said stumblingly, 'I'm – not sure. I ... don't know...'

'Please don't put my wife under pressure like this,' begged Richard.

'Did you perhaps hear Diana telling Richard that it would be better if he talked to you?'

Alice looked from Pearl to her husband, then nodded slowly. 'Yes,' she whispered. 'Yes. She was saying something about it being better if you explained, Richard, rather than her.'

'So you heard Diana pressing Richard to be honest,' said Pearl. 'But about what? Surely from such a conversation you might have suspected that they were having an affair? But that cannot possibly be so, because we now know that it was Christopher who Diana loved, Christopher she had intended to marry. Christopher who was waiting for her in the background.'

Pearl looked from Christopher Hadley to all those assembled in the room. 'Cleaners and accountants have one thing in common,' she said. 'They're both in positions of trust. They understand those they work for and Diana, as an accountant, would have understood her clients' spending habits.' She addressed Richard. 'Two withdrawals totalling ten thousand pounds might not represent a great fortune, but those sums would have been noticed by your accountant because they were cash withdrawals. What were they for?'

'I planned to take Alice away,' Richard told her. 'To Venice. We stayed at the Cipriani. It's a wonderful hotel and I wanted it to be a memorable experience.' He paused. 'When we returned, I also had to pay for some repairs that had taken place at the surgery.'

'But you didn't claim this as a deductible expense,' Pearl noted

'No. I paid in cash.'

'Why?'

'The workman said he preferred it.'

'But he failed to give you a receipt?'

'I ... wasn't thinking clearly at that point. I was distracted. Alice ... my wife wasn't in good health at that time.'

Pearl nodded, accepting this and moved on. 'And so we come to the final Christmas card – the one left by Martha. Something about it troubled me from the moment I found it beside her body. The message, cut out in newsprint just like all the others, read: *I know what I did was wrong.*' Pearl shrugged. 'Why not simply: *What I did was wrong?*'

She left the question hanging and turned to McGuire. 'And then I learned that the words that formed the messages had been taken from a local newspaper – the *Courier.* All except those on the final card. On that, three words had been cut from another newspaper. A daily newspaper. Why? Everything else was the same but for the words "I" and "was wrong". But what if those words had been added later and the original message had read differently?' She turned, now addressing the vicar. 'What is the missing sin?'

'Lust,' said Rev Pru.

'Is that how Martha might have a viewed a summer romance between a young man and an older married woman? An instance of lust?' Pearl turned around, this time to Alice Clayson. 'What happened? Did Martha catch you together one day?'

Alice looked at her husband then hung her head in shame.

'My love...' began Richard, pained.

'The last card was for you, Alice,' said Pearl. 'The Scout Post deliveries had ended on Friday so Martha had to deliver it herself, but that was no problem because she knew she could bring it with her to work and leave it for you.'

Alice shook her head slowly. 'But she didn't. I don't know what you're talking about. Martha always arrived for work with us on Tuesdays, promptly at nine a.m., but I was at the beach hut that last morning, working on my sketch. Richard came down.' She turned to him in desperation. 'You saw me.'

He nodded. 'I did. It's true. Straight after I finished morning surgery.'

Pearl held the doctor's gaze. 'But then you returned from the beach, entering from the garden, through the sliding glass doors – to see what? Martha leaving the card before she left by the front door?' Pearl waited. 'She didn't see you, did she? But you opened the envelope and read the message and assumed that she'd left the card, not for Alice – but for you. *I know what you did.* That was the original message, cut from newsprint from the *Courier,* like all the others. Martha had been referring to Alice – and the young man, Michael Arthur. But you, Richard, assumed the message was for you – and that Martha knew what you had done.'

'Richard?' asked Alice, concerned, but her husband remained silent.

'You knew Martha didn't drink alcohol,' Pearl continued, 'but she had a very sweet tooth. So you took a gift to her that you knew she would find irresistible. Martha left the back door unlocked as usual, and on your way home from afternoon surgery you checked to make sure she was dead and you took the card she had left for Alice in order to alter it in Martha's home. Why? Because it would be important to use the same adhesive. The one thing you hadn't bargained for was that Martha had used only the *Courier* newsprint for her messages. You altered the message to make it look like an admission of guilt, a possible suicide note – *I*

265

know what I did was wrong – and then you left.'

The silence that followed was palpable. It was broken by Alice Clayson's voice.

'It's not true,' she said weakly. 'It can't be.' She pleaded with her husband. 'That would mean you killed Diana – and you had no reason to.'

'But he did have a reason,' said Pearl, looking directly at the doctor. 'Diana came to your home that last evening and warned you to be honest with Alice – because she knew you were being blackmailed.'

'Blackmailed?' echoed Alice.

Ignoring her, Pearl carried on. 'What did Diana say to you?' she asked Richard. 'That if you failed to tell Alice, she would have to do so herself? It was to be a Christmas for home truths. She said that herself on the night of the fundraiser. I remember she looked at us all: at Giles and Stephanie, at Bonita and Simon – but also at you and Alice. Was she giving you a warning, a deadline until after the Christmas holidays?'

'But I don't understand,' Alice persisted. 'Who on earth would want to blackmail you – and about what?' Her husband failed to reply.

'I never understood why Cassie arrived to spend Christmas in Whitstable alone,' Pearl said to Dolly.

'There's nothing wrong with wanting to spend time on your own,' her mother argued.

'But at this time of year – in Whitstable? Why not in summer when the light is so wonderful? Surely that's the time when any photographer or artist would want to be here, to enrol for a watercolour class, perhaps – like the ones you taught, Alice?'

Dolly shrugged. 'I told you, Pearl. Cassie said she came because a friend had been here and recommended it.'

'Someone who had clearly enjoyed their stay,' said Pearl. 'Michael Arthur. He's the reason for all of this.'

Alice Clayson looked lost. 'Michael?'

Pearl turned to face Richard Clayson. 'I understand how you couldn't bear the thought of losing your wife to him.'

Alice looked at Richard in disbelief as Pearl went on, 'You knew how she felt about Michael Arthur – how they felt about each other. What happened, Richard?'

Pearl waited for his response and finally, it came. Richard Clayson spoke softly but directed his speech only to his wife. 'I found his number on your phone and one afternoon, one hot summer's day, I called him and asked him to meet me. I'm not sure what he expected, I simply explained.'

'Explained what?' Alice asked breathlessly.

'Everything,' said Richard calmly. 'How I couldn't live without you – nor you without me.'

Alice frowned at this but Richard went on, holding her attention as though they were the only two people in the room. 'You'd been through so much, Alice. I know how desperately you wanted a child...'

Alice tried to break in. 'Richard...'

'No. You have to understand this – how hard it's been for me to stand by and see you suffer so much disappointment.' Richard took a deep breath. 'I told him everything. I explained how ... fragile you are. How much you need protecting.

And I asked him how he imagined he could ever possibly give you that protection – how he could take care of you as I do.' Richard shook his head. 'I knew he might have persuaded you to leave, but he was just a boy – a young boy with nothing to his name. I knew you loved him, Alice, and I learned that day that he loved you, because he understood. He listened to me and when I had finished, he agreed he would never take you from me. He did that before I even offered him a penny.'

'You … offered him money?' Alice's voice was a mere whisper.

'Five thousand pounds,' said Richard.

Alice Clayson closed her eyes.

'Not a bribe, but a gift – to see him on his way, though I'd have given him ten times more if I had had to.' Richard raised a hand to wipe his mouth. 'He promised he'd leave and never come back.' Clenching and unclenching his hands as he spoke, Richard's voice still remained calm. 'He said I would never hear from him again. And he was true to his word. He loved you enough to disappear.'

In the silence that followed, Pearl took up the story. 'So you whisked Alice away to Venice … to forget. And just when you thought it was all behind you, someone else got in touch.'

Pearl paused for a moment. 'Detective Chief Inspector McGuire discovered today that Michael Arthur had exhibited some of his work in a summer arts festival in Yorkshire.' She turned to Alice Clayson. 'He was still in love with you, Alice, so he couldn't help confiding to someone he had met during the same festival – a friendly young photographer called Cassie Walker.'

Dolly's hand went to her mouth at the mention of Cassie's name but Pearl was still addressing Alice.

'You're a married woman with a successful husband who had provided you with a beautiful home and a standard of living that Michael Arthur could never hope to match. And Michael had deserted you for the very best of reasons, but he felt that he had compromised himself by taking money from your husband. Now he felt guilty for doing so.' She went on: 'Cassie was also an artist, living off what she earned from her photographs – which wasn't much. But she was also canny, an opportunist who shamelessly seized any chances that came her way – to take photographs from the porch of a stranger's beach hut? Except you weren't a stranger to her, Alice. She had heard all about you from Michael Arthur and she recognised very clearly your husband's dilemma: he had done everything he could to keep you – and succeeded – but how might you react if you were told that he had bought off the young man you had fallen in love with?' Pearl said to Richard: 'Is that how Cassie phrased it when she contacted you for money?'

Richard Clayson looked away guiltily.

'So you gave it to her,' said Pearl. 'To keep her quiet and to prevent your wife knowing the truth, you gave Cassie Walker five thousand pounds because you couldn't risk Alice finding out that Michael Arthur still loved her, still wanted her and had only left her because of you.'

'Yes,' he said resignedly. 'I gave her what she wanted.' His expression hardened and he stared around as though for a means of escape but found none. 'At the same time Diana began asking me to account for the money. She was suspicious but I ... trusted her to keep quiet and so I told her what had happened.' He looked helplessly at Pearl. 'She was my accountant and a good friend. She was bound by confidentiality, just as I am with my patients, but she said that blackmail was a crime – and she warned me that it would never end.' He looked back at his wife. 'She said that if I didn't explain everything to you – then she would do so.' He closed his eyes for a moment. 'Why didn't she listen to me? I couldn't let her do that, Alice. I couldn't risk losing you again.'

'So you murdered Diana?' she whispered, horrified.

Richard Clayson nodded slowly. 'But she was right,' he said. 'It was never going to end.'

Pearl spoke up. 'True – because you discovered that the girl who was blackmailing you was actually here, staying in Whitstable for Christmas. She came to your house the day that Alice fainted at the beach hut and was impressed by what she saw ... seeing it as rich pickings...'

Richard broke in bitterly. 'And she phoned me and said she wanted more money. Then I knew she was never going to stop, not until I had lost everything.'

Pearl filled the silence that followed. 'The last time I saw Cassie alive, she was returning from Seasalter on her bike. You were there, with Alice, and so were Bonita and Simon. They were just heading into town when Cassie made a point of giving me a message. Do you remember what she said? "The very least that should go to those who've lost someone they love, is the truth." I thought at the time it was an odd thing to say. I assumed she was referring to finding the murderer, but later I recognised it wasn't a message for me but for someone else who had been present. She had intended it for you, Richard – a warning that if you didn't give her money, she'd go to Alice.'

Alice looked at her husband in disbelief. 'I would have forgiven you, Richard,' she said. 'I could have forgiven you for Michael – but not for this.' She managed to utter finally, 'Not – murder.'

Richard watched his wife take a step away from him. Pearl noted how they were still standing close – but a million miles apart.

McGuire took this as his cue, moving forward to take control. 'Richard Clayson, I am arresting you for the murder of...'

But he got no further, for in a flash of movement so fast it was almost unnoticeable, Christopher Hadley had seized Richard Clayson, his strong arm held firmly against the doctor's throat.

It was an action that caught everyone by surprise and Pearl saw that Hadley showed no emotion – only a focused intention. McGuire approached slowly, his voice remaining calm as he ordered, 'Let him go.' But Christopher seemed not to hear anything except the desperate effort Richard Clayson was making to breathe. McGuire moved closer still and said softly, 'He took her life, but you still have yours.' McGuire recognised that there was a message for himself in the following words as he spoke them. 'Don't waste it,' he said finally. 'Live it for her.'

Another timeless moment passed before Christopher Hadley's gaze shifted to McGuire. The detective gave a silent nod of his head and, as if acting under orders, Hadley released Diana Marshall's murderer from his grasp. As the doctor began gasping for air, Pearl, too, felt herself begin to breathe again.

Chapter Twenty-Two

Christmas Day, 7.45 a.m.

Pearl gently opened Charlie's bedroom door and saw that he was fast asleep. As she had feared, his flight from Berlin had arrived late and it had been almost 1 a.m. before mother and son had finally arrived home after the twenty-minute drive from Manston airport. In Pearl's absence, Dolly had worked hard to tidy Seaspray Cottage so that not a shred of evidence remained of the drama that had occurred that evening. Instead, Pearl returned to find her table set in readiness for Christmas dinner the next day, with plates and cutlery, napkins, candles and Christmas crackers.

Pearl and Charlie had shared only a single glass of corn schnapps together before her son had succumbed to fatigue. His room was now dominated by an unpacked rucksack and suitcase, clothes scattered haphazardly around on the 'floordrobe' but Pearl was in no mood to nag him. Instead, she closed the door quietly and let her son sleep on.

On meeting Charlie at the Arrivals gate, Pearl

saw that he had lost weight but Christmas would surely provide a way of making up for that. Having been up for almost two hours this morning, she had busied herself making chestnut stuffing and gravy, and preparing vegetables for roasting. Sprouts were to be stir-fried with lemon and pine nuts, and red cabbage spiced with cinnamon. Once the turkey was placed in the oven, Pearl was confident that the smell of Christmas would soon lure Charlie from his bed.

Downstairs, she smiled at the sight of two creatures nestled together in a basket by the fire. At 9 p.m. on Christmas Eve, Martha's cats had been delivered to Seaspray Cottage by the local refuge and had taken immediate cover beneath Pearl's sofa until a saucer of poached tuna had finally tempted them out. A full investigation of the property and some gentle strokes from Pearl had persuaded Pilchard and Sprat that there was nothing to be feared about their new owner – or her cosy, warm environment. Taking charge of her two new companions helped Pearl to feel that she had gone some way towards paying an outstanding debt to an elderly lady.

Looking at the lights of her Christmas tree, Pearl's thoughts turned to McGuire. A Christmas card had been the premise for his return, but murder had brought them back together again. Dr Richard Clayson was in police custody and would pay for his crimes, for while acting out of love for his wife, he had deprived others of those they loved – and for them, the price he paid would surely never be high enough.

In his Best Lane apartment that overlooked the River Stour, McGuire stood beneath a hot shower. He had slept badly, still wired with adrenaline from the night's events, but the hot water was helping him to relax. The case was wrapped up with a full statement and confession from Richard Clayson, but Welch was already asking difficult questions about McGuire's involvement with a smalltown private investigator, and answers would have to come later. Contrary to McGuire's earlier expectations, he would not be on duty at Christmas. For the first time since Donna's death, he was about to celebrate the season with a family.

He raised his face, allowing the water to waken him properly, reminding him of the heat that day in Venice when he and Donna had left the hotel near the Rialto and breakfasted in San Marco. Afterwards, they had wandered the narrow streets, not talking much, just being, and in the afternoon, when the heat had become oppressive, they had returned to the hotel, lying together, facing the breeze that entered from the open windows, feeling at one but entirely separate from the life going on outside. Gondoliers had ferried tourists while other craft transported produce along the canal to markets, much as the visitors and traders beyond McGuire's window in Canterbury used St Peter's Street or the Stour River. But it wasn't the same.

McGuire switched off the shower and instantly the heat faded. Pulling a towel around himself, he walked into his empty living room, unable to clear his mind of that last afternoon with Donna – and not wishing to. The past came to him regularly. At the Lido, he had remained on the beach while she had gone to swim, wearing a black swimsuit with a silver clasp at her cleavage. It had glinted in the sunlight as she turned to him at the water's edge, one hand raised above her auburn hair. It was a picture he had seen in his mind's eye many times over the past year, like an after-image burned into his memory but now, and for the first time, he saw Donna's face being slowly eclipsed by Pearl's.

In the kitchen at Seaspray Cottage, Pearl checked the turkey that was roasting in the oven. A Christmas pudding steamed on a backburner. Everything was prepared and the day finally under control. It was time to wake Charlie and to get herself ready. She pushed her tangled curls back from her face and smiled to herself, but the smile quickly faded as she realised she had forgotten one thing. She began searching for her mobile phone.

McGuire had just put on some trousers, black but casual, and slipped into a clean white shirt when he looked beyond his window, noticing that the city seemed strangely quiet, with none of the familiar sounds of the usual busy mornings, no appetising smells wafting across the river from the pizzeria: warm prosciutto, oregano, basil and freshly baked dough. Today was a day unlike any other. It was Christmas.

He fastened the last button on his shirt as the joyful sound of cathedral bells suddenly rang out. For a moment they reminded him of the bells of San Marco – but the text that arrived just then on his mobile phone left him in no doubt as to where he was. Reading the message, his face broke into a smile. *Don't be late, and bring brandy!*

An hour later, a loud bang sounded and a champagne cork flew up to hit a piece of cornice on Pearl's living-room ceiling. She quickly filled the glass in Charlie's hand. 'Shouldn't we wait for McGuire?' he asked. After wallowing in the bath, Pearl's son was now dressed in clean jeans and a new T-shirt with the message *Christmas is for Life.*

'What for?' asked Dolly, who waited for no one and took a sip of her own champagne, together with a bite from a triangle of rye bread topped with smoked salmon, cream cheese and capers. 'There's plenty more where this came from.' She tossed her Christmas feather boa across her shoulder before raising her glass to Pearl, who was just about to take a sip from her own glass when an oven alarm sounded. 'I'll be right back,' she said, quickly heading off.

In the kitchen, Pearl switched off the oven, reflecting for a moment that with her turkey cooked, she had everything ready for Christmas – except brandy and McGuire – but soon he would be here and on the one day that mattered, she had actually found time to put on some make-up, style her hair and slip into the vintage white crepe dress with tiny glass beads that caught the light like falling snowflakes.

'Can someone give me a hand?' she called.

Charlie and Dolly entered quickly and Pearl handed them warm serving dishes. 'Take these in,' she said briskly.

Without question, Charlie and Dolly did as they were told while Pearl transferred the turkey to a platter, garnished with continental parsley. As she settled the bird in prime position, Pilchard and Sprat came forward to investigate.

'Right,' said Pearl, lighting tall candles in their silver holders. 'Everything's ready.'

'Apart from some music,' said Charlie. 'What would you like to listen to?' But before Pearl had time to respond, the doorbell sounded.

Pearl stopped in her tracks but Dolly commanded, 'What're you waiting for? Go and let him in while I carve.' She took up her daughter's best knife.

As Pearl reached the door, her heart rose in expectation only to fall again when she heard the sound of children's voices chattering outside before the first strains of 'Silent Night' were sung.

The candles on Pearl's table had almost guttered in the cold draught so she slipped the latch and pulled the door closed behind her. Four children stood on her doorstep, wrapped up against the cold in scarves, gloves and mittens with carol sheets in their hands. They continued their singing without missing a beat and with such earnest expressions that Pearl felt compelled to give them all her attention.

The youngest child, a boy no more than six years old, sang from memory, his face raised to Pearl, singing so intently, as though his young life depended upon it. Pearl let go of every expectation, allowing the magic of Christmas to wash over her like the high tide washing up on the shore. As the song continued, nothing else seemed to matter, only this moment, pure and simple, an impromptu Christmas gift delivered by these few young souls

277

singing their hearts out on Pearl's doorstep.

When the final chorus came to an end, the youngest boy raised an empty chocolate tin towards Pearl but it was another hand that leaned in and made the donation. As the children hurried off, Pearl turned to see McGuire. He was wearing his dark overcoat, his eyes firmly fixed on hers, noting that she looked beautiful, not stressed or anxious but calm and somehow strangely serene. She took from him the bottle he offered, noting it was a fine Cognac, but before she could thank him, he handed her something else.

Pearl opened the envelope and took from it a card that spilled no glitter but showed a red pillar box on its front cover. The message inside stated simply *I'm glad you got in touch*.

She looked up and McGuire smiled. 'Merry Christmas, Pearl.' Taking a step closer, he pulled her gently to him, holding her in a warm embrace and Pearl hesitated only for a second before she felt herself respond, her cheek pressed against his strong shoulder. And then she looked up to see that something magical was happening: snowflakes were falling, melting on McGuire's blond hair, disappearing into his overcoat.

As they broke apart, McGuire recognised her look of childish wonder before she smiled and replied, 'And to you, McGuire.'

A moment later, the door to Seaspray Cottage opened wider beneath her hand and McGuire and Pearl entered to take their place at the Christmas table, while outside, children's voices echoed from another doorstep on Island Wall.

'All is calm. All is bright.'

Acknowledgements

I am very grateful to Cllr Paula Vickers and Rev Peter Doodes for some very timely research and to Mark Salisbury, Police Chief Superintendent (retired), for his valuable advice on police procedure.

My thanks, as ever, go to Michelle Kass, Alex Holley, Taran Baker and Nicola O'Connell for their continued support and to Florence Partridge and Kate Doran at Little, Brown for all their hard work in promoting the Whitstable Pearl series.

This Large Print Book for the partially sighted, who cannot read normal print, is published under the auspices of

THE ULVERSCROFT FOUNDATION